A Magical Bakery Mystery

Spells and Scones

Bailey Cates

New York Times Bestselling Author of *Magic and Macaroons*

OBSIDIAN

$7.99 U.S.
$10.99 CAN.

ISBN 978-0-451-46743-0

9 780451 467430

5 0 7 9 9

S ▷ EAN

PRAISE FOR THE
NEW YORK TIMES BESTSELLING
MAGICAL BAKERY MYSTERIES

"Katie is a charming amateur sleuth. . . . With an intriguing plot and an amusing cast of characters, *Brownies and Broomsticks* is an attention-grabbing read that I couldn't put down."
—*New York Times* bestselling author Jenn McKinlay

"Cates is a smooth, accomplished writer who combines a compelling plot with a cast of interesting characters."
—*Kirkus Reviews*

"Full of delicious recipes and descriptions of food . . . [a] charming and magical mystery."
—Kings River Life Magazine

"If you enjoy books like Ellery Adams's Charmed Pie Shoppe Mystery series, and Heather Blake's Wishcraft Mystery series, you are destined to enjoy the Magical Bakery Mystery series."
—MyShelf.com

"[A] subtle blend of magic and mystery."
—Cozy Mystery Book Reviews

"[This series] just keeps getting better and better!"
—Book of Secrets

"With a top-notch whodunit, a dark magic investigator working undercover, and a simmering romance in the early stages, fans will relish this tale."
—Gumshoe

"Complex and intriguing. If you like a little magic, you will want to read this series."
—Fresh Fiction

"Ms. Cates has most assuredly found the right ingredients . . . a series that is a finely sifted blend of drama, suspense, romance, and otherworldly elements."
—Once Upon a Romance

Spells *and* Scones

A Magical Bakery Mystery

Bailey Cates

AN OBSIDIAN MYSTERY

OBSIDIAN
Published by New American Library,
an imprint of Penguin Random House LLC
375 Hudson Street, New York, New York 10014

This book is an original publication of New American Library.

First Printing, August 2016

For more information about Penguin Random House, visit penguin.com.

ISBN 9780451467430

Printed in the United States of America
10 9 8 7 6 5 4 3 2 1

PUBLISHER'S NOTE
This is a work of fiction. Names, characters, places, and incidents either are the
product of the author's imagination or are used fictitiously, and any resemblance to
actual persons, living or dead, business establishments, events, or locales is entirely
coincidental.

Penguin
Random
House

Acknowledgments

I am very lucky to have so many talented and hardworking people who helped to get this book in front of readers. A big thanks to Kim Lionetti of BookEnds Literary Agency and another to Jessica Wade, who is the best editor an author could hope for—smart, insightful, and patient. The talented and hardworking team at Penguin Random House also includes Isabel Farhi, Ashley Polikoff, Eileen Chetti, Danielle Dill, and Julie Mianecki. I can't possibly name all the individuals in the writing community at large who inspire me, but a special shout-out goes to the ones who review my work and give me both advice and tough love: Mark Figlozzi, Laura Pritchett, Laura Resau, and Bob Trott. And, as always, I'm grateful to Kevin—for everything.

Chapter 1

"I can't believe I actually get to see her!" Margie Coopersmith bounced on her chair with excitement.

"Mmm-hmm," I managed around a bite of sweet potato and brown butter scone. The rich flakiness melted on my tongue, and I made a mental note to add a bit more sage to the next batch.

My friend had stopped by the Honeybee Bakery after taking her kids to Friday-morning story time at the Fox and Hound Bookshop next door. Aunt Lucy had immediately shooed me out of the kitchen for my first break since arriving at five a.m. to start on the day's baking, and I'd joined Margie at a small table near the front windows. The Coopersmiths lived next to my little carriage house in Savannah's Midtown, so most of our conversations took place over the fence between our backyards. Lately we'd both been so busy that there hadn't been many of those chance encounters, and it was nice to have this opportunity to catch up.

Margie's blond ponytail swished as she shook her head in wonder. "I've called in to Dr. Dana's radio show twice but never thought I'd have the chance to meet her face-to-face. I can hardly wait for her signing tomorrow night."

Twice? Really? But I just smiled.

The door to the bakery was propped open to the sixty-five-degree morning, and a pleasant breeze wafted inside. The Ohioan in me loved the change of seasons, even if they weren't nearly as marked in Georgia. I welcomed the caress of the mild, humid air after months of air-conditioning, happily clad in my usual skirt-and-T-shirt work uniform. Margie wore jeans and a light sweater with a denim jacket and sneakers—practical mom garb heavy enough to ward off what she considered chilly weather.

Margie's five-year-old twins, Jonathan and Julia—the JJs for short—ignored their mother's enthusiasm. Sitting next to her at the table, they bent flaxen heads together over their newest book purchase, oatmeal cookies clutched in their right hands. Baby Bart snoozed in his stroller on her other side. Though he was nearly two years old, I suspected the youngest Coopersmith would be called Baby Bart until he was old enough to drive. Baby Bart and the JJs. It sounded like a band from the seventies.

As the JJs turned the page, I saw that the book gripping their attention was *The Night Before Thanksgiving* by Natasha Wing. The holiday was only a week away, and I was looking forward to a big traditional turkey dinner with Aunt Lucy, Uncle Ben, my boyfriend, Declan McCarthy, and as many of the members of the spellbook club and their families as could make it. I hadn't decided on my culinary contribution to the festivities yet. Lately all my spare attention had been devoted to working with Lucy and our part-time employee, Iris Grant, on providing plenty of delicious snacks for the very author event Margie was waxing on about.

Work or not, it was awfully fun. Not only did the occasional catering job give us an excuse to play around with new recipes, which was one of my favorite things to do as a co-owner of the Honeybee, but we could also explore how to bring the right kind of kitchen magic to the table.

Literally.

Soon after I'd moved to Savannah and started the bakery with Lucy and Ben, my aunt had delivered the bombshell that hedgewitchery ran in our family. The term came from the women who used to cross the hedges that protectively surrounded many villages. They would venture into the wild forests and fields to collect plants, which they then used to help and heal the townspeople. Of course, one of the other "hedges" my kin had access to was the veil between this plane and the next, which provided us with unusual intuition, especially in relation to our herbal skills.

That was all on my mother's side. My father was descended from a long line of Shawnee medicine men and had also passed on magical talent to his one and only daughter. Of course, I shared their physical characteristics as well. My short auburn bob was darker than Mama's fiery red hair, and my eyes a lighter green. Her pale Irish complexion had lost out to Daddy's richer skin tones, though she'd seen fit to sprinkle a few freckles across my nose nonetheless.

After I'd eventually come around to the idea of being an actual, you know, *witch*, complete with a Cairn terrier as my animal familiar, my aunt had brought me into the spellbook club. It was a real book club with regular meetings, but it also turned out to be an informal coven.

The four other ladies had welcomed me with open arms and kindly offered to train me in their various magical specialties.

However, the ancient knowledge of herbal magic that ran through my DNA had required only a bit of reminding from Aunt Lucy, and now almost everything baked in the Honeybee kitchen featured sprinkles of positive, supernatural intention mixed in with the sweet and savory flavors of our rotating selection of pastries.

I took a sip of spicy chai to wash down the rich, buttery scone. "Well, Dr. Dana's based here in Savannah, so it's not exactly surprising that she'd have a book signing in town. And heaven knows the timing is good. Croft—you know, the owner of the Fox and Hound?"

Margie nodded.

"He's hoping this big-name event will bring in lots of early Christmas shoppers."

The espresso machine behind me roared to life as Uncle Ben pulled a shot for a customer, so I almost missed Margie's response. Almost, but not quite, because her exclamation was louder than the whine of the over-pressure valve.

"Oh, it will! Katie, she's *famous*! People listen to her radio show all over the country! And for good reason, too. Dr. Dana is super smart." Margie brushed crumbs from her lips with a napkin and sat back in her chair. The solid, tanned planes of her face reflected Scandinavian roots, but the softly rounded edges of her words revealed that she was a born-and-bred Southerner.

She continued. "Practical, you know? No nonsense. I just adore that about her. No wonder she's so dang popular. I bet Croft is going to sell out of *How to Do Marriage Right* in no time." She pointed to her diaper bag, and I saw the author's photo staring up at me. "That's why I bought my copy early."

I ventured a noncommittal smile. The one time I'd heard Dr. Dana Dobbs, radio psychologist extraordinaire and one of Savannah's more modern claims to fame, I'd been unimpressed. The suggestions she'd made to her call-in clients had struck me as staid and unimaginative—except for when she told a woman whose father didn't like her new husband to cut off all ties with daddy and not look back. That seemed like an awfully severe solution, and honestly I'd been a little shocked to hear a therapist suggest something so drastic based on such limited information. After all, I'd had difficulties with my mother because she'd kept my heritage as a hedgewitch a secret from me, yet over time we'd worked it all out. Now we not only got along, but she'd started practicing the Craft again as a result.

Margie stood. "Come on, kiddos. We've got to hit the grocery store before your naps." She helped Julia down from the chair and handed Jonathan his baseball cap, then looked over at me. In a conspiratorial voice, she said, "Date night after their bedtime, and I'm making Redding his favorite supper—grilled ham steak with red-eye gravy, buttermilk corn bread, and sweet-and-sour green beans."

I blinked. Margie's usual idea of cooking was to order pizza.

Her grin turned into a laugh. "I know, right? His mother gave me her recipes, so I'm going to give them a go. What's the worst that can happen?"

A sudden vision of the house on the other side of my driveway reduced to a smoldering pile of ash flashed across my mental movie screen.

"I'm not going to attempt dessert, though. The only thing I can reliably pull off is my Coca-Cola cake." Pronounced *Co-cola*.

"Which is amazing," I said with feeling.

"I do love it," she admitted. "But I'm relying on you for something sweet tonight."

I snapped my fingers. "Oh! I have just the thing. Eggnog pecan Bundt cake."

Her eyes flicked to the tall chalkboard behind the register where we listed the current Honeybee offerings. "That's not on the menu."

"Which is why it's a good thing you know the proprietors." I grinned. "Between catering Dr. Dana's signing and the upcoming holidays, it's time to shake things up. So Lucy and I were playing around with some new recipes this morning. We'll bring some of them to the bookstore tomorrow night and gauge the responses, but this one is so good we already know it'll go on the menu. Best of all, there's an optional bourbon glaze for the grown-ups."

Her eyes lit up. "Darlin', I am all over that!"

Happy to contribute to Margie's evening with her husband, I hurried into the kitchen and grabbed a square box emblazoned with the stylized logo of an orange tabby cat—Lucy's familiar, Honeybee, who had inspired the name of the bakery. A phalanx of cupcakes surrounded the perfectly formed Bundt on the counter, along with a scattering of crumbs left from our taste testing.

I pointed to the cake. "Okay if I give that to Margie? Date night with Redding," I explained to a startled Lucy.

Beneath the gray-blond mop of hair piled up on her head, my aunt's eyes flashed amused understanding. Quickly, she bent over the cake and muttered a few words. Then, with a wide smile, she helped me load it into the bakery box, and I took it out front to my waiting neighbor.

I kept the incantation Lucy had said to amplify the romantic effects of the cloves and nutmeg in the cake to myself.

The next day was Saturday. After we'd closed the Honeybee at five, Uncle Ben set up the rented buffet table next door in the Fox and Hound Bookshop. Lucy and I covered it with a periwinkle blue cloth and began arranging platter after platter of goodies for the anticipated crowd. There were fig muffins and cranberry coconut cookies, buttery pecan sandies covered with powdered sugar and a variety of sweet and savory scones. Brightly frosted cake pops beckoned next to red velvet whoopie pies and miniature sticky buns laced with citrus peel and cardamom.

Dr. Dana Dobbs wasn't due to start her reading until six o'clock, so Ben took his time setting out the big jugs of mulled cider and peach sweet tea, pausing every time the door opened to see if he recognized whoever was entering. More often than not, his gentle brown eyes lit up behind his glasses, and he raised his hand in an easy wave. My guess was that by the end of the evening, he'd have added even more people to his considerable list of friends. Ever since retiring as Savannah's fire chief, my uncle had happily indulged his extroverted nature—a boon for a customer-oriented business like the Honeybee.

However, six o'clock came and there was no sign of the author. A few people looked at their watches and marched out the door five minutes later, but most of her fans continued to chat and browse. At six thirty, the owner of the Fox and Hound, Croft Barrow, caught my eye and wove his way toward me through the milling

fans. When he reached my side I could see stress in his
pinched forehead and the lines carved around his thin
lips. He ran his fingers through a shock of white hair,
and his worried expression deepened with yet another
glance at the door of the shop.

"No one's seen her?" I asked.

He shook his head.

"Do you have her cell number?"

"She didn't answer." Frustration infused his words.

His phone rang, and he whipped it out of his pocket
like it would reveal the secrets of the universe. "It's her
assistant," he said to me as he thumbed the screen.
"Phoebe! Is everything all right? Where are you?"

Hearing the urgency in his voice, a nearby couple
turned toward us with curious expressions.

Croft wiped his brow and sidled to the deserted corner by the magazine display. As he moved away, I heard
him say, "Yes, that works. We'll see you in a few minutes." His relief was palpable.

Breathing my own relief, I hurried back to the table,
where Aunt Lucy and Uncle Ben were busy dispensing
snacks. Dr. Dana Dobbs was the biggest celebrity Croft
had ever booked, and I knew he wanted everything to
be perfect. His store was doing better than some inde-
pendently owned bookshops, but it was still a bit of a
struggle at times. However, I had high hopes for lots of
sales. Lucy and I had done what we could by adding a
bit of cinnamon to the snickerdoodles and poppy seeds
to the lemon pound cake to encourage prosperity. The
grande dame of the spellbook club, Mimsey Carmichael,
specialized in flower magic and had supplied small vases
of Peruvian lilies to attract money. We'd set those among
the pastries.

"Katie, could you grab some more cups?" Lucy asked

as she handed a cranberry walnut scone to an angular woman.

My aunt's consistent, Zen-like calm instantly dissipated the nervous energy I'd picked up from Croft. Tonight she'd twisted her mass of wavy hair into a loose French braid, and her skirt, blouse, and vest reflected the russet tones of autumn leaves and emphasized her petite figure.

"Sure," I said, and bent down to the bin I'd stashed under the table earlier. Liquid brown eyes looked back at me. Mungo, my Cairn terrier, was guarding the extra supplies. "Good boy," I murmured before straightening with a sleeve of disposable cups in my hand.

Lucy handed me a scone studded with flecks of rosemary, Kalamata olives, and nuggets of salty feta. "Any news?"

I took the scone gratefully. We'd spent the whole afternoon baking and setting up for the event, and I hadn't eaten much since the ham and tomato omelet Declan had whipped up for breakfast that morning.

"The good doctor's assistant just called," I said. "It sounds like they'll be here soon."

"Good." Ben filled a cup with fragrant apple cider and handed it to a waiting customer. He smiled as the woman took the cup, and the corners of his eyes crinkled behind his glasses. In the two years since he'd retired from the fire department, a few white hairs had worked their way into his ginger hair and short beard.

"The last thing Croft needs is for this shindig to fail," he said after the customer had moved away to peruse a display of Dr. Dana's tomes of relationship advice.

Looking around, I saw several patrons already carried stacks of books. "Oh, I don't know. A little extra time to shop, especially with Christmas coming up, can't be bad for business." Nearly swooning with hunger, I took a big bite of the scone and continued to watch the milling crowd.

Croft Barrow had been one of the first people I'd met when I moved to Savannah a year and a half before. Excited about opening a bakery with Ben and Lucy, I'd traveled down from where I was living in Akron. After searching for a name, we'd decided to name it after Honeybee, Lucy's orange tabby cat. Of course, that was before I knew anything about witches' familiars, or that Honeybee was Lucy's. My aunt and I had worked out recipes while Ben searched for the perfect location for the shop. He'd found it next to the Fox and Hound, the quaint, brick-faced bookstore established in Savannah's historic district by Croft's father, Randall Barrow, in 1964.

The inside boasted warm brick walls, a high ceiling, and a crackling fireplace where patrons could settle into comfy chairs and warm their feet during the chilly months. The large children's section was well regarded among parents, not least because two times a week one of Croft's employees, a grandmotherly sort with a talent for voices, read stories aloud to the kiddos.

On the other side of the Honeybee, Annette Lander ran the Fiber Attic yarn and knitting store. Once the bakery had opened, Croft and Annette had seen their traffic pick up, and heaven knew their customers often dropped in for a tasty treat in our establishment. Often they'd settle in with a new book or a knitting project while nibbling on a pastry and sipping coffee. It was a perfectly symbiotic business relationship.

Annette hadn't been able to attend Dr. Dana's talk, but I recognized many of those who had come. Of course, Margie had already ensconced herself in the front row of folding chairs arranged in front of the podium. The kids were nowhere to be seen, and she'd ditched her practical mom uniform for a pretty, floral-print dress. Her sandy hair hung in ringlets down her back. They swung over her shoulder when she turned to smile and give me a little wave.

I put a slice of lemon pound cake on a paper plate and made my way over to her.

A petite, dark-haired woman was sitting next to Margie. Her gaze flicked up to me as I approached, and as our eyes met, she tipped her head slightly to one side. Did I know her? She looked a few years older than my twenty-nine and wore skinny jeans, a cream-colored T-shirt, and a short leather jacket that matched her brown boots. Before I could decide if I should recognize her from the Honeybee, she bent her head over her copy of *How to Do Marriage Right*.

Shrugging, I sat in the empty chair on the other side of Margie. "How did date night go?" I asked with a conspiratorial grin, and handed her the treat.

"Thanks! And thanks for the Bundt cake—it was the highlight of the meal last night." She wrinkled her nose. "I didn't burn anything too much." She shrugged. "Except for the corn bread. That was sort of, you know—black. And honestly, I don't think I'll ever get the hang of making gravy that doesn't look like kindergarten paste. Luckily, Redding doesn't expect me to cook like his mama—and date night involves a lot more than supper." She waggled her eyebrows suggestively, a girly Groucho Marx.

My mouth opened in a silent laugh. "Why, you naughty girl!"

A blush crept into her cheeks. "We are married, you know."

I looked down at the copy of *How to Do Marriage*

Right she held on her lap. "And it sounds to me like you already know how to 'do it right,' too." The extra romantic oomph Lucy had added to the Bundt cake probably hadn't hurt, either.

She smiled and ducked her chin. "Redding and I are good together. You never know, though. I bet Dr. Dana has some real gems in here. I've been too busy to take a look yet."

Rising, I put my hand on her shoulder. "I'm going to check on the buffet table. Catch up with you later?"

She nodded and turned to face the podium with an air of expectation.

Back at my station, a soft tongue licked my ankle, which was bare beneath the long, crinkled skirt I'd donned for the evening. I stepped back and looked down to see Mungo eagerly gazing up at me. My familiar's nose twitched, and he broke eye contact to stare at the last bite of scone in my hand with the laser focus of a brain surgeon.

"You already had your supper," I said.

Boy, had he ever. Ben had indulged him with leftover fried chicken and mashed potatoes from Mrs. Wilkes' Dining Room, and Mungo had even tucked into some stewed okra, a Southern delicacy he happened to love but for which I had yet to develop a taste. Thinking about what my dog had had for supper made my own stomach growl, despite the Greek scone.

Now he made a sound low in his throat and cocked his head to the side, eyes still riveted to the pastry remnant I held.

Ben laughed. "The little guy just wants a bit of dessert to go with supper."

The dog's nose twitched, and he grinned a canine grin.

"Okay, fine." I bent and offered the final bite to him.

He stepped forward and daintily extracted it from my fingertips before wolfing it down in a single gulp.

I rolled my eyes, and Ben laughed.

A portly man with a graying comb-over and blue suspenders approached the buffet table and began examining the pastries on offer. He clutched a Craig Johnson mystery in one hand and I wondered briefly if he was there to see Dr. Dana or had inadvertently stumbled into the festivities.

He pointed at a platter and said, "Whatever that is, it looks mighty tasty. Mind if I try one?"

"Bacon jalapeño corn pones." Ben's eyes lit up as he handed the man a small paper plate and napkin. "By all means, take two." He waved at Lucy and me. "These ladies are geniuses in the kitchen, but I have to tell you that delectable concoction was my idea—which, of course, they implemented to a spectacular degree."

The man took a healthy bite, his eyes widening as the spicy, salty, smoky, and slightly sweet combination hit his taste buds. "Whoo-ee! That is *good*! I believe I will have another. Where did you say these came from?"

"The Honeybee Bakery," Ben boomed. A few heads turned. "Right next door."

"I might just have to try one of those myself," a familiar voice said.

I looked up to see Declan McCarthy grinning down at me. Moving out from behind the table, I wrapped my arms around him in a hug and bussed his cheek. "Nice of you to finally show up."

He donned an expression of mock hurt but couldn't keep it up for more than a few seconds. His blue eyes drank me in as I resisted running my finger along his square jaw. His dark, wavy hair had grown almost long enough to challenge fire department regulations, and I had a hard time not touching that, too.

Keeping myself under control, I squeezed his arm and reached for a corn pone. Handing it to him, I gestured toward the rapidly filling seats. "You might want to find a place to sit down before the festivities begin."

"I'd rather hang out with you." He looked around. "Where is this relationship guru?"

"On her way," Croft muttered as he passed by. "At least that's what Phoebe said."

"Phoebe?" Declan asked as he watched the stressed older man walk away.

"Dr. Dana's assistant," I said.

"Her sister, too, from what I've heard," Lucy chimed in.

"Really? I wonder what it would be like to work for your sister," I mused. As an only child, I sometimes wondered what it would be like to even have a sister.

"Well, I don't know that I'd want to work with mine," Lucy muttered under her breath.

I stifled a laugh. She was talking about my mother, Mary Jane Lightfoot, and I had to agree with her.

The man popped the last bite of his second corn pone into his mouth and tugged at his suspenders as he chewed. He swallowed and took a swig of the tea Lucy had handed him. "Thank you, ma'am. You put on a nice spread here. Too bad it's for that sham of a therapist."

Lucy and Ben looked at each other.

"What do you mean?" Declan asked.

"Relationship guru," the man grated out. "My foot, she's a *guru*. You know that radio show she has? The one where people call in and talk smack about their husbands or wives or relatives?"

I nodded. "Sure. *The Dr. Dana Show*. My friend loves

it." Glancing over, I saw Margie staring a hole in the door to Broughton Street as if she could bring the tardy author into the Fox and Hound by sheer willpower.

"*Dr.* Dana. Right. Well, first off, she gives crappy advice." His voice was loud.

A curly-haired woman with dark eyes was browsing a rack of new releases nearby. When she heard him, the side of her mouth turned up, and she gave an indulgent shake of her head. Moments later she had come over to join him.

He put his arm around her and continued his diatribe. "Really horrible advice. I did what she suggested, since she's such an *expert* and all, and you know what?"

"What?" Declan asked. His eyes shone with curiosity. Who says men don't like gossip?

"My Sophie here almost left me." He gave the woman a squeeze.

My boyfriend blinked. "Really? Geez, what did Dr. Dana say to you?"

I glanced at Margie, who didn't seem to be tuned in to our conversation. However, the dark-haired woman sitting next to Margie had twisted in her seat to watch us. Her eyes slowly narrowed. In anger at the stout gentleman sharing his story with us? She looked down at the book she held in her hand, and her lip curled.

No. She doesn't like Dr. Dana, either.

A bad feeling settled across my shoulders, sifted down through my chest, and took up residence in my solar plexus.

The man's face had grown ruddier by the second. "Lots of things," he said. "Mostly about keeping tabs on everything my darlin' Sophie did. But the worst thing was she told me to make my fiancée quit her job."

The woman next to him—presumably darlin' Sophie—rolled her eyes. "Can you believe it? In this day and age?

Not to mention we have our own business. It's not like I could quit that, even if I wanted to."

My aunt's eyes widened, openly curious. "But why on earth would Dr. Dana say that?"

"She said for the first year of marriage the wife should stay home." He snapped his suspenders for emphasis.

I felt my jaw slacken. "You've *got* to be kidding me."

Sophie laughed. "He got his mind right. We've been married for six months now."

He shook his head. "I checked into her background after what happened. Her psychology license in the state of Georgia is expired, but it hardly matters since she doesn't practice privately anymore. Just gets on that radio show of hers and tells people she's never met what they should do to fix their lives. Heck, the woman wrote a book about child rearing, and she doesn't even have any children."

"But how can—," I began, but the murmur of voices rose. The front door had opened, and all eyes turned toward the woman who entered.

Chapter 2

A tall, slender woman about my age entered the Fox and Hound. Her shiny brown hair brushed the shoulders of a button-down oxford shirt tucked into black jeans. She kept her hand on the door as her eyes searched the crowd. When they lit upon Croft, she lifted her other hand to get his attention.

Something like joy crossed his usually gruff face, then drained away as he hurried over to her. I held up my finger to Declan and sidled close enough to hear their exchange.

"What's wrong?" Croft asked in a stage whisper. "Is your sister still coming?"

So this must be Phoebe, the sister/assistant.

"She's right outside," the woman responded in a soothing tone. "I'm just checking to make sure everything is ready for her. She doesn't like waiting." Her eyes flicked to the podium. "Is there bottled water? Did you crack the seal as I asked?"

"Of course," Croft said, impatient. "Everything has been ready for an hour now. People are starting to get restless. If she doesn't get in here, they're going to start walking out."

Phoebe's smooth demeanor cracked. "I'm sorry, Mr. Barrow. We've been behind schedule all day, and tonight we were particularly late because there was a . . . situation . . . my sister had to take care of."

What does she mean by "particularly late"?

Did Dana Dobbs always arrive late to author events? From what I'd read in the *Savannah Morning News*, *How to Do Marriage Right* was her fourth book, and she was on the radio three days a week. Busy, I could understand, but keeping people waiting for this long was downright rude.

"Well, get her in here," Croft said, equally unimpressed.

The doctor's sister nodded, her gaze sweeping over the crowd. Then she turned and opened the door, gesturing to someone out on Broughton Street. The room grew quiet as everyone realized the star was about to arrive.

Suddenly, the door was jerked wider, and Dr. Dana Dobbs clicked into the Fox and Hound on four-inch heels. Her golden hair was sculpted into a retro flip, and she wore a light blue, long-skirted wool suit that looked like it was from the fifties. Mascara, salmon pink lipstick, and a dusting of rouge completed the *Mad Men* look.

A couple of steps inside, she paused. Her large brown eyes scanned the eager crowd, and despite her very put-together look, I sensed anxiousness. A split second later it was gone, and her lips curved up in a regal smile.

Croft hurried forward, holding out his hand. "Here she is! Welcome, Dr. Dana! Everything's ready."

She shook his hand twice, then let it drop. "Thank you so much, you dear man. I'm delighted to be in your little bookstore." Her words drawled out sweetly, but there was just enough condescension in her tone to make me frown.

I saw the skin tighten across Croft's features and knew he'd caught it, too.

Behind Dr. Dana, a man filled the still-open door to the street. He wore a blue sports coat over an open-collared white shirt and dark blue jeans and carried a leather folio bag with a handle. His chestnut hair curved toward his collar, accenting the handsome lines of his face. Phoebe hustled toward him and put out her hand. He nodded, reached into the bag, and handed her a sheaf of papers, then ambled to the seat she pointed to.

Croft hurried behind the podium and turned on the microphone. I winced as his voice thundered throughout the room. "The woman you have all been waiting for has arrived." He turned the volume down to a more bearable level. "I'm sure you're all quite familiar with her work, both on the radio waves and in print. So without further ado, please give a warm welcome to Dr. Dana Dobbs!"

Applause smattered from the audience. The author marched up to take Croft's place behind the podium and surveyed the room. Phoebe scurried up and handed her sister the papers, then faded to the side. Everyone else settled in their chairs, including the man who had been regaling us with the sad tale about his fiancée. Declan came around to where I stood. He leaned against the wall, and I leaned against him. He put his arms around me and rested his chin against my temple.

"Thank you all so much for coming. I know there are a lot of places you could be on a Saturday evening, and I'm honored that you chose to come to . . . to . . . here," Dr. Dana finished with a little smile.

"She doesn't know the name of the bookstore," Declan murmured into my ear.

"I bet she's been to so many that they all run together,"

I whispered back, trying my best to be charitable. "Besides, her sister probably sets it all up." Never mind that since she lived in Savannah, she should have been familiar with all the local bookstores.

Dr. Dana reached under the podium and drew out a bottle of water. She removed the cap and lifted it to take a sip. When she saw the label, the smile on her face froze, and she slowly lowered the bottle again. Her eyes sought out her sister, whose eyes widened when she saw the water. The celebrity's delicate nostrils flared.

Phoebe hurried to the man who had followed them in from the street. With a wry look, he reached into the leather bag at his feet and handed her a bottle of water. Quickly, she twisted off the cap and took it to Dr. Dana.

"Sorry!" Phoebe whispered. "I told them which brand, but—"

Dr. Dana's eyes narrowed, and she grabbed the bottle. After taking a delicate sip, she placed it under the podium.

I twisted my head to look up at Declan. "What was that all about?"

He rolled his eyes. "She probably only drinks rare water from an underground spring in the south of Monrovia."

I gave him a gentle pinch. "Be nice."

"I'm not the one who showed up late, insulted Croft, and then makes everyone wait while she gets her special beverage."

Ben shifted on one foot to lean closer to us. In a barely audible voice, he said, "I'm with you, Deck. Let's get this show on the road. It's getting late, and I've got an eight o'clock tee time at Crosswinds tomorrow morning."

"Now, where was I? Oh, yes. Thanking you, my dear readers—and listeners," Dr. Dana said. "How many of you listen to my nationally syndicated radio program?"

Half the hands in the audience shot up, including Margie's.

"Wonderful! So that means many of you are already familiar with my husband, Nathan Dobbs, whom I often talk about on the program." Her arm extended in a royal gesture as she smiled at the handsome man who had followed her inside. "Nate, the love of my life, and the reason I felt compelled to write this book."

One side of his mouth turned up in a half smile.

"You see," Dr. Dana continued, "we've been together for twenty years, and during that time we figured out how to do marriage right! Every day we are so happy and grateful to have each other, and I wanted to pass on how we make that happen so that every one of my readers and listeners can unearth the same kind of bliss in their own relationships."

Declan gave me a squeeze and whispered in my ear, "I'm going to have to pick up a copy of that book."

"I don't think we really need someone to tell us how to get along," I replied.

"Maybe it's different once you're married," he said.

I patted him on the arm but didn't reply. Lately he'd hinted a lot about moving in together and sometimes mentioned future plans that included children. However, after my last disastrous engagement—a major reason I'd left Akron for Savannah—I was inclined to move a bit slower.

"The key," Dr. Dana went on, "is complete honesty."

Well, duh.

"Trust. *Radical Trust.*"

The way she said it made me envision the term followed by a trademark symbol.

"My husband and I have no secrets whatsoever. I know everything he does all day long, and he knows everything I do."

Okay . . .

The short woman who was sitting next to Margie laughed. Margie turned to look at her, mouth automatically pursed into a *shh* as if the stranger was one of her children. The woman ignored her.

Dr. Dana looked down at the front row. Her eyes widened for a fraction before she licked her salmon-tinted lips and continued in a distracted tone. "We have GPS trackers on each other's phones. We have lists of each other's passwords—for everything imaginable."

The petite woman turned to look at the author's husband. My gaze followed hers in time to see the unguarded look of distaste on his face before it was replaced with a smooth mask of disinterest.

"And we regularly check each other's texts and voice mails," Dr. Dana said.

The woman next to Margie shot to her feet. "That's crazy!"

The author blanched, then quickly recovered her poise. "On the contrary," she replied. "It's honesty."

"It's an invasion of privacy!" the portly man who had so enjoyed the bacon jalapeño corn pones said. Unlike the dark-haired woman, he remained seated. However, his voice was deep and loud enough for everyone to hear. "And pretty awful advice, by the way. Just like the rest of your relationship wisdom. My fiancée was so insulted when I ran a background check on her— which, among other things, you advised me to do on your radio show—that our relationship nearly *ended*. Luckily, I backed off, and we're married now. But I can just imagine what she'd think if I started reading her private e-mail."

I saw Sophie duck her head as if embarrassed.

"Now, folks." Croft started forward. "Let's just settle—"

Dr. Dana cut him off with a raised palm, and he stopped short. "No, no." She shook her head at her detractor. "You don't understand. Only by being completely honest and open with one another can you really make marriage work. Your wife must have been hiding something." She nodded sagely. "In fact, she probably still is."

Now Sophie turned bright red.

Declan murmured, "I take it back. We definitely don't need her book."

The petite woman next to Margie stabbed the air with her finger. "Well, I called into your radio program, too. And I was dumb enough to follow your advice to tell my husband about something in my past. You know what, Miss Smarty-Pants marriage expert? I'm divorced now." She sat down again and folded her arms across her chest.

Margie stared at her seatmate with a wounded, bewildered expression. I knew later I'd hear my neighbor's strong opinions about someone crashing a book reading for no better reason than to heckle the author—probably over a glass of her favorite pink wine. At least I hoped so. In fact, I wouldn't have minded a glass of it right then. I cast my attention around the room, trying to get a feel for where things might go next. Ben was frowning, and Lucy's face was worried. None of us were particular fans of Dr. Dana's, but we all wanted things to go well for Croft's sake.

The talk show host shook her head and looked sympathetically at her critic. "Dear, I'm so very sorry. But a successful marriage cannot tolerate secrets of any kind. I'm afraid your divorce was—"

Mungo let out a loud *yip!* and suddenly ran out from

under the buffet table. Stunned, I watched him beeline toward the podium.

Midsentence, Dr. Dana looked down and saw him coming toward her. Her eyes grew wide, and her mouth formed an O of surprise before she opened it wider to scream.

Chapter 3

I bolted out to retrieve my dog. "Mungo! Get back here!"

Croft had been leaning against the endcap of a bookshelf near the front of the room. Now he pushed himself upright, his expression livid. "Oh, for Pete's sake, Katie!"

"I'm sorry," I said, feeling the heat of embarrassment in my cheeks. "So sorry." Bending to scoop up Mungo, I paused for a second in surprise. He wasn't looking at Dr. Dana at all. His eyes were riveted on the dark-haired pixie who sat next to Margie.

She stared at him as well, her face suddenly as pale as mine was red.

Confused, I grabbed him tightly into my arms and went to stand by Declan again.

"Now, everyone, let's settle down and let Dr. Dana speak," Croft boomed without the aid of the mic, while at the same time aiming a vitriolic look at me.

Dana Dobbs managed a wavering smile, took another drink of water, and gathered herself. Soon the psychologist was reading from the introduction to her book, which, from what I understood in my distracted state, explained in detail how to track another person's every move.

Mungo wiggled in my arms. I tucked him closer to my shoulder and whispered, "Do you know that woman sitting next to Margie?"

He nosed my chin, then nuzzled into my neck.

I tried to listen to Dr. Dana drone on about how spouses—and significant others if they were really, you know, *significant*—should exchange passwords for e-mail and social media, as well as grant each other access to voice mail. But I couldn't stop thinking about how I'd found my little Mungo.

Of course, he'd actually found me. I'd later discovered that's how it works with familiars, after he'd wiggled his furry behind into my new life on my very first day living in Savannah. That was before I even knew I was a witch. Cute as a button, he'd bounded down my driveway and then kept mysteriously showing up in the backseat of my Volkswagen Bug when we were getting ready for the grand opening of the Honeybee. It hadn't taken long before it was clear the little terrier and I were destined to be a team.

My attention returned to Dr. Dana as she began to describe the difficulties she and her husband had been having before she'd discovered the joys of Radical Trust. My gaze slid to his face. How must it feel to have your spouse share your personal life in print and on the radio?

Finally, the author finished and stepped away from the podium, water bottle in one hand and signing pen in the other. Her assistant led her to the table Croft had set up near the front of the store, and the audience rose to form a ragged line. Nate Dobbs moved to stand behind his wife, while Phoebe went to talk to Croft.

Ben poured a cup of peach sweet tea and took it over to Dr. Dana. Leaning down, he said something to her.

She smiled and put her hand over his, then shook her head. He said something else and came back to the buffet table.

"No sale on a pastry," he said. "She seemed pleased to get the sweet tea, though."

I noticed she was drinking her water, though, while the paper cup Ben had taken her was untouched.

A woman wearing a bright pink-and-orange Mexican poncho and a long blond braid down her back entered the bookstore. Her gaze swept the room and landed on the podium. A sour expression twisted her mouth, and her eyes narrowed. She saw Phoebe then, adjusted the purse strap on her shoulder, and threaded her way through the crowd to the author's assistant. They spoke for several seconds, Phoebe shooting looks at her sister the whole time. Then the newcomer gave Phoebe's arm a squeeze and marched over to cut in front of the fan at the head of the line, her Mexican poncho nearly knocking over the cup of sweet tea. Dr. Dana's eyes widened in alarm, and she flinched when the woman leaned over to say something into her ear. Then the woman straightened and walked back out of the bookstore.

The author looked visibly shaken. Phoebe hurried over and opened another bottle of water for her. Dr. Dana took a sip and motioned the next person in line forward.

A few minutes later, the portly man who had dished the dirt on Dr. Dana grabbed one more corn pone with a quick wink at Lucy, purchased his mystery novel, and exited the front door with Sophie. I saw Margie moving up in the queue. She seemed to be purposely avoiding her erstwhile seatmate, whom Mungo had seemed so interested in. After the woman had made such a scene, I couldn't blame my neighbor for distancing herself.

Still, I had serious reservations about Dana Dobbs' advice. The whole concept of Radical Trust sounded like exactly the opposite, more like the doublespeak one might expect from a prevaricating politician than from a professional therapist offering relationship tips.

I murmured into Mungo's ear, "If I put you down, will you stay here behind the table?"

He huffed.

"No? Well, I guess I'll have to run you next door to the Honeybee." He came to work with me nearly every day, and not once had he ever misbehaved. Now he wiggled in my arms, trying to get down.

"What is the matter with you?" I hissed.

He kicked, and I had to stoop quickly to set him on the floor so he wouldn't fall. He scooted away. I grabbed for him, but he was too fast. Just beyond my reach under the buffet, he whirled to face me, sat down, and tipped his head to one side as if to say, *See? I'm being good.*

Lucy and Declan approached. "Everything all right over here?" my boyfriend asked.

I regarded my familiar suspiciously. "Fine and dandy. Right, Mungo?"

The dog delivered a soft grunt and grinned up at me.

I gave him a hard look.

He kept grinning.

Taking him at his grunt, I left Declan to chat with Ben while I set out a few more savory Greek scones. I inhaled the scent of rosemary and admired the pretty flecks of green in the golden triangles. Rosemary promoted fidelity, among other things, but Lucy and I hadn't cast any spells to trigger that element of the plant. Now, looking around at the avid faces of Dr. Dana's fans, I wondered if they were all having trouble in their relationships, and I wished we had focused on that aspect of the herb.

Margie moved to the head of the line and eagerly handed her book to the author. Relief settled over me. My neighbor and her husband were obviously head-over-heels in love even after three children and a trucking job that took him away for days at a time. Margie was simply starstruck by meeting a celebrity, and, more than likely, others were here to see Dr. Dana for the same reason.

At least I hoped so.

A few minutes later, I looked up to see Dr. Dana's pixie-haired female heckler, the one Mungo had been so interested in, marching up to the head of the line. Unlike everyone else, she wasn't holding a book.

"Hey! Wait your turn!" a man who had been standing patiently for several minutes protested. Margie, who had been excitedly discussing something with her idol, fell silent.

The dark-haired woman whirled to face us with her hands on her hips. "My name is Angie Kissel, and I'm here to tell you that this woman is a fraud, people! She has no up-to-date qualifications as a therapist, and her *doctorate* isn't even in psychology, for heaven's sake. Dana Dobbs is a sham whose goal is simply to take your money, not help you with your marriage."

Dr. Dana's face went stark white, and even from across the room I could see the bottle of water in her hand was shaking.

Margie's lips parted in surprise, and then anger flared in her eyes. "Listen here, lady," she started, but Dr. Dana interrupted her.

"You horrible woman!" She stood and pointed her

finger. "I'm warning you. Leave me alone, or I'll get that restraining order we threatened. I'm not kidding, Ms. Kissel. I will see you behind bars if you continue to harass me."

As she spoke, Nate Dobbs took a step forward. He looked furious. Across the room, Phoebe started hurrying toward her sister.

Croft Barrow stepped in. "I'm going to have to ask you to leave, ma'am," he said with a scowl, and reached for the interloper's arm.

Angie Kissel jerked away from him and marched to the front door. Yanking it open, she stepped across the threshold. At the last moment, she turned and regarded the silently watching group. "I'm just trying to help. Don't let her fool you." She pulled the door closed and was gone.

"Thank you," the author said to Croft in a shaky voice. Then she cleared her throat, took a sip of water, and turned back to Margie. Slowly, her husband stepped back to lean against the wall again, while Phoebe whipped out her cell and began murmuring into it.

"Wow. Quite the drama," Declan said in a low voice.

"No kidding. I hope it doesn't hurt sales," Ben said.

"Mmm-hmm," I said, watching Mungo. He was on his feet, gazing at the front door as if there was bacon on the other side of it. His furry brow was wrinkled in a frown.

I bent and rubbed his head. He glanced up at me, then back at the door.

"What's up with him?" Declan asked.

At the other end of the table, Lucy was watching the dog, too, and flicked a concerned glance my way.

I straightened. "I'm not sure."

"Looks like she's about done," Ben said as two young

couples exited the bookstore. The line in front of Dr. Dana had dwindled to three stragglers, and the piles of her books had all but disappeared. "Let's start cleaning up."

Together, we dove in. Lucy packed up the remaining pastries, and Declan loaded them into a plastic bin. Ben started breaking down the folding table, and I went out to police any paper plates and cups that careless patrons had left lying around.

Dr. Dana finished and rose. Her husband, who had stopped hovering behind her and now sat on a folding chair with a spy novel, began gathering his belongings. Croft hurried over to the author, and I heard him ask if she'd mind signing some of the stock he still had in the store.

"I'd be delighted," she said with a gracious air.

"I have another case in the back room." Croft smiled a rare smile. Sales must have been good after all.

Dr. Dana followed the bookstore owner as he wended his way through to the back room. Moments later he returned to the register to help the last two customers. They paid up and left. As they exited I heard them chatting about the unexpected excitement that evening.

Nate Dobbs had returned to his seat and opened his book again. Dr. Dana's sister, Phoebe, sank onto the chair next to him. He gave her a sympathetic look.

Ignoring it, she took a deep breath and stood again. "I'm going to see if I can find a closer parking space so Dana won't have to walk so far on those silly heels."

Nate stood. "I'll come with you." The look he directed around the room was rueful. "I could use the fresh air."

I stifled a smile.

She shrugged. "Suit yourself." Her lack of enthusiasm was palpable.

I turned away to pick up a stray plate.

Margie passed by me with her signed book under her arm and a grin on her face. "Hi, Katie! Wasn't she wonderful? She must have talked with me for five whole minutes!"

"Glad you enjoyed your night out," I said, and gave her a hug made awkward by my full hands.

She grabbed one of the few remaining volumes by the psychologist—this one an earlier advice book about raising children: *How to Do Kids Right*. "I'm getting this one, too. She probably has all kinds of good ideas for how to deal with the JJs. I bet I can still get her to sign it, too." Before I could respond, Margie headed toward the back of the store, where Dr. Dana was signing Croft's extra stock.

Huh. Just as I'd always thought of Margie and Redding as having a great marriage, I'd been in awe of the ease and wisdom she displayed as a mother. Why on earth would Margie need advice on either front?

I dumped the detritus I'd collected into the trash bag Declan held out for me; then he put a lid on the tub of leftovers. He'd promised to drop them at the homeless shelter after we were done. Lucy had already folded the tablecloth and put it in a bag to take home and wash, and Ben had tucked the table against the wall for the rental company to pick up the next morning. I was tired as all get-out and wanted nothing more than to go home and relax on my back patio with a light, late supper and my boyfriend. Our conversation that evening was bound to be interesting.

A scream echoed from the back room, and my chin jerked up. Mungo started barking, loud and urgent, and took off like a shot toward the sound.

I wasn't far behind him, and Declan was right on my heels.

We barreled through the open door, nearly knocking Margie over. I caught myself on the doorframe. Gently, I pushed my friend to one side and stepped up to stand beside her. Adrenaline thrummed through my veins as my mind scrambled to process what I was seeing: dim light, cartons stacked on metal shelving units on either side, a haphazard pile of books on a small table, and a box half-full of more volumes on the floor. Straight ahead, the door to the alley hung open, and a slight breeze stirred the air.

Between where I stood with Mungo quivering at my feet and that open door, Dr. Dana lay sprawled on her back beside an overturned chair. And hunched over her was the woman Croft had kicked out of the bookstore.

Angie Kissel.

Chapter 4

"Ohmagod!" Margie rushed forward.

Angie held up her hand. "No. Don't come any closer."

"But she's sick!" Margie protested. "We have to get her to the hospital."

The other woman met my eyes. Slowly, she shook her head.

"Are you sure?" I asked, understanding at once.

"I'm sure." She stood. "I was just feeling for a pulse."

Margie gaped. "But . . . but . . . are you saying . . . ?"

Declan shouldered past me. "If you don't mind, I'd like to take a look." He looked over at my uncle. "Try to keep everyone from coming in here."

Ben nodded.

Angie Kissel looked peeved but took a step back. "She's not breathing, and her heart isn't beating."

Beside me, Margie let out a small hopeless sound.

"He's a fireman," I said. "With medical training. He just wants to make sure."

She gave a nod and stepped back farther.

Declan quickly knelt beside the author and checked her with a professional air. Then he looked up at me and shook his head in confirmation.

Behind us, I heard voices becoming louder, and then a shout. "That's my wife! Let me through!" Nate Dobbs pushed through the door, despite my uncle trying to stop him. He saw his wife on the floor and stared in disbelief. "Dana?" He looked around with bewildered eyes. "What happened?"

Declan stood. "I'm afraid she's gone, sir. I'm very sorry."

Nathan Dobbs blinked a few times, then rushed toward his wife and kneeled beside her.

"Dana?" Phoebe said from behind me, and pushed forward. "Dana! What happened?"

"Sir, I apologize," Declan said to Nate, "but I think it might be best if we cleared the room."

Something in his voice. I felt the skin tighten across my face.

"I'm very sorry," Declan continued in the smooth, calming tone he reserved for the worst emergencies. "But it's possible the authorities will deem this a suspicious death. We all need to go out front until they arrive."

Angie's mouth dropped open at the same time I heard Phoebe's sudden intake of breath. Nate rose as if in a trance and shambled over to stand with the rest of us huddled just inside the room.

So I hadn't misunderstood the meaning in Declan's tone. He didn't think Dr. Dana had died of natural causes. From my vantage point, I could see that her face and one hand were flushed a dark crimson, but I couldn't tell if there was any evidence of injury. Still, my boyfriend knew his stuff.

I stifled a sad sigh. Since moving to Savannah I'd learned that I was not only a hedgewitch, but also a catalyst and a lightwitch—meaning things sort of *hap-*

pened around me. In practice, that meant I stumbled into an unusual number of wrongs that required righting.

Wrongs that involved murder, unfortunately. And more often than not, some kind of magic.

But this was getting ridiculous. I'd already been involved in five murder investigations in less than two years. Now this? I had no connection to Dr. Dana, at least not that I was aware of. I bowed my head and sent an intention of grace to the soul who had so recently departed for the next plane. And then I allowed myself to hope that my presence this time was plain old coincidence.

I mean, a girl can hope, right?

"The police and ambulance are on their way," Ben said from behind me. I glanced back to see Phoebe and Croft Barrow crowded in the doorway. Phoebe stared at her sister without blinking, tears slowly welling in her eyes.

Declan held out his hand in a silent gesture to Angie Kissel. She frowned but picked her way around the exterior of the room to where we stood. Declan was right behind her.

"You okay?" he asked me in a low voice.

"Uh-huh," I said. "But I don't think Margie is." My neighbor's face had gone waxy beneath her tan, and her pupils were huge. Her breathing was fast and shallow.

Suddenly, she lifted her hand and pointed at Angie Kissel. "She killed Dr. Dana! Arrest her! She killed her!"

Declan put his arm around Margie's shoulders. "Let's get you out of here."

The fight seemed to drain out of my friend. She let out a long sigh, then obediently allowed him to lead her away. Declan looked back over his shoulder and mouthed, "Shock."

I turned to see the Kissel woman watching Margie, her eyes wide and one hand on her throat.

"Now, I think we should all step back for right now," I heard my uncle say. "Let's all wait out here in the bookstore for the police to get here. Croft, how about we put some of those folding chairs back out for folks to sit in."

Croft's voice rumbled something like agreement.

Phoebe stared at the overturned chair as if dreaming. Suddenly, she shook her head and passed her hand over her face as she left to join the others. I had a feeling Declan would be treating her for shock next.

Ben came up behind me. "I'll stay here and keep an eye on things."

Angie Kissel turned her head as if considering a quick bolt through the open door to the alley, then took a deep breath and set her jaw as if making a decision.

Mungo whined. She looked down at him, and a small smile tugged at the corner of her mouth. With my familiar in the lead, we went out to join the others.

"I'm Angie," the woman said to me in a low voice.

"I heard," I said in a wry tone. "I'm Katie Lightfoot."

"Katie, I didn't kill *anyone*. I mean, I'd never . . ." She trailed off.

"Okay," I said. "So did you see anyone else?" Dr. Dana was still warm, and yet I couldn't keep myself from asking questions. I wasn't proud of that.

Angie shook her head. "I came in from the alley right before that woman started screaming. Dana was bright red, and I thought maybe she'd choked. But her mouth . . ." She blanched. Licked her lips and tried again. "I didn't want to admit it, but that fireman might be right. I think she was poisoned. And Lord knows there were plenty of people who wanted her dead."

Including you?

It was a quiet group who waited for the police to arrive: Lucy, Ben, Declan, Margie, Nate, and Phoebe. And Croft, of course. And me and Angie.

Declan had seated Margie in the corner and was talking to her in a low voice. He'd slung Ben's jacket around her shoulders, and a half-full glass of water sat within easy reach. She still looked dazed and pale, but she seemed to be responding to his questions.

Dr. Dana's husband and sister stood by the front window. Nate put his hand on Phoebe's shoulder and gave it a squeeze. She shrugged it off without looking at him.

My aunt was perched on the edge of a chair and sprang to her feet when she saw me. "Is it . . . ?"

"She's gone," I said, holding out my arms for a hug.

"I know that," Lucy said, sounding almost annoyed as we embraced.

I blinked in surprise. She was usually a bit of a delicate flower. Still, I knew what she was getting at. "We don't know what happened yet," I said noncommittally, and stepped back.

Her eyes shot to Angie, and her eyebrows rose. "What are you doing here?" Lucy's unusual bluntness spoke to her state of mind.

Angie looked uncomfortable. At Lucy's question, all eyes in the room had gone to the woman Croft had asked to leave the premises.

Croft himself looked livid, his face dangerously red. "Well?" he demanded. "I'd like to know that, too."

Angie Kissel held up her palms. "I only wanted to talk to Dr. Dana."

Silence greeted Angie's statement, stretching into

several seconds before being cut by the sound of approaching sirens.

Lucy whispered in my ear. "I'll be right back."

My surprise turned to understanding as she headed toward the restroom. Then it turned back to surprise as I saw her veer toward the back room, where Ben was keeping an eye on the body.

But Croft was already hurrying to open the front door for a bevy of uniforms, and no one else was paying attention.

What is my dear aunt up to? I wondered.

"I came back to talk to her," Angie was saying again, this time to Detective Peter Quinn. "She needed to understand the kind of damage she could cause when she gave terrible advice to people who respected and trusted her. Heaven knows how many relationships she sabotaged. But I never would have . . ." She trailed off.

Quinn quirked an eyebrow but didn't look up from the old-school notebook he was writing in. I'd met him for the first time shortly after moving to Savannah. He'd tried to pin the murder of a horrible old lady on Uncle Ben, and no way could I sit still for that. Over the last year and a half the detective's hair had become significantly more salt than pepper. If anything, it made him even more debonair. He always dressed well, and tonight he wore a suit that matched his gray eyes, and a crisp white shirt. His shoes gleamed with fresh polish.

Soon after he'd arrived, Lucy had strolled casually from the back of the store, Ben close behind her. Quinn had talked to Ben and Margie so far, which hadn't taken long but had certainly turned his attention on Angie. Now he was interviewing her, while I sat unobtrusively on a stool behind the Fox and Hound checkout counter.

Perhaps I moved and drew the detective's attention, or perhaps he'd known all along that I was sitting there, but he looked up and snagged my gaze. When he'd first walked into the bookstore and gave me the evil eye, I'd been a little worried. After all, this wasn't the first—or even the second—time he'd answered a homicide call to find me nearby. We'd butted heads a few times, yet I'd also helped him clear some cases. The result was a tenuous friendship built on conflict, mutual respect, and the occasional bribe of a Honeybee pastry.

Now a ghost of a smile passed across his face, and he shook his head ruefully. That was much better than a scowl and an eye roll.

"Katie, why don't you wait over there?" He tipped his head toward the cluster of chairs.

I balked for a second but knew it was useless. As I slid off the stool and started toward where Lucy and Ben sat huddled with Margie, I heard Quinn ask Angie about her previous interactions with Dr. Dana.

Declan had gone out front to talk with some of his co-workers, who were wrapping things up from the perspective of the fire department. Ben's 911 call had brought out a ladder truck and an ambulance, just in case. However, the body would be transported to the morgue in a county van, and a pot of beef stew was waiting for the firefighters back at the station. In the meantime, Nate Dobbs had requested to see his wife, and two officers had led him to the back room. Phoebe went with him but returned after only a few minutes. Now she stood looking out the window like she'd been hit with a stun gun. The expression on her face brought a lump to my own throat as I turned toward my neighbor.

I sat down next to Margie and put my arm around her shoulders. "How are you doing, hon?"

She looked at me with a bewildered expression, but she nodded and gave me a little smile. "I feel better. That boyfriend of yours is good at his job."

Warmth flooded through my chest. "He sure is. I'm glad you're feeling more yourself. Have you talked to Redding?"

"Uh-huh. He wanted to come downtown, but I told him to stay home. It's too late to call our regular babysitter, and his mother lives out toward Pooler. I'll be able to leave soon, won't I?"

"I sure hope so," I said, eyeing the slight tremble in her hands. "Maybe I should give you a ride home."

I thought she'd pooh-pooh the notion, but instead she nodded in relief. "That would be great."

My heart ached for her. My neighbor hardly ever got away from her family to do something just for her, and now this had happened. I gave her another squeeze.

"Are they going to arrest that horrible woman?" she asked.

I glanced over to where Quinn seemed to be finishing up with Angie. "I don't know. Did you see her doing something suspicious?"

Her lips turned down in a thoughtful frown. "Like what? She was right there, kneeling over the poor thing when I walked in. But she wasn't supposed to be here, not after Croft told her to leave. She was so *mean*. You could tell she really hated Dr. Dana."

"Katie, may I speak with you a moment?" Lucy said.

I patted Margie on the hand. "Detective Quinn will be done with us soon, okay?"

She nodded gratefully.

Lucy led me to the reading alcove in the children's section and spoke in a low voice. "Do you smell that?"

I sniffed. "The mulled cider?"

"No! Almonds."

I tried again, then shrugged. "Sorry."

She sighed. "I guessed you must not be able to. From what I've heard, not everyone can."

My brow knit. "Lucy, what on earth are you talking about?"

Her eyes softened. "I'm sorry, sweetie. I'm not being very clear. After all the ruckus in the back room, I smelled almonds. But we didn't bring any pastries made with almonds, or even almond extract. Ben said Dr. Dana may have been murdered, so I got to thinking. I went back there, and Ben let me close enough to her body to make sure. The smell was much stronger the closer I got to her." She gave me a knowing look.

"I still don't . . ." I flashed on an image of Sherlock Holmes. Yes, the Benedict Cumberbatch version, thank you very much, even if the Conan Doyle tale that came to mind was one of the old classics: *A Study in Scarlet*.

The scent of almonds, which only certain people were able to smell . . .

"Cyanide? Lucy, are you serious?"

Her grim expression showed just how serious.

Flushed face. And something about her mouth.

"No one uses cyanide anymore," I said.

A stubborn expression settled on her face. "Well, I'm going to tell Peter Quinn."

Suddenly a stuffed animal fell off the bookshelf above and bonked me softly on the head. I bent to pick it up, and my breath caught in my throat.

It was a poufy dragonfly, complete with smiling face and fat blue-and-yellow wings.

Silently, I held it out toward Lucy. Her eyes widened.

She'd been the one who'd explained to me that the drag-onfly was my totem. They'd been attracted to me my whole life—a handy thing in mosquito-y Savannah—and since I'd come into my own as a witch it had served as a kind of metaphorical tap on the shoulder when they appeared.

Pay attention.

"Dang," I said. "Coincidence?"

She gave me a look.

"Yeah, okay," I sighed. "You should definitely let Quinn know. Gosh, Lucy. That's something, you putting that together."

My aunt smiled but still looked sad as she peered around the end of a bookshelf. "He's done with that woman. I'm going to tell him now." She strode toward Quinn with a purposeful set to her shoulders.

I sidled over to where Angie Kissel now hovered alone near a display of Harry Potter books. She looked up at me with wide brown eyes, and I realized she was terrified.

Because she'd just committed murder? Or because she was innocent? I got the feeling that either way, it hadn't gone well with Detective Quinn.

Mungo had been shadowing me around the book-store, and I hadn't had the heart to ask him to sit out of the way. Now he made a noise in the back of his throat. Angie looked down at him, and her gaze softened. He had that effect on a lot of people. There was something different about her response, though. I couldn't put my finger on what.

"Are you okay?" I asked.

Her head bobbed yes, but her eyes still said she was anything but okay.

"Can I get you some cider or something?"

She shook her head.

Well, this is going nowhere.

We were silent for several long seconds, watching the hustle and bustle of uniformed men and women.

"That detective thinks I did it," she said.

My eyes cut sideways to her. "You sure didn't like her."

"No, I did not. Not a bit. But I wasn't the only one."

"From what I understand, that's true," I said.

We were quiet for a few beats. I debated what to say next. Probably my best option was to say nothing at all. It wasn't any of my business who killed Dr. Dana. I didn't know her, and I sure didn't see any connection to magic in her death. Still . . . Mungo was gazing up at me with an urgency that bordered on hunger.

And I couldn't help being curious. So I asked, "Care to tell me why you disliked her so much?"

She looked down at Mungo again. Smiled. Then she bent at the knees and ran her fingers lightly down his back.

He beamed at her, looked at me, and then returned his attention to Angie.

Well, he sure doesn't seem to think she's a murderer.

I realized then that I couldn't read Angie Kissel at all. I can occasionally get intuitive hints from people, especially if I really try. It wasn't any kind of real clairvoyance, more of a feel for who they were or their emotional state, and usually I interpreted it in terms of flavors— bitter, sweet, salty, and the like. It came in handy at the bakery when a customer needed a little enchantment in her life. But try as I might, Angie was . . . flavorless.

She gave Mungo another pat and stood, then answered my question in a low voice. "I was having problems with my husband. It was just the usual stuff couples go through, I suppose, but we'd only been married a year. I wanted it to be like it was when we first got together, all lovey-dovey and moonlight and wanting to be with each other all the time."

"The honeymoon phase," I said without thinking. *Like I know.* I glanced over at Lucy and Ben. He had his arm around her shoulders as she spoke with Peter Quinn. Those two had never known anything *but* the honeymoon phase, so maybe it didn't even exist.

Then I looked at Declan, tall and in charge yet so gentle and easy with Margie. A little thrill went through me as I watched him talking with a crime scene tech. By now I knew his many sides, and other than a tendency to be a bit of a slob, he was a flat-out gem. Would that thrill I felt fade away if we were to marry? Or even if we didn't?

Angie nodded. "There's a good reason they call it the honeymoon phase, of course. We still loved each other, don't get me wrong. There was nothing really wrong, just that all those falling-in-love chemicals were fading and life was getting back to the everyday, and while my husband was fine with all of that, I was having a hard time with it." She sighed. "I occasionally listened to Dr. Dana on the radio, and for some reason that day—it was a Tuesday, I remember—I called in. She was just starting to tout her whole Radical Trust philosophy, and she asked me if I had any secrets from my husband."

My eyebrows raised a fraction.

"I told her no."

"So what was the problem?"

Angie hesitated. She looked down at Mungo, licked her lips, and then met my eyes again. "She persisted. And there was something; something from my past. She insisted that I tell my husband whatever it was, and that honesty would bring us closer together."

Little spikes of excitement mingled with my curiosity now.

She squared her shoulders. "So that night I told my husband of a year that I used to be a practicing witch."

Chapter 5

My mouth dropped open. Angie laughed, and I saw Quinn turn his head to eye us speculatively.

"He reacted like that, too. At first. Then he got really angry. Accused me of devil worship and a bunch of other stuff. Wouldn't even listen when I tried to explain what modern witchcraft is really like."

"Sounds painful," I ventured. "Wait—you said you *used to be* a practicing witch," I said, and as I spoke I realized something else that didn't quite fit.

"I stopped," Angie said. "Before I got married. That's why I didn't think it was relevant to my marriage."

Confused, I blurted, "Why did you stop practicing?" I personally didn't know if that could be possible. After all, my own mother had turned her back on her magical heritage for decades in an attempt to keep me safe in the small town of Fillmore, Ohio, but in the long run even she had come back to what was in her blood.

Maybe Angie wasn't a hereditary witch. Maybe she had just been a dilettante, dabbling in the Craft for a little fun.

Now she looked down at the floor and shrugged. "I have my reasons."

"Angie," I said.

She looked back up, her eyes as dark as chocolate ganache.

Surprised, and a little uncomfortable, I said, "You don't know me at all. Being a former witch isn't usually the kind of thing you'd tell a stranger."

She didn't look away, but her eyes grew even wider. I pressed on. "So why did you just tell me all that?"

She blinked. "Because you're a witch."

Someplace in the background voices rose and fell, but my world had collapsed to a few square yards in the Fox and Hound children's area.

After trying twice to swallow and finally succeeding, I managed, "Why on earth would you think that?"

"Because of Mongo."

Yip! It was a small sound, a doggie whisper rather than his usual vibrant bark. Not understanding why my heart was pounding against my ribs a mile a minute, I watched him look from me to her and back at me again.

"Mongo?" I asked, feeling stupid.

She raised her eyebrows. "Is that what you call him? I called him Mongo. Pretty close. When I saw him, I knew you had to be a witch."

I stared at her, unable to speak.

"He was my familiar," she said, and as the words flowed over me, I felt something *crack*. "When I stopped practicing he ran away. I guess he found himself a new witch." Her smile wavered. "You."

I felt myself sway. Her hand flashed out to steady me. She looked over my shoulder.

"Katie?" Lucy's voice came from behind me. "Are you all right?"

Angie's hand fell away as I slowly turned to look at my aunt.

"I'm . . . I'm fine," I stammered.

She didn't look like she believed me, but she let it drop. "Peter's ready to talk with you."

"Okay." I bent, scooped Mungo up, and walked away without looking back at Angie. But I could tell my familiar was still watching her.

It didn't take long for Detective Peter Quinn to interview me. After all, this stuff was getting to be old hat for us, so I ran down what had happened in record time. But then he asked about what Angie Kissel and I had talked about, the expression on his face letting me know he was somewhat peeved we'd talked at all.

"Just this and that," I told him. It wasn't like I was going to share what she'd told me about being a witch. Not just a witch, but my little Mungo's former witch. I'd held him tightly in my arms the whole time Quinn and I talked. Bless his little canine heart, he seemed to understand and hadn't wiggled once to be let down.

"You two seemed to know each other." He'd obviously been watching us.

I shrugged. "Just met her."

"Your neighbor seems pretty sure Kissel killed the psychologist," he said.

"Well, she was kneeling over the body when Margie went in," I said. "But Lucy told you about the almond smell, right?"

He pressed his lips together.

"You can't smell it either, can you?"

A sigh, and he shook his head. "One of the techs could, though, so your aunt might be right. We'll see if it's really cyanide."

Citing my dragonfly confirmation would only make him think I was crazy. I said, "Well, it if was poison, it was something that works quickly. She didn't seem at all ill before she went into the back room. How quickly does cyanide kill?"

Quinn looked grim. "It's one of the most lethal and fast-acting poisonous substances out there."

"Well, Dr. Dana was back there by herself for fifteen minutes or so. Er, *presumably* by herself," I corrected myself. "And you have no idea how she ingested it?"

"Not—" He stopped himself with a grimace. "Listen, Lightfoot. I know you fancy yourself an investigator, but unless you have something to add to the information I have right now, we're done."

"Hmm." I thought for a moment. "I'm still kind of reeling from the whole thing."

He glanced up at me. "Of course. I sometimes forget you don't run into this kind of thing as often as I do."

I held up a finger. "Hang on." I told him about the mix-up regarding the bottled water and how the one Croft had mistakenly provided had been open for at least an hour by the time the author arrived. "Her little entourage brought along her favorite brand, though." I gestured subtly toward the victim's sister and husband. "That's what I saw her drink. Of course, it's possible she sipped from the pre-opened bottle at some point, even after she was such a prima donna about the whole thing. I didn't see her do it, but I wasn't watching her all the time."

He nodded. "Someone else mentioned that. Don't worry. We're sending all the containers to the lab. Did you see anyone touch either of the water bottles?"

"Just Nate and Phoebe and Dana herself. And presumably Croft opened the one that sat behind the podium until they got here." I snapped my fingers. "And she had a cup of peach sweet tea by her when she was signing books for people." I left out that Ben had been the one who'd brought it to her. Quinn had already accused my uncle of murder once, and I wasn't going to invite him to do it again. "I don't know if she drank any of it or not, though."

"Okay. Did Ben tell you I'm sending all your leftover pastries to the lab, too?"

"What?" Dread stabbed through me.

Quinn frowned. "If the victim was poisoned, it makes sense to test everything she might have consumed."

"Yes. Yes, of course. But you don't think anyone at the Honeybee had anything to do with her death, do you?"

He suppressed a smile. "I'm fairly sure you didn't off the radio psychologist, Katie. But a nice scone would be a perfect delivery vehicle for poison—don't you think?"

I grimaced. "Well, I didn't see her eat a thing while she was here."

"We have to check."

"I know." The thought that someone might have used one of our goodies to commit murder made me downright angry. It didn't help that someone had done something similar once before.

Quinn stood. "I'm sending everyone home now. I'll let you know if I have any more questions."

Relieved, I went to grab my stuff. An exhausted Croft Barrow started shutting off lights. I heard Nate offer to take Phoebe home, and she nodded. She looked as if she'd aged ten years in the course of the evening. Angie Kissel left, and Ben went to get the car. Margie was still pretty shaky, and more than ready to go home to her family.

"If you want to get a little air, I'll be right out," I told her as I shrugged into my jacket. "I just want to check in with Deck."

"Okay," she said, and I heard her relief at getting out of the bookstore. I hoped it wouldn't stop her from bringing her kids in for story time in the future.

Declan came toward me carrying an empty plastic bin. "Lucy told me to grab some of the leftovers from next door since the police took everything from the signing. We don't want to disappoint the folks down at the shelter."

"Good idea. Trust her to think of it. You want some help?"

He held up a key. "Nah. I borrowed this from Ben. You get Margie home, and when I'm done at the shelter, I'll be over. Okay?"

"More than okay."

He smiled, then gestured at my neighbor standing out on the sidewalk. "She's better?"

"Seems to be."

"What about you? You've seen so many dead bodies at this point—"

"Hey!"

"—that I kind of assume you're fine," he finished. "Are you?"

"Sure."

His eyes narrowed. "Really? You seem . . . something."

I hesitated. "I got some weird news this evening."

"In the middle of all this?"

Putting my hand on his arm and giving it a squeeze, I smiled with my eyes. "Don't worry. I'll tell you all about it when we get home."

He nodded his agreement and, with one last look over his shoulder, went out.

Lucy bustled up to me, a surprising twinkle in her eye. "Don't you worry, Katie. The spellbook club will meet at the Honeybee tomorrow afternoon after we close. I've already called the others."

"Luce," I said. "I don't think—"

"Now, don't argue," she said. "You know we need to talk about what to do about this latest murder, and the sooner the better."

"I'm sure Quinn can handle this one," I said, but I didn't even manage to convince myself. After all, having the primary murder suspect be Mungo's ex-witch lent a paranormal element to Dr. Dana's death. Or did it? After all, Angie wasn't even a witch anymore. Still, if she was innocent, she might need my help.

If she was innocent. And whether I wanted to give her that help? That was yet another matter.

"Pffft." Lucy broke in to my thoughts. "You always say that. You're a catalyst *and* a lightwitch, and if you're here, there must be a good reason. When this kind of thing has happened before, there was usually magic involved. You know Peter Quinn can't—or won't—pay attention to that aspect of his cases."

"But—," I said.

"Bye, honey! See you bright and early." And she was out the door.

As I turned onto Abercorn Street, I glanced over at Margie. She sat in the passenger seat of my Volkswagen and stared straight ahead without blinking.

That morning I'd placed a tiny bouquet of basil and lavender in the Bug's narrow bud vase. It was a combination I often used because of the two herbs' many magical associations. Basil was a standard for protection, but tonight I was glad it also dispelled confusion and calmed fear. Margie and I could both use some of that. Lavender, which grew here and there throughout my gardens at home, also afforded protection, as well as healing and peace. Steering around Lafayette Square, I casually reached out and adjusted the herbs in the vase, squeezing them enough with my fingertips to release their combined aroma into the air.

"Do you want to let Redding know we're on our way?" I asked.

"I called him when I was waiting for you."

She looked down at the books in her lap. Dr. Dana's face was on the cover of both of them, her retro look the same on both volumes. I wondered whether the rather outdated advice she'd provided stemmed from a fifties sensibility as well.

"You don't think she did it, do you?" Margie asked out of the blue.

"I assume you mean Angie Kissel? I have no idea."

Mungo made a noise in the backseat. I ignored him.

She turned in her seat. "I saw you talking with her. It seemed pretty intense."

Not for the first time I fervently wished my discussion with the former witch hadn't been so public. Everyone seemed to think we were buddy-buddy now.

"You're going to try to prove she's innocent." Margie couldn't keep the disgust out of her voice.

"Now, why would you think that?" I asked.

Movement in the rearview mirror drew my attention. Mungo had apparently decided not to stay in my tote bag as usual. Instead, he leaned on the back of my seat with his front paws and bored a hole in the back of my head with his eyes.

"Mungo, will you please sit down back there?"

He blew hot breath in my ear but did as I asked.

Margie said, "Oh, you don't talk about it much, at least

not to me, but I know you've been involved in murder cases before. I've seen that Detective Quinn at your house a bunch of times. And then there was all that business about voodoo and Mother Eulora a few months ago."

"They don't even know for sure that Dr. Dana was murdered," I hedged.

She made a rude noise. "Your own boyfriend said it was a crime scene."

"*Possible* crime scene."

"Whatever. She was too young for it to be a heart attack or something like that. And she was a health nut, too. Talked about it all the time on the radio."

"Talking isn't the same as walking." I turned toward our neighborhood in Midtown, already thinking about a plate of pasta and a salad.

From the corner of my eye, I saw Margie roll her eyes.

"Okay, it was probably murder," I said. "More than probably, in fact. Poison. And Ms. Kissel definitely had a problem with Dr. Dana."

"I'll say," Margie muttered.

Yet Angie's dislike of the psychologist didn't necessarily translate to a murder motive. "That other gentleman who was there tonight didn't like her, either," I said. "He confronted Dr. Dana in front of everyone, too."

"He left and didn't come back, though."

"Maybe. But we can't know that for sure. And he's not the only one. That back door to the alley was open. Anyone could have come in that way."

In fact, Nate and Phoebe had gone out to move Dr. Dana's car closer. Together. Could they have conspired to kill her? From what I'd seen, Phoebe didn't much care for her brother-in-law. Besides, if one of them had dosed the water bottle, he or she wouldn't have had to come in from the alley anyway, which made their absence from the bookstore at the time Dr. Dana died completely moot.

I shook my head, feeling confused.

Margie pressed her lips together and blinked slowly. "I guess you're right about the alley door." She didn't sound convinced, though.

However, I wasn't trying to convince her. I was only playing devil's advocate, right? For all I knew Angie Kissel had indeed murdered Dr. Dana.

But the former witch's voice echoed in my mind. *I didn't kill anyone.*

I pulled into my driveway. It ran between my little carriage house and the Coopersmiths' far larger home. Margie got out at the same time that her front door opened, and Redding's substantial figure filled the frame. I let Mungo scramble down to the asphalt and grabbed my tote bag from the backseat. Margie's husband came down the steps, backlit from inside. He had Baby Bart on one hip and a glass of Margie's favorite pink wine in his other hand.

Now, *that* was a good husband.

I gave Margie a big hug. "Detective Quinn will figure it all out."

She stepped back. "Or you will. After all, if that Kissel woman didn't kill Dr. Dana, then I certainly don't want her to go to jail." Her expression hardened. "I still think she did it, though. And whatever happens now? Well, that's not going to bring back Dr. Dana, now, is it?"

I shook my head sadly.

Redding ambled across their lawn and handed his wife the wine. She took a gulp before tipping her face up for a kiss.

"Thanks, hon."

"Lordy, sweet pea. What'd you get yourself into?" he asked.

Bart blinked up at his mother with wet eyes, then down at Mungo. His face brightened. "Puppy!"

"Oh, golly. It was awful," Margie said. Then her mom instincts kicked in, and everything else fell away. "Why's the little one up?" She handed me the wine and the books and reached for her son. Redding handed him over, and I handed the wine and books to him. He did a double take when he saw the titles.

"What's this nonsense?" he asked. "I thought she was a talk show host."

Margie's face crumpled at the mention of Dr. Dana. "She was. On the radio." Then she gathered herself and looked back at Bart. "Wha's a matter, baby?"

"Mamamamamama," he intoned in a sleepy voice and laid his head on her shoulder.

"Just fussy," Redding said. "Doesn't seem to be sick or anything. Misses you, I expect."

"Oh, go on with you. He's probably getting a tooth." She started to walk away, then stopped and called over her shoulder. "Thanks for the ride home, Katie."

"Yeah, we appreciate it," Redding echoed, and then I heard him ask his wife if she was really all right.

I didn't hear her response, but being with her family seemed to be the best medicine for Margie.

"Come on, little guy," I said to Mungo.

Chapter 6

Mungo trotted across the grass to the tiny porch of the carriage house. I'd found it while helping Lucy and Ben get ready to open the Honeybee and had jumped at the chance to live in such a cute place. It had once been part of a large estate, all the rest of which was long gone and the land subdivided for residential homes. My lot was the same size as those on either side, but because my house was so small that meant both my front and back yards were expansive.

Good thing, too, because a significant part of hedge-witchery takes place in the garden as well as the kitchen.

Trailing my fingers along the wrought-iron railing of the porch, I inhaled the night smells of sweet Daphne and the mustiness of fallen leaves beginning to rot. At a little after nine, the temperature had dipped a few degrees below sixty. The air was soft with cool humidity. The magnolia by the corner of the house cast crazy shadows in the moonlight as I unlocked the door and reached inside to flip the light switch.

The living room bloomed into view: peach walls, worn wooden planks beneath my feet, built-in bookshelves to the right, and beyond that the short hallway that led to the bedroom and bathroom. Straight ahead, my vintage purple fainting couch backed against the far wall. To the left of it, French doors opened out to the small covered patio and extensive gardens beyond. Narrow stairs led to the loft above, where a futon served as guest quarters and a drop-lid secretary's desk kept my altar tidy—and hidden from general view.

I loved coming home to this place. Even though Declan spent a lot of his time here, it was mine, bought and paid for with the money I'd so carefully saved for the house my fiancé and I had planned to move into after our marriage. But shortly before our wedding day, Andrew had gotten cold feet and called everything off.

Very shortly before.

His fear of commitment had been the best thing that had ever happened to me. Sure, there was rejection, heartbreak, and anger. But in the end I'd moved to Savannah, which I absolutely loved, opened my dream business, and bought this adorable house—not to mention discovering my true witchy nature and finally understanding why I'd always felt so different from everyone else. And if it hadn't been for Andrew canceling our wedding, I'd never have met Declan, and I wouldn't have the amazing group of friends I had now.

I wasn't usually one to think that absolutely everything happens for a reason. However, many things seem to, and when it came to getting married versus moving to Savannah, the trade had been worth all of the pain of the journey.

Mungo barked, bringing me back from my wandering thoughts. He ran to the kitchen and looked back at me expectantly.

"Okay, okay. I'll get the pasta going." I tossed my tote on one of the two wingbacks that sat across from the purple couch and turned back to close the wooden shutters over the front windows.

In no time a pot of salted water was heating on the stove, and I'd laid out asparagus, lemon, garlic, tarragon, and mustard for an easy sauce. I'd make a quick salad after Declan got there, but first I wanted to have a little chat.

With my dog.

"Come in here, Mungo."

He made a noise in the back of his throat and looked at his place mat in the corner of the kitchen.

"You can eat later. With us." I turned and walked into the living room and sat down on the couch. A few minutes later he followed, only once glancing back at the kitchen and its treasure trove of people food.

I patted the seat beside me. He jumped up and put his front paws on my lap, his brown eyes now riveted on mine.

"That Angie woman told me you used to be her familiar."

He licked my chin.

"Is that true?"

Yip!

"And . . . you ran away?"

Yip!

I slumped against the sloping back of the couch. My day had started at four thirty a.m. I'd baked and served customers and then baked some more. I'd set up for a book signing and witnessed bad behavior on many fronts, and once again a dead body had turned up on my watch. But here I was in my living room, having a rather emotional talk with my canine companion, and my stomach was tied in worse knots than I'd felt all day.

Apparently, meeting your familiar's . . . ex trumped murder on the anxiety scale.

Mungo's forehead scrunched, and he climbed all the

way onto my lap. He dipped his head and pushed it into my hand. I stroked his soft ears, and he looked up at me from beneath his doggy eyebrows with such sweetness that my heart melted.

"And you picked me," I whispered.

He grinned. *Yip.*

"Is your real name supposed to be Mongo?" I asked around the lump in my throat.

He sneezed and shook his head vigorously.

"So it's really Mungo?"

Yip!

I didn't know how that was supposed to work, but I was willing to go with it.

Taking a deep breath, I said, "I got the feeling tonight at the bookstore that you still, um, like Angie."

He blinked, as if surprised that I'd even ask that question. *Of course he does.*

"She's a murder suspect, you know."

His lips pulled back to expose his teeth in a fierce look. I knew it wasn't directed at me. Then he dropped the snarl and gave me a look I knew well.

I want something, and I want it now. Right now. I need it now.

Usually that look was about peanut butter or sausage gravy or carrot cake. But this time I knew it was about something else.

"You want me to help her."

Yip!

I kept the expletive that came to mind to myself.

Little mind reader that he was, Mungo frowned at me anyway.

Suddenly the little dog's ears perked up, and he shot off the couch, skittering across the wooden planks to meet Declan as he came through the door.

"Hey!" he greeted the wee beast wiggling at his feet, and reached down to pet him. "Settle down, son. You're acting like you haven't see me all day." He straightened and regarded me. "You look like you could use some TLC."

I got off the couch and met him halfway across the room. Folding into his arms, I muttered, "I look that bad, huh."

"Nah. You're always gorgeous. But I'm right, aren't I?"

I nodded into his shoulder, inhaling the smell of the dryer sheets they used at the firehouse and relishing his solid muscles as my form melted into his. My hand moved up to run through his dark curls.

"Water should be ready for the pasta," I murmured.

He laughed. "I'll cook."

"That's not fair. You cooked breakfast."

"You cooked all day."

We separated and headed toward the kitchen, Mungo practically dancing now that supper would be arriving in his bowl soon.

"I'll make the salad," I said. "I harvested a few things from the garden yesterday."

"Deal."

Declan chopped asparagus and sautéed it in butter and olive oil with minced garlic. I rinsed baby spinach and sliced a yellow tomato, scallions, and baby carrots. He zested a lemon and tossed that in the pan, along with lemon juice, mustard, and a bit of cream. I added an avocado to the salad, along with a handful of walnuts and a few sprinkles of blue cheese, then dressed it with a quick vinaigrette of olive oil and vinegar cut with a drizzle of honey, salt, and lots of black pepper. Within fifteen minutes we were taking plates of pasta and salad out to the patio table. Declan carried Mungo's dish—no salad for him, just a few sliced carrots—and a bottle of wine under his arm, while I grabbed the wineglasses. He turned the radio in the corner to an oldies station, and soon we were tucking into our repast.

"I hadn't realized how hungry I was," I said after plowing through half my meal.

"Sure hits the spot." He sat back with a satisfied sigh and took a sip of wine. Eyed me speculatively. "So Ben told me that Lucy thinks Dr. Dana was poisoned with cyanide."

"Honey, we're eating."

He shrugged. "I was just wondering."

"She said she smelled something like almonds, and she told Quinn." I paused.

His eyes narrowed. "And?"

I sighed. "And a stuffed dragonfly fell on my head right after she told me."

One corner of his mouth turned up. "Ah. I see."

He took a bite of tomato from the salad and chewed slowly. "Hmm."

"What?" I asked.

"I'm just wondering if Dr. Dana was some kind of a witch. She sure seemed to have some of her fans under her spell."

"Declan! That wouldn't be ethical."

"Well, duh. But neither is stalking your partner. *Radical Trust*." He started to blow a raspberry but stopped himself. "Sorry. Respect for the dead and all. But isn't there usually some kind of magical aspect to these, er, situations you get caught up in?"

Situations. That was one way to put it.

"I don't think Dr. Dana had any connection to the Craft," I fudged, not quite able to bring myself to talk about Angie's link to Mungo. "But you never know."

"Yet you're still involved."

"Who said I'm involved?"

He looked skyward. "Oh, let's see. You were there when someone was killed . . ."

"Deck—"

". . . again. And given how that's worked out in the past, I'm pretty sure you'll be up to your neck in suspects and magic in no time."

I put down my fork. "Hey, I know you don't like it when I get involved with this kind of thing, but I can't help it if I'm a lightwitch. Just like you can't help, well, you know."

His look sharpened.

My jaw set. If he was going to be like that . . . "Connell. You can't help the spirit of your leprechaun great-great-whatever-uncle from borrowing your body every once in a while." So there. And Lord knew, it was disconcerting when it happened.

He sat back and crossed his arms. "For the record, when is the last time that happened?" he asked.

"It's been a while," I admitted.

"It's been months, and you know it. I told you after the last time it happened that I confronted him. I explained how much the prospect of waking up next to him instead of me upset you, and he agreed to keep to himself." He uncrossed his arms and leaned forward. "Didn't you believe me?"

"It's not that . . ." I trailed off.

"What, then? Connell might be a strange character, but he gets it. He likes you. A lot."

That was what I was afraid of . . .

"Does he still watch over you, though?" I asked.

A rueful look descended on Declan's features. "No way he'll stop that. But it's kind of nice, you know. To have met your guardian angel, in a way."

I was quiet for a long moment. "I'm sorry. It was nice of you to do that for me."

"I did it for me, too. The point is, I know the lightwitch thing is part of who you are. An important part."

Shaking my head, I said, "Not necessarily. One of the lessons I've learned about being a lightwitch is that I have a choice." I smiled. "Maybe I'll just choose not to jump into the middle of things this time."

Mungo bounded to his feet and glared at me.

Declan followed my gaze. "What was the deal with him tonight? He seemed to have some kind of problem with that woman. The one who found the psychologist." His eyes widened. "The one who Margie accused of killing her. He's a smart pup. Do you think he knew what she planned ahead of time?"

I bit my lip. Could that be true? But my Mungo, *my* familiar, would have alerted me if he'd known a murder was about to take place. Then again, how would he know, even if Angie used to belong to him? He was, as Declan said, "a clever pup," and I sometimes joked that he was a mind reader, but he couldn't actually . . . could he?

I looked over and saw him blink at me from the shadows.

"Earth calling Katie," Declan said.

I rubbed my hand over my face and met his eye. "Angie Kissel was Mungo's former owner."

My boyfriend looked nonplussed. "Oh. Well, I didn't expect that. Is that the weird news you mentioned at the bookstore tonight?"

Bless his heart. Declan might occasionally channel his not-quite-dead ancestor, but he didn't practice magic and didn't have a familiar. So he didn't make the connection.

"He was her familiar," I said. As I heard the words,

a pang shot through me. With horror, I identified it as jealousy.

That was what I'd been feeling ever since Angie had told me about Mungo. Mongo. Whatever.

Jealousy.

It was an awful feeling. I'd never felt it over a man, including Andrew, probably because he hadn't taken up with his new girlfriend until after I'd moved to Savannah.

And, I realized, it was clouding my judgment about whether to help Angie or not.

Declan was watching me with a wary expression. "So she's a witch. And she just showed up out of the woodwork, publicly denounced the good doctor at her book signing, and then Dr. Dana is murdered." He whistled. "Well, I guess that explains the magical element."

"Former witch," I muttered.

"What?"

"She doesn't practice anymore. That's why Mungo left her." I shoved aside my plate, suddenly not hungry anymore. "Can we change the subject?"

He blinked. "Sure. But I just want you to know I'm on your side. I admire your abilities, and all that magic stuff you do." He grinned. "Even if you did almost kill me."

My mouth dropped open. He'd never brought that up, not once, since it happened. And now he was teasing me about it?

I stood and said airily, "Only the one time, dear." And then I gave him my own mischievous grin. "So far."

His laugh was tinged with a tad of uncertainty.

"Oh, please." I ruffled his hair. "Like you have to worry about me doing you any harm."

Still, his smile in response seemed the tiniest bit strained.

Chapter 7

After dinner, we'd started watching *Tremors* for the ump-teenth time to let the day wind away. Declan had dropped off in the middle of the movie, but it had taken me a long time to get to sleep. The events at the Fox and Hound kept rolling over and over in my mind. It also didn't help that I could sense Mungo staring at me in the dark.

My entire life I'd had a kind of sleep disorder that kept me from sleeping more than an hour or two most nights. It didn't affect my energy level, and it wasn't a bad thing for a baker who had to hit the ovens at o'dark thirty most mornings. So Sunday morning I woke up bright-eyed and ready to go, but Declan was still snoring through his requisite seven hours at four a.m. I'd quietly showered and dressed, bundled Mungo into my tote bag, and sneaked out in the cool of the predawn morning.

Two and a half hours later, Iris Grant and I were fin-ishing up the cream cheese frosting on a batch of pump-kin spice cookies in the Honeybee kitchen as the sun began to glint off east-facing car windows out on Brough-ton Street. Ben was off playing his weekly round of golf, so it was Lucy who opened the blinds and tidied the poufy chairs and sofa that were arranged around the coffee

table in the reading area. Light jazz came on the stereo
system, right before my aunt opened up the front door at
seven. A couple of weekend regulars were waiting outside
for their Honeybee fix, and a few moments later I heard
my aunt revving up the espresso machine.

"Katie?" she called.

I looked up and saw a customer at the register. I
stripped off my plastic gloves as I hurried out from the
open kitchen to ring up one of the daily specials: a delicate miniquiche packed with onions caramelized in
balsamic vinegar and flecked with fresh thyme. I'd
already set one aside for my own breakfast.

Once the customer had gone, I grabbed a cup of drip
and leaned my hip against the counter to drink it. Lucy
had returned to the reading area and was rearranging
books on the shelves. The volumes were roughly orga-
nized by subject, but the reason to it varied on who was
doing the organizing. There was fiction and nonfiction,
a fair amount of self-help, poetry, and inspirational
fodder, as well as the occasional magazine. Regardless
of the contents, most of our selection had been chosen
by the ladies of the spellbook club, each witch somehow
knowing that a particular book might help a Honeybee
customer. A few had even helped me, though not always
in the way one might think a book helpful. Other books
had been supplied by Honeybee customers who wanted
to share what they'd been reading. I'd wondered at first
whether Croft would view a super-informal lending
library like ours, right next to his bookstore, as compe-
tition. He'd taken one look at the eclectic contents and
assured me with a small laugh that there was no overlap.

The amber walls around me reached to high ceilings.
Fans suspended from the dark beams kept the air moving. The single burnt orange wall behind the register held

the tall blackboard where we listed the rotating menu items. I loved the color combination with the blue-and-chrome tables and the shiny kitchen mostly open to public view so patrons could see us making the pastries they loved.

Of course, that open design also meant any hedge-witchery had to be performed with discretion.

I returned to where Iris bent her head over a cookie, pastry bag in hand. The tip of her tongue protruded from the corner of her mouth in concentration. I smiled at her earnestness. We'd hired her a few months before, a Goth girl with spiked black hair, black clothes, and black fingernail polish. Or so we thought. Since then she'd gone natural with her makeup and grown her hair out enough to form a stubby ponytail for work. The month before, she'd dyed it flamingo pink in honor of National Breast Cancer Awareness.

She inhaled deeply and a grin broke across her face. "Mmm. The allspice is so intense, but I can still detect the milder taste of ginger, too."

"Remember that allspice is uplifting and healing," I said.

The first time I'd met Iris I'd known she had power, and it hadn't been long after she came to work for us that Lucy and I revealed the special elements we added to our baked goods. She'd asked us to train her in kitchen magic, and, delighted that the universe had sent her to us, we'd happily complied.

Now she nodded. "And ginger speeds and intensifies any spell. Do you have an incantation?"

I shook my head. "Not yet. Why don't you make one up?" In truth, Lucy and I didn't use incantations all the time, instead simply directing our intention into the food as we mixed and formed and baked, with the knowledge that we were triggering and intensifying the natural magical elements of the herbs. It couldn't hurt, though, and Iris needed the practice.

Her eyes lit up. "Just . . . make one up? Really?" She did a little two-step. "What should I say? I mean, I've noticed sometimes yours and Lucy's rhyme, and sometimes not."

"It doesn't really matter how you say it, or even the specific words you use, as long as you get your point across. Spells focus intention, and the verbal aspect of them simply narrows that focus to intensify their power. Your power."

She pointed her finger at me. "Right. Okay, let me think about it."

I nodded with a smile. "Okeydoke. But do it quietly—and don't take too long. I bet customers are going to snarf up those cookies with their morning coffee."

The phone rang, and I grabbed it off the wall behind the register. "Honeybee Bakery."

"Katie? Quinn. I tried your cell."

"I forgot it in the back," I said, scooting through to the office and shutting the door for a little privacy. Mungo was snoozing on the club chair where he reigned most days. "You're up early."

"Never made it home."

"Ouch." And yet I knew he'd look fresh and cool, no doubt in one of the starched shirts he kept at the office. "Dr. Dana?"

"Yes, though there's only so much I can do during the night on that. There's another case I'm working, too. One where you *weren't* on-site when it happened."

"It's not like I try to find dead bodies, Quinn. What's the other case?"

He sighed. "Katie, honestly. Over time I've learned

that when you're mixed up in one of my cases, as much as I dislike a civilian sticking her nose into things, I'm probably going to clear it. But that doesn't mean you need to know details about all the homicides in Savannah."

"Well, gosh. I was just wondering."

A few seconds of silence. "Sorry. I'm just tired. The other death is pretty cut-and-dried, clear motive and opportunity. Still takes a while to dot my i's and cross my t's."

"Pulling an all-nighter is no fun." And Quinn, vital and suave as he appeared, was no youngster, either. He also insisted on working alone ever since his erstwhile partner, Franklin Taite, had gone out of the picture. "So . . . why are you calling? Are you dotting i's and crossing t's on the Dr. Dana case, too?" Meaning: Had he already arrested Angie?

Mungo leaned forward as if trying to hear Quinn on the other end of the line.

"I wish," he said. "We have our suspect, though, so I hope to be able to wrap up things soon—and without your help. I called to let you know that your aunt was right about the cyanide."

I sank onto the desk chair. "Ugh." I hadn't necessarily liked Dr. Dana, or how she treated people, but she sure hadn't deserved to die like that.

But would Angie Kissel agree? I wondered whether she still believed in the Rule of Three from the Wiccan Rede since she no longer considered herself a witch. The Rule basically held that anything you do comes back to you threefold—good or bad. I thought of it as the Golden Rule on steroids.

"Not that cyanide is readily available," Quinn went on. "It's pretty hard for the average Joe to access anymore. Highly regulated."

"So there's no chance it was an accident."

"Zero. It had to be deliberate. There were no traces of poison in either of the water bottles we confiscated, nor in the full, unopened one provided by the sister."

"Really?" I had been thinking all along that someone had dosed one or the other of them. Then I remembered the other alternative. "What about the food items from the Honeybee?"

"Not there, either. That's the other reason I called."

Kind of buried the lede, didn't you?

Still, I took a deep, relieved breath. "Thank heavens for that. So how . . . ?"

"That cup of sweet tea. Did you see her take it to the back of the store with her?"

I shook my head, then realized he couldn't see me. "There was a lot going on right then. I didn't notice."

"The empty was on the floor, and the lab confirms traces of cyanide. The medical examiner will let me know more about stomach contents later today."

Eww.

He said, "But she had to have drunk it after she went to sign the extra books. So the drink was either dosed with the poison before she went in the back, and she hadn't sampled it yet, or someone came in and put the cyanide in the drink after she was already back there."

"You said there's a suspect. But really there must be plenty of suspects. I mean, lots of people disliked Dr. Dana," I said.

"Yet only Ms. Kissel made it her business to try to ruin Ms. Dobbs," he said. "It wasn't the first time she'd confronted the victim in public. The sister, Phoebe Miller, called the precinct when Kissel showed up last night."

Thinking back, I had seen her talking on her cell right about then. "She called the cops on Angie?"

In the pause that followed I realized I'd made it sound like Angie and I were best buddies.

"There was no actual threat made, so Ms. Miller was told she could come in and file a report today." He cleared his throat, and when he spoke again his tone was firm. "Katie, Angie Kissel had clear motive and obvious opportunity. I just have to figure out how she got the cyanide."

"And how she convinced a woman who loathed her to let her close enough to poison her sweet tea," I said.

He was silent.

"Are you looking at anyone else? Remember the man I told you about who also heckled Dr. Dana?" The one who liked the jalapeño corn pones so much.

"He left well before the victim went in back—"

"Detective Quinn! First off, Ben gave . . . Dr. Dana had the sweet tea beside her the whole time she was signing. People were walking by and milling around, and she was distracted by her adoring fans. Plus, anyone could have come in from the alley before Angie came in and found the body. Including that guy. Do you even know his name?"

Quinn sighed. "No. If he bought something, we'll get around to questioning him. Croft gave us a list."

"His wife is named Sophie," I offered. "And what about Dr. Dana's husband and sister? They weren't in the bookstore when she apparently took the poison. One or both of them could have sneaked around back—"

"Now, come on, Katie. I'm not an idiot. I checked on their story about moving the car closer so Dana Dobbs wouldn't have to walk three blocks after the signing. The timing is right, and several patrons who were sitting in the front window of the Chive Restaurant saw them get in the car and go back toward the bookstore." He paused. "I thought you said you didn't know Kissel."

"I don't."

"So what's your stake? You have no reason to fight the obvious like this. You might have been helpful before—somewhat helpful," he quickly corrected himself. "But now you're just being contrary. I'm disappointed in you, Katie."

"Quinn, you're not—"

"Seriously. This is one you can leave to the professionals. Good-bye, Katie."

Mungo tipped his head and looked at me with worried eyes.

"Well, heck." I thumbed off the phone. "Little guy, maybe Angie did do it."

His forehead wrinkled.

"I know, I know. But there is a lot of evidence." I frowned. "But there was against Uncle Ben, too, and we all *knew* he didn't kill Mavis Templeton. Is that how you feel about Angie?"

He responded with a quiet but intense *Yip!*

I made a decision. "Okay, then." I softly stroked his ears. "I'll do what I can."

When I returned to the kitchen, Iris whirled around from where she was unloading the dishwasher.

"Holy cow, Katie! Lucy just told me about what happened last night in the Fox and Hound. You didn't say a word about it earlier."

"Sorry. We were pretty busy . . ."

She waved her hand. "Never mind that! She said you were back there talking to a *detective*?"

I nodded. "Detective Quinn. You remember me telling you about him last August."

"Of course! Are you going to solve the murder like you did then?"

Lucy made her way back from the register. "There are customers out there, and they can hear you, Iris."

"Oops! Sorry," she stage-whispered.

"Katie, what did Peter have to say?" my aunt asked in a low tone.

"Well, you were right about the cyanide."

Iris' eyes widened.

"And our pastries were all untainted," I said. "So were the water bottles. Someone put it in the sweet tea Ben gave her, and Quinn is sure as anything that Angie Kissel did it."

Lucy looked thoughtful. "Hmm. She was pretty obnoxious at the signing, and then she came back." Her eyes cut toward our helper. "But we can talk about all that later this afternoon. After we close." She didn't refer to the spellbook club, but she'd already told me that everyone would be there by one o'clock.

Iris' face fell.

One of our regulars came in for her weekly loaf of sourdough bread, and I went to help her.

"Hello, Mrs. Standish," I greeted her. "One loaf or two?"

Edna Standish had been one of the Honeybee's very first customers and continued to support us on an almost-daily basis. A tall and broad-shouldered woman, she wore wide-legged woolen trousers in soft gray and a silken tunic covered with depictions of sailing ships. Her precise gray curls were covered with a pink scarf that wound twice around her neck and then tied at her throat.

"Katie Lightfoot!" she said in her loud and nasal voice. "How are you this fine day?" She leaned forward and put her finger alongside her nose. "Though it certainly isn't a fine day for Savannah's most famous radio show host, is it?"

I absolutely adored this woman, but she was the biggest gossip imaginable.

"So you heard," I said.

"Oh, Lord, child. *Everyone's* heard. It's all over the papers this morning—though I did manage to hear about it before then." She gave me a conspiratorial grin. "I do declare, my dear. There is so much excitement that happens in this little block of Broughton Street, and you always seem to be in the middle of it."

"Mmm," I said without enthusiasm.

"Well, I must tell you, though of course I shouldn't, that I am just the teensiest bit jealous. *Not*, of course, that I want anyone to die. Heavens no! *But*, since there are so many murders in this neighborhood, it does seem like at least once I would be nearby."

I blinked, not knowing how to respond to that.

"Anyway, is there any news regarding who did the horrible deed?"

"Not really," I said. No need to feed the beast.

"Well, I'm afraid I simply don't know much about this Dr. Dobbs person, other than she was famous. From what I understand, she specialized in relationship therapy, and heaven knows Skipper Dean and I don't need that!" She laughed loud enough that the couple sitting by the window stopped talking to stare at us.

Smiling, I said, "Glad to hear you and Dean are doing so well."

"Not half as glad as I am!" She squinted and looked into the distance. "Say, I don't suppose you know that doctor's husband's name, do you?"

"Nathan Dobbs," I said.

A smile broke across Mrs. Standish's mannish face, and I found myself leaning forward in anticipation.

"I knew I was familiar with that surname!" she exclaimed.

A shiver ran like a mouse down my back, but I forced myself to wait for her to continue.

"You remember when I decided I wanted to be a big real estate mogul last year? When I bought the Peachtree Arms?" she asked.

I nodded. The woman Uncle Ben had been accused of killing had owned the wretched apartment building, and Mrs. Standish had stepped in to save the structure and the tenants, and even managed to benefit the local no-kill animal shelter.

"I tried to buy that commercial complex on the edge of Ardsley Park—on the corner of Bull and Victory Drive." She peered at me to see if I knew the one.

"I pass that place all the time on my way to Lucy and Ben's town house," I said.

She stabbed the air with her finger. "Right. Perfect location, well away from the tourist hustle down here in the historic district, but close to lovely neighborhoods where residents would like to be able to shop closer to home. The upper floor was big enough for a nice-sized fitness center, too."

"What happened?" I asked.

"I was soundly outbid, my dear. By Mr. Nathan Dobbs." She shook her head and tsked. "Not that he's done anything with it since. It needed a lot of work, but he's let it just sit there empty. A moneymaking opportunity like that! Makes me a little ill, truth be told." She took a deep breath and brightened. "Oh, well. All water under the bridge. Now, I'll take two loaves of your delectable sourdough today, and oooh, those sticky buns look just perfect for our afternoon tea."

"Coming right up," I said absently, thinking about what she'd just told me.

Why would someone buy a business building and then do nothing with it? Luckily, I knew just who to ask.

When Mrs. Standish had gone, I returned to find Lucy asking Iris about her classes at the Savannah College of Art and Design. She was taking a lot of different subjects because she hadn't decided what she wanted to focus on yet. They were unloading the dishwasher, and the topic soon turned to one of Iris' instructors.

"He's such a jerk," Iris said. "Never smiles. Gives us a ton of homework. And he's really sarcastic."

"He doesn't sound like a very happy man," Lucy said. "Maybe you should take him some cookies." My aunt thought a sweet treat would fix the majority of unpleasant situations.

"Probably wouldn't even eat one," Iris grumbled.

"Well, it couldn't hurt to try," Lucy said. "Or maybe a scone." She gazed out the window, thinking. "With dried bits of tangerine, or maybe a tangerine icing." Her attention returned to Iris. "Tangerine facilitates cheerfulness and optimism."

That was news to me. I made a mental note.

"Boy, he needs both of those," Iris said with an eye roll. "But I don't think there's enough tangerine in the world to change him."

"Lucille!" trilled a voice from out front. "Katie!"

We turned to see Mimsey Carmichael, her blue eyes twinkling with good humor. The blue bow affixed to her straight white pageboy was the same color as her eyes. She owned the Vase Value flower shop and practiced color and flower magic. Blue was her favorite color, among other things representing wisdom, counsel, and guidance—quite fitting since she was the oldest of our group at seventy-nine, and our de facto leader.

I looked at my watch. It was twelve thirty. We closed at one, so the other spellbook club members would be arriving soon.

Good thing, because I sure need their help.

"Lord love a duck, you two! Another . . . ?" Then Mimsey noticed the customers sitting at nearby tables, who were all watching her. With an impish grin, she drew her finger and thumb across her mouth as if zipping it closed. "Never mind. I'll just wait over in the reading area until the others arrive."

Lucy hurried toward her. "Of course, hon. Can I get you something?"

The bell over the door rang as Jaida French came in next. She waved at Iris and me and went to join Mimsey and Lucy. A slight smile curved her vermillion lips, and her wise eyes conveyed both respect and affection for the older witch. I always associated the smell of cinnamon with Jaida, a lawyer who shared an office—and a home—with a male witch named Gregory. Since it was Sunday, she'd ditched her usual formal business wear for an electric blue, tie-dyed tunic over leggings and high boots. A chunky gold necklace gleamed against the chocolate brown skin of her throat, and a matching bracelet dangled at her wrist.

As the two women settled into the poufy chairs in the reading area, Mimsey with a straight Americano and Jaida with a caramel mocha, I looked up to see Dr. Dana's sister hurrying by on the sidewalk outside.

Chapter 8

Phoebe looked like she was on a mission, head forward and shoulders hunched. Her hands were jammed deep into the pockets of her peacoat.

"I'll be right back," I heard myself say as I scooted to the door and looked out.

She'd stopped in front of the Fox and Hound and was peering through the window. She knocked, her knuckles loud enough on the glass of the front door that I could hear them several yards away. She didn't seem to notice me.

The door opened, and Croft stepped halfway out with a ring of keys dangling in his hand. Shook his head. Shrugged. Then the two of them went inside.

I hurried back to the kitchen and grabbed a waxed bag. Opening it, I layered several of the pumpkin spice cookies between slices of parchment paper and folded down the top.

Lucy followed me to the door as the others looked on with a mixture of curiosity and surprise. "What's going on?"

"Phoebe just went into the bookstore," I said. "I want to take her some cookies."

My aunt nodded vigorously. "That's a good idea. I bet Croft could use one, too."

I went out to the sidewalk. Hopefully, Iris had added a nice *zing!* of power to the healing and uplifting qualities of the allspice and ginger, but just in case, I added an arrow of my own intention to the sweet concoctions.

In the distance, a guide on one of the ubiquitous tour buses extolled the foresight of General James Oglethorpe, Savannah's founder and designer. He was the one responsible for the unique arrangement of more than twenty parklike squares in the historic district. The city's deep and fascinating past, along with its beauty, its architecture, and the success of what locals simply called The Book—known by the rest of the world as *Midnight in the Garden of Good and Evil* by John Berendt—attracted travelers from all over the world. Tourism had become quite the industry in my adopted home, and I'd learned to embrace it.

The sound of a growling car engine on the street drew my attention. I looked over to see an Audi A7, shiny gray and chrome, slowly driving by. A hand snaked out and waved at me. Surprised, I stopped on the sidewalk and began to raise my own hand.

Then I saw who it was.

Steve Dawes gazed out at me from the open window, his brown eyes drinking me in the same way I remembered from the first time we'd met. His honeyed hair, which he'd always worn in a ponytail, was now cut short on the sides and longer on top so it flopped down across his forehead, accenting his tanned, patrician features. He grinned, and white teeth flashed at me.

My smile faltered as my heart did a thumpa-thumpa in my chest. Steve—journalist, druid, and erstwhile suitor—had left town suddenly back in August. Now, seeing him out of the blue like this, I was unprepared for my visceral reaction.

The light changed, and the car drove away, that grin still lingering in the rearview mirror. When had he gotten an Audi? He'd had a Range Rover ever since I'd known him. And that short hair. What was up with that? Though I had to admit it looked good on him.

Apparently a lot of things had changed. But if that look he'd given me was any indication, that didn't include his feelings for me. Declan would not be happy to learn his former rival had returned to Savannah.

And that turnover in my chest? Well, that was just because I was happy to see Steve was okay. His self-imposed exile hadn't been because of me—at least not directly. But I hadn't heard a word from him since August, and none of my texts had been returned. I'd been worried, was all.

Nothing else.

Shaking my head, I turned back to the bookstore and strode to the door. I could follow up with Steve later, find out what he was doing. Never mind that he was back in town and hadn't contacted me. But for now I had other things on my mind. Like cookies to salve the hurt of tragedy.

And a few questions.

The CLOSED sign was up in the window, which gave me pause. Croft was usually open on Sundays, especially this time of year, when the tourists were thick and the holidays were approaching. Perhaps the police had asked him to remain closed. Or perhaps Croft, gruff curmudgeon that he was, was still reeling from the turn of events at the biggest signing he'd ever had in his store.

The Fox and Hound was dim inside, but I saw a sliver of light through the glass. Cupping my hand to the window, I saw a flash of yellow crime scene tape and movement toward the rear of the store. I pushed the unlocked door open and went inside. The office door behind the counter was open a crack, and I heard a noise on the other side. The air still held the faint scent of mulled cider from the night before, but for the life of me I could not smell anything resembling almonds. Of course, that might have faded away since the night before, and Lucy said it had been much stronger in the back room, where Dr. Dana had died.

The place felt sad, the fire in the hearth dead and the only illumination coming from the shafts of light arrowing through the windows. Dust motes danced in the filtered sunshine.

"Hello?" I called.

The sound of a drawer closing came from behind the office door.

"Um, the bookstore's closed," a voice said from the rear of the store.

I squinted and saw Phoebe walking toward me.

"I figured it was. I'm Katie Lightfoot, from the Honeybee next door." I moved toward her, my eyes adjusting to the low light.

She nodded slowly, though the gesture seemed to cost her effort. Her crisp shirt and jeans of the night before had been replaced with a pair of faded khakis and a shapeless sweater under the felted peacoat. Her hair fell lank around her pale face, and dark circles surrounded her blue eyes.

"You're the baker," she said.

I nodded and held out the bag of cookies. "I know it's not much, but it's what bakers do in times of crisis—offer food. I'm so very sorry for your loss."

Her mouth opened, then closed. Then: "Thank you. I'm still having trouble believing that she's really gone."

I stepped forward and patted her on the shoulder. "Of course you are. Such a horrible thing." I opened the bag and held it out again.

She looked at me gratefully and took a cookie. "I suppose I ought to eat something. Thanks." When she took a bite, I thought the pain behind her eyes lightened a fraction.

Light cut into the area where we were standing as Croft opened the door behind the counter and bustled out to join us.

"Katie." He frowned. "What are you doing here?"

"I brought over some cookies."

His frown deepened as he looked at the bag. "I'll pass, thanks."

I grimaced. "How long do you have to keep the store closed?"

"Until tomorrow, at least. Maybe longer." He glanced meaningfully at Phoebe. "It's not a big deal."

I knew it was a big deal, but he didn't want to make her feel bad.

He held his hands out, palms up. "I'm sorry," he said to Phoebe. "No one turned in a wallet."

"Darn it! Just what I need right now—to have to cancel my credit cards and deal with the DMV."

"I'm so sorry," Croft said. "I'll keep a lookout for it."

"Maybe I lost it on the street when I went out to move the car." Her voice cracked on the last two words. "The last time I saw her, Dana was signing books and talking to her fans. It was one of her favorite parts of the job."

I patted her on the shoulder again, feeling completely

ineffective and hoping at least the half cookie she'd eaten had sparked some healing.

But her face clouded as she took another bite. She swallowed and said, "I hope they put that woman away for a long time."

I looked at Croft, whose lined face was filled with concern for the young woman standing between us.

"Don't you worry," he said. "From what I can tell, Detective Quinn is collecting plenty of evidence against her."

"Um," I said. "Are you talking about Angie Kissel?"

They both glared at me. "Of course!" Phoebe said.

I pasted a noncommittal look on my face. "Well, your sister did mention something about a restraining order."

Phoebe nodded vehemently. "We hadn't gotten one yet, but after that horrible creature showed up yet again last night, I was going to apply for one today." She faltered.

"Again? So Kissel had been a problem before?" I asked. Leading the witness. And I would have felt bad about it if Phoebe hadn't seemed to be so willing to talk about it. She certainly seemed more energetic, thinking about someone to blame.

"Oh, Lord yes. Dana had seen that woman following her three or four times, and she showed up at a previous signing. She didn't say anything to my sister then, though, or I would have tried to have her removed before Dana began speaking last night." She passed her hand over her eyes, and when it dropped they were blazing. "And that's not all. Kissel harassed her in other ways."

I leaned forward. "Like how?"

Croft's eyes narrowed. "Katie, don't you have a bakery to run?"

I smiled at him.

But Phoebe jumped at the chance to tell me more about Angie. "She was starting a letter-writing campaign. First it was just her. She wrote letters to the station manager at WMBK-AM, where Dana recorded her show, trying to get him to drop her. Like that was going to happen! Even if it did work, another station would have stepped in. Dana was terribly popular, you know? But that woman just kept trying. She threatened to solicit other people to write to affiliate stations across the country, too."

"Really?" I asked.

Croft took the bag of cookies and set them on a nearby table. "Thanks, Katie."

I was being dismissed.

A small smile tried to find a place on Phoebe's face. "I'd better be going. There are arrangements to make, and I'm the arrangement maker, you know." Her expression turned thoughtful, and she said as if to herself, "Some kind of memorial—I wonder what would be the most appropriate thing to do? Maybe something her fans could participate in? And then there are all those cancelations . . ." I could see Dana's sister had thrived on her job administering her sister's day-to-day activities. Thinking about logistics seemed to center her.

The phone rang. Croft looked torn.

"I have to get going," Phoebe said, and headed for the door. "Thanks, Mr. Barrow."

Croft grabbed the phone, calling after her, "You take care, now. I have your number." And then into the phone: "Hello?"

I grabbed the cookies and trotted after her. "Here. Take these."

She smiled, but it didn't reach her eyes. "Thanks."

I pushed the door closed behind her and turned back to Croft.

His tone was dangerous as he spoke into the handset. "I have no interest whatsoever in talking with you, or anyone else, about what happened last night. Now, stop calling!" He slammed the phone into its cradle, making me jump.

"Who was that?" I asked.

"Reporter. He's left four messages on my voice mail. Maybe he'll get the hint now." His eyes met mine. "What a mess."

I wanted to give him a hug, but he was not a huggy kind of guy. So, I plunged in with the other reason I'd come next door.

"Croft, you remember the big guy who confronted Dr. Dana? The one who said he'd almost lost his fiancée?"

He nodded.

"Do you know his name?"

"He's not a regular."

"He bought a book," I said. "Can you look up the transaction and see if he paid with a credit card?"

His lips pressed together. "Maybe. If I knew what book it was." A wry look crossed his features. "I assume it wasn't a Dana Dobbs title."

"I don't know the title, but it was one of Craig Johnson's mysteries."

"Why do you care about that guy?" he asked.

"We were chatting over at the buffet table, and he said something about needing some catering." The lie came with disturbing ease. I tried to mitigate it with a little truth. "Plus, I'm curious. After all, he harassed Dr. Dana, too."

He snorted. Still, he moved behind the counter and began pushing buttons on the computer. "Hmm. Only one Johnson book sold yesterday. To an Earl King." He looked up. "That must be your guy."

"Thanks, Croft. I'll give you a finder's fee if he ends up hiring us." *Stop making it worse!* I looked at my watch. "I've got to get back and help Lucy close. I sure hope you'll be able to open up tomorrow."

"From your mouth to God's ear."

Chapter 9

When I returned to the Honeybee, the last two members of the spellbook club had arrived. Bianca Devereaux towered over the others, her long black hair worn loose, and an elegant, mauve-colored maxi-dress draped on her willowy frame. Of all of us, she looked the most like a traditional witch—Mimsey actually looked more like the fairy godmother in Disney's *Cinderella*. Bianca also had quite the talent for making money in the stock market, which nicely augmented the income from Moon Grapes, her wine shop on Factors Walk. I saw her familiar, a white ferret named Puck, stick his little pink nose out of the pocket of the jacket she'd slung over the back of her chair.

Cookie Rios was the last and youngest member of the group, and even though I knew familiars chose their witches, I couldn't help hoping that she'd left her king snake, Rafe, at home. She was originally from Haiti, her background in voodoo, but she'd turned away from that element of her life to focus on the kinds of magic the rest of the spellbook club practiced—until very recently, that is. Now she was slowly delving back into some of Savannah's voodoo culture despite the concerns of her husband of less than a year.

She'd worked as a commercial agent for Quartermaine Realty for more than six months, and though she'd changed jobs every three months when I first met her, so far she wasn't showing any signs of restlessness. Today she wore leggings as well, though unlike Jaida's simple black ones, Cookie's were leopard print and worn with metallic leather ballet slippers and a swirling ochre top studded with fake jewels. It made her look older; though I had only a few more years than her twenty-six, I tended to think of her as a bit of a youngster. Still, she was a settled, married woman, while I'd practically been left at the altar in Akron.

I dashed over and gave them each a hug. "Hey. Thanks for coming on such short notice."

"Lucy said you needed us," Bianca said with a smile, and that said enough.

"We just need to close things down so we won't be interrupted," I said. "Then I'll fill you in on what happened last night."

"Oh, I've already done that," Mimsey said. "At least all the information your aunt gave me."

"Well, that'll save some time," I said wryly. "But I might have a few tidbits to add."

"Do tell," Jaida said, her curiosity evident.

"Oh, I will," I said, and headed into the kitchen.

It was almost one o'clock. Of course, we could have added a few sales to the register if we'd stayed open on Sunday afternoon, especially in late November, but we had decided to draw the line. After all, if we'd stayed open until ten at night we would have garnered traffic from the after-dinner crowd, too, but there had to be some kind of a limit. Maybe we'd rethink things when we could hire another full-time employee. As it was, Lucy and I worked a lot of ten- and twelve-hour days. That was one of the reasons why being able to add Iris to our roster had been such a boon. I loved my work—I mean, I *loved* it—but I couldn't work twenty-four-seven.

The spellbook club usually met on Sunday afternoons, and often at the bakery. We'd had a few meetings since Iris had been hired, but Lucy and I hadn't mentioned anything about a meeting today, and her interest was obviously piqued. As she chopped a pile of candied orange peel and dried cherries, she eyed the ladies in the reading area again and again.

"Better watch what you're doing," I teased, donning a vintage apron from my collection arrayed on the back wall. "That knife's sharp."

She blushed. "What's going on over there?"

"A little impromptu meeting," Lucy said as she breezed by. "Why don't you go ahead home when you're done there, dear. We'll finish closing up."

Iris looked disappointed. "I can stay if you need me."

"Nonsense. You go on and enjoy yourself," Lucy said.

The younger woman grimaced. "If you call doing homework enjoyment."

I laughed. "It can be. I used to love coming up with recipes for class when I was in pastry school."

"Sure. I bet you liked taking tests, too."

Actually, I had, but I knew better than to say so. "What homework's on your docket this afternoon?"

She sighed. "I have to write a short story."

"Really? I thought you were taking metalsmithing."

"And graphic arts. And photography. And creative writing."

I smiled. "Sounds like you're dipping your toe in a lot of waters."

"I just can't make up my mind." She sounded frustrated as she scooped the chopped fruit into a lidded container and set it aside on the big steel worktable.

"You'll figure it out. And you know how many times I've said you have a knack for baking—especially our kind. Those pumpkin spice cookies worked wonders this morning."

She brightened. "Yeah?"

I nodded. "For the sister of the woman who was killed last night."

That sobered her. "Well, that's nice to know." She hesitated. "It's just that there are so many choices. What if I make the wrong one?"

Lucy passed by with a roll of paper towels and the disinfecting cleaner we used on the tables. "You'll make a new choice. Don't worry about it. Some of your decisions are going to be wrong. That's okay. Life teaches you how to live it the longer you do it."

I stared after my aunt. Was that directed at Iris or me?

Lucy and I quickly tidied and cleaned after the last customer left. I'd already set up the sourdough levain to rise overnight in the refrigerator for a quick pop into the oven the next morning. Iris left, and we locked the front door and flipped the CLOSED sign.

Finally, I let Mungo out of the office, loaded a tray with goodies from the display case, poured myself a cup of drip brew, and joined the ladies of the spellbook club.

Lucy had already removed her Birkenstocks and tucked her feet under her on one end of the sofa. Her orange tabby was curled up in her lap, purring contentedly.

"Well, hello there," I said to the feline. Mungo put his front paws on the chair and the two familiars touched noses.

My aunt smiled. "Ben brought her by after his golf

round. I feel like I haven't spent enough time with her lately. Will you be okay?"

"Of course!" I said, though I could already feel a tickle in my nose. I adored Honeybee. It wasn't my fault I was so allergic to cats.

Mimsey sat in the smallest chair, her sensible heels barely brushing the floor. Cookie lounged sideways in the other one, her legs draped over the arm. Jaida had settled in next to my aunt. They had been working out logistics for Thanksgiving dinner—which was coming up fast.

Lucy smiled at me. "Guess what. For the first time, we'll all be together for the holiday. Mimsey here was just telling us that Wren is spending the week with her mother in Europe." Wren was Mimsey's granddaughter. My aunt continued. "And Cookie and Oscar have decided not to travel to Florida this year, so they'll be joining us, too."

I couldn't help grinning as I looked around at my fellow witches. "That's terrific."

"Ben will smoke the turkey," Lucy said. "And I'll make the corn bread dressing and mashed potatoes with collards."

Mimsey said, "I'll bring my sweet potatoes with bacon and pecans. It's actually my mama's recipe."

"That sounds fantastic!" Cookie said. "I'll bring salade russe—a beet salad that my family always makes for the holiday. I imagine you're on dessert duty, Katie?"

I set the tray of pastries on the coffee table. "Sure. We'll have plenty of pies to choose from. And count on me for sourdough rolls, too."

"God," groaned Bianca as she eyed the tray of pastries. "All this talk of food, and then you tempt us with all those yummy muffins and cakes. I love this place, but sometimes I wish you and Lucy had started a health spa or a juice bar. You two are murder on my waistline."

I rolled my eyes and didn't even bother to comment. Bianca was tall and slim enough to be a model, with a natural elegance that simply would not permit any damage to her figure. It wasn't that she ate like a bird; she simply enjoyed her food slowly and deliberately. Now I watched as she licked a bit of maple buttercream from the edge of a peach cupcake and rolled it around in her mouth.

I, on the other hand, was often so busy baking and serving that I forgot to eat. My stomach grumbled, and I snagged one of the Greek scones that were my current favorite before taking my place on the other end of the sofa next to Jaida.

Jaida leaned forward and put her empty mug on the table. "Okay, Katie. Spill."

I took a deep breath. "You know Dr. Dana was murdered, and that Lucy figured out she was poisoned by cyanide."

Mimsey nodded enthusiastically at my aunt. "Well done, dear."

Lucy smiled. "It was just luck."

Bianca tapped her temple. "And smarts."

"Detective Quinn confirmed her, uh, diagnosis earlier today," I said, and filled them in on our conversation.

Cookie impatiently jumped in. "Katie, why have you been called to remedy this situation?" The vestiges of a Haitian accent lilted around her words.

I was quiet.

Lucy's eyes narrowed. "You've been keeping something from me."

I looked at Mungo. His eyes urged me to tell them.

"Margie Coopersmith found Dana Dobbs."

Cookie waved her hand. "Yes, yes. Your neighbor."

"And Angie Kissel was kneeling over the body," I said.

"Right," Jaida said. "Sounds like she's the prime suspect. Do you think she did it?"

I looked at Mungo. "No."

Her gaze sharpened.

I said, "Unfortunately, not only did Angie confront Dr. Dana in front of her fans at the Fox and Hound last night, but I found out she'd followed her several times and attended at least one other event."

"When did you learn that?" Lucy asked.

"Just now. Next door. That was Phoebe walking by on her way to Croft's," I explained to the others. "She was looking for her lost wallet. Anyway, I went over to offer my condolences, and she told me that she'd been planning to get a restraining order on Angie."

Lucy nodded. "Dana Dobbs said something about that last night."

"Right. Well, Phoebe also told me that Angie had been writing letters to the radio station here in Savannah where Dr. Dana records her syndicated advice show. Angie was trying to get the manager to dump the show." Then I told them about the letter-writing campaign Angie had threatened.

"Okay, motive for sure," Jaida said. "Though I admit it's a pretty long way from writing letters to killing someone."

"I agree," I said. "But then Croft kicked Angie out, and she came back, only to be found in a rather suspicious position over Dr. Dana's dead body."

"Opportunity," Jaida said. I could tell the lawyerly part of her was enjoying this bit. "So what was Kissel's beef with the victim?"

I related what Angie had told me about how Dr. Dana's advice had ended her marriage.

Bianca's lips pressed together, and I could tell she was thinking of her own ex, who had left when she'd developed a strong interest in Wiccan spell work and moon magic.

Jaida nodded decisively, adding that bit of information to the rest. "What else haven't you told us?"

Lucy, as patient as Job, slowly raised her eyebrows. "There's a magical connection, isn't there?"

Mimsey swung her legs like a little kid. "Of course there is."

"Angie Kissel is a witch." I looked down at Mungo. "Or rather, was a witch."

Lucy's eyes grew wide, while Jaida simply looked speculative, adding this new information into the equation. Cookie whistled.

Mimsey, however, frowned. "Do you think she might have used magic to murder Dr. Dana?"

I snorted. "Only if cyanide is magic. Last I heard, it wasn't."

"However," Lucy said thoughtfully, "it might be possible for a witch, say, an experienced hedgewitch with knowledge of plant extraction techniques, to obtain cyanide."

Surprised, I asked, "How?"

"Oh, it exists naturally in apple seeds and peach pits, as well as other stone fruit seeds—like cherries and apricots."

"I guess I've heard that. But only in tiny amounts," I said. "Nothing lethal."

"There are ways to extract it and concentrate the effects—both mechanically and magically."

I blanched. "Good heavens."

"So," Jaida said, and reached for a brown butter

scone. "More opportunity to go with the motive if Ms. Kissel specialized in hedgewitchery. Do you know?"

I shook my head.

She tipped her head to the side, her wise eyes boring into mine. "Do you think you're being called to right a wrong involving this Angie person? Because I have to say, you don't seem all that enthusiastic about it."

I looked away.

"Katie, how do you know she's a witch in the first place?" Lucy asked the question no one else had thought to.

"She told me."

"Why?" Cookie said bluntly.

I washed down the scone with a swig of lukewarm coffee, taking my time. "Because she figured out right away that I'm a witch."

Alarm crossed all their faces.

"Because of Mungo."

All eyes turned to him. He responded with a panting grin.

"He used to be her familiar."

Complete silence descended over the group.

Puck nosed his way out of Bianca's sleeve to look at Mungo. Rafe coiled out of Cookie's bag to run up her arm and take a look at my dog over the edge of the chair. Honeybee sat up on Lucy's lap.

"Well, I'll be dipped," Mimsey breathed. She looked around at the other ladies. "Have you ever heard of such a thing?"

As one they shook their heads.

"Not ever in all my years," Mimsey went on, "have I known a witch to give up a familiar and then have it go on to find another witch." She seemed truly disturbed as she turned toward Mungo.

Yip!

Normally that would have brought a smile to my face, if not everyone else's, but not this time.

"The relationship between witch and familiar is like a marriage," Lucy said in a low voice.

A few beats, and then we all smiled. Not because she was right, but because we all knew that our connections with our familiars were stronger than marriage. They were a part of us. I couldn't imagine in a gazillion years what it would feel like to lose Mungo. It would be like losing an arm, or a piece of my soul.

And Angie had just given him up.

"So . . . now what?" Jaida asked, ever the practical one.

"Mungo assures me Angie Kissel is innocent. Quinn thinks she's guilty and told me to stay out of this one."

Lucy and Mimsey exchanged glances. "Like when he was going to arrest Ben for killing Mrs. Templeton?" my aunt asked.

Bianca said, "Peter Quinn dismisses anything at all paranormal as 'woo-woo nonsense.' It's a blind spot." She looked at me. "A blind spot you can see."

"Mungo wants me to help Angie," I said. "He made that pretty clear."

In confirmation, he jumped up on the sofa with me. Normally, he wouldn't dream of doing that, since I'd explained that there were people who were allergic to dog hair. But right now I needed the comfort of my little dog in my arms, and he knew it. Heck, he might have needed a little comfort himself. It was a pretty awful situation we were talking about, after all.

The other witches were looking around at one another again, troubled.

Mimsey, though, nodded emphatically. "Of course.

There is a reason you were there when it happened. Ever since you've learned you are a lightwitch with a calling to the light, you've done the right thing."

"That's because I felt like I had to." My former mentor, Franklin Taite, had told me I had no choice but to serve the light. Recently, I'd learned he had greatly exaggerated that obligation.

Exaggerated as in *lied*.

"But I thought if it happened again I'd have a choice. That I could walk away from the darkness of murder."

Mimsey made a rude noise. "My dear, dear Katie. You need to pull your head out of the sand. Of course you have a choice. Everyone has choices, for heaven's sake. But just because those choices are there for the making doesn't mean there isn't a right one *to* make."

Well, that gave me pause.

"Why don't you think of it as helping Peter Quinn," Lucy said in that utterly reasonable tone of hers. "In the end, you want justice—and so does he. If Angie is innocent, you're probably one of the best people to prove that. Besides, you've already started, what with following the victim's sister into Croft's and questioning her."

"Hey, I wasn't . . ." I trailed off.

Jaida snorted a laugh. "Oh, I saw you hightail it out of here as soon as you saw her. You might as well admit it. Even if you think you don't want to investigate, you probably couldn't help yourself in the long run."

I sighed. "Well, when you put it like that . . ."

Mungo jumped up and licked my chin. I laughed and pushed him down. He ran back to his bed on the bottom bookshelf, and in doing so he dislodged a thin volume from the shelf.

I reached over to pick it up and paused. Then I held it up for them all to see.

It was one of the coloring books designed for adults that had become all the rage. Every single picture in it was of a dragonfly.

Cookie swung her legs to the floor. "All right, then. That's settled. Now—what do we do first?"

Chapter 10

I shook my head. "I'm not sure. Do you have any ideas?"

"The radio station manager," Mimsey said with authority. "His name is Bing Hawkins, and I've known him for years. Old Savannah family. His grandmama and I went to school together, and before he managed the station he was their advertising manager. He still handles my account." Mimsey still worked at her flower shop most days. She said it kept her vital. Since Lucy assured me she didn't use magic to keep her youthful vigor, I was prone to believe her claim.

"I'll give him a jingle tomorrow," she went on, "and tell him you might be in the market for some radio advertising."

"Oh, Ben won't like that," Lucy said. "He's the one who handles all the marketing for the Honeybee, and he thinks radio is too expensive."

Mimsey shrugged. "It works for me, especially around the holidays. And it won't hurt to talk to Bing. You don't have to buy anything, honey. Just get in the door."

"And find out about those letters Angie wrote," I said.

She pointed her finger. "Exactly."

"Want some company?" Jaida asked.

I grinned at her. "I'd love some."

"My schedule is busy, but a lot of it's paperwork right now. Let me know when you want to go, and I'll see if I can get away."

"Deal." I turned to Cookie. "Do you happen to know anything about the sale of that commercial building on the corner of Victory and Bull?"

Her perfectly shaped eyebrows rose. "That was before I started working in the business. I don't even know if my company handled it. Why?"

"Because Mrs. Standish told me Dr. Dana's husband bought it, but he hasn't moved forward with leasing spaces," I said.

Mimsey and Lucy exchanged a look.

An ironic smile curved Cookie's lips. "I can tell you why, but it has nothing to do with my job. Oscar told me."

I frowned. Her husband worked for a company that tested for environmental hazards. Things like . . .

"Asbestos?" I breathed.

"Nothing so dire," she said. "Not so great, either, though. Black mold. It's expensive to fix, and afterward there will likely need to be significant repairs to the affected areas."

I winced. "Sounds horrible. I'll have to tell Mrs. Standish she lucked out on that deal."

But as I rose to clear away the dishes, I had to wonder what Dr. Dana had thought of her husband's business dealings. Something told me she wouldn't have approved.

The ladies left, and Lucy and I shut off the lights. She locked the door that led to the alley and put the cash bag into the safe in the office, while I checked the pans of sourdough that were slowly rising in the industrial fridge. As I came back out with Mungo firmly ensconced in my tote bag, I saw someone silhouetted in the light coming through the front window.

Someone very short.

"Hi, Katie."

I flipped the lights back on to see that we'd neglected to lock the front door after the spellbook club had left, and Angie Kissel had let herself in. Mungo wiggled and grinned at her. Lucy came out of the office and joined me, her brow wrinkled.

"I saw the closed sign, but it looked like you were having some kind of a meeting."

Yeah. About you.

"I didn't want to disturb you, but then those other women left so I thought maybe . . . well, I wondered . . ."

"If Katie could help you?" my aunt asked.

I stifled a groan.

Surprise flickered across Angie's face. "Help me? How would . . ." Her eyes narrowed. "Ah, perhaps that's it."

Lucy shot me a look, then turned her attention back to our visitor. "Why don't you two sit down? I forgot something in the back."

Angie sank into a bistro chair. She wore an above-the-knee skirt with tights and boots and a light cabled sweater—all in brown. According to Mimsey, brown was the color of grounding, protection of familiars, and special favors.

Is she invoking color magic? Or does she just like earth tones?

"Why don't you tell us why you're here?" I asked, taking another chair and lowering Mungo down to the floor.

He peered up at me with a question in his eyes, and then hesitantly padded over to Angie.

Her face broke out in a grin, and she actually laughed as she reached down to scratch under his chin. "I came to see Mungo."

That horrible feeling of jealousy pierced through me. I set my jaw against it and reached down to pat my familiar's back. As I touched him, I felt a *zip!* of electric energy hiss through me. Angie and I jerked our hands back at the same time.

Eyes wide, I raised my head to see Angie had the same expression on her face that I imagined was on mine. As one, we looked back down at Mungo. He distributed an impish grin between us.

"Why, you little dickens," she said.

I tipped my head to the side. "Yeah?" I asked him. *Yeah,* his look said.

"He says you're innocent," I said. Because along with the electric rush had come a deep knowledge that Angie was not a murderer. It hadn't exactly come *from* Mungo, but *through* him—as if he was a conduit between us.

"He 'says'?" Angie seemed confused.

Perhaps whatever had happened hadn't worked both ways. Or perhaps they'd never been as deeply connected as Mungo and I were—and had been from the beginning of our relationship.

"Just trust me," I said.

She sat back. "You know? I do. I can't explain it, but I feel like we met for a reason. I assumed it was because of Mungo here. But perhaps there's something else. The other woman—your aunt?—said something about help." She blew her bangs off her forehead. "And Lord knows, I could use some help. That detective seems pretty determined to pin Dr. Dana's murder on me. He's already called my parents and my ex-husband, trying to see if I have any access to cyanide."

"Do you?" I asked.

She glared at me. "No."

"Good." I saw Lucy coming back. "I don't think you were really introduced last night. This is my aunt, Lucy Eagel."

The nodded at each other.

"Do you mind if I ask you another question?" I asked.

"Go ahead."

"What kind of witch were you before you stopped practicing?"

She inclined her head toward Lucy. "You're one, too. Of course. Hereditary." And then to me, "That was a coven meeting, wasn't it?"

I didn't answer.

"Fair enough. I was a green witch. I still work at Chatham Garden Center."

Lucy and I exchanged a glance. Once again, my aunt was right. Green witch was another term for hedgewitch. And for once, it was a good thing that Quinn didn't know about any of it, because if he'd known Angie could squeeze cyanide from a peach pit, so to speak, she'd be awaiting trial.

"Do you know what a lightwitch is?" I asked.

She shook her head.

"Well, to put it simply, it's someone called to right wrongs, and in my case to work against evil. That might be secular, but it's sometimes the evil of dark magic."

"In your case. You mean . . ." She whistled. "Mungo sure found himself a powerful witch." She bit her lip. "So do you think you can help me?"

I took a deep breath. "I don't know. But I'm going to try."

I meant to go straight home, I really did, but I still couldn't resist a side trip on the way. Instead of taking my usual route toward Midtown on Abercorn, I turned left and then right, and soon the Bug was crawling down Bull Street toward Ardsley Park. It was an older neighborhood, more upscale than some, but still quintessentially Savannah. Green expanses of lawns sprawled in front of stately homes, which were interspersed with more modest 1920s bungalows. Live oaks arched overhead, dripping with the Spanish moss ubiquitous to the area.

Ben and Lucy lived on the edge of Ardsley Park, in a lovely three-story townhome with a low-maintenance rooftop garden. They shopped downtown and occasionally at the Southside shopping malls, all of which were within easy access. Still, as I pulled up in front of the L-shaped building that I'd passed numerous times on my way to their home, I could see Mrs. Standish's point. The right businesses in this location would attract tons of traffic. The bottom floor would be prime for retail, and possibly a restaurant and bar. The upper level offered a walkway with exterior access to each unit. The space on the long side of the L looked like one big expanse, perfect for the neighborhood fitness center Mrs. Standish had imagined.

A parking lot large enough to accommodate a double row of spaces sat between the curb strip next to where I was parked and the building. Potholes crumpled the asphalt, and the painted stripes delineating the individual spots were faded where they showed at all. Two vehicles sat nose-in at one end of the building. One was a PT Cruiser, and the other obviously a work truck, complete with utility racks and a sign on the side that read LINCOLN BARD, GENERAL CONTRACTOR.

Checking the rearview mirror to make sure there were no cars coming, I slowly backed up along the curb until I could see the license plate on the passenger car.

DOCDANA.

Well, that seemed pretty clear. Was this the car Phoebe and Nate had moved after the signing so Dana wouldn't have to walk far on her high heels? Honestly, I'd imagined a Caddy or a BMW. For someone who was afraid of being stalked, it seemed like she'd want to keep a lower profile. On the other hand, the murder victim had possessed a rather obvious narcissistic streak.

I turned off my car, thinking. Who was driving her car? Possibly Phoebe, but why would she be here? Was she involved in the Dobbs' real estate venture as well? Either way, it seemed awfully coldhearted to be conducting any kind of business less than twenty-four hours after a loved one's death.

A wide-shouldered man wearing work pants and a canvas jacket came out of a downstairs unit. The angled late-day sun struck his face, highlighting two days' worth of grizzled stubble on his sturdy chin. He carried a flip-top notebook and stopped in the middle of the parking lot to make a note with a short stub of pencil.

"I'll be right back," I murmured to Mungo. He stood on his back paws and watched out the rear window as I exited my car and approached the man.

"Excuse me," I said.

He looked up and nodded in a friendly way. "Yes, ma'am? What can I do for you?" His deep drawl curved around the vowels in delicious curlicues, and I couldn't help returning his smile.

I pointed to the truck. "Is that you, or are you the owner?"

Subtle, Katie.

"That's me. Lincoln Bard, at your service."

"You must be a hardworking man, Mr. Bard. Here on the Sunday before Thanksgiving."

"Yes, ma'am." He winked. Coming from most men, it would have made me cringe, but the gesture fit him to a tee. "But not as hardworking so's to work on the Sunday *after* Thanksgiving."

"Good for you. Say, what can you tell me about this place?" I asked, trying for casual.

He shook his head. "Oh, now. You'd need to talk to the owner about that."

"Mmm-hmm," I said, raking the building with a skeptical look. "I know about the black mold. Are you here to, what do they call it?"

"Abatement," he said with a slow nod. "That's not my business, but I'll be working with the folks who do that. Gonna have to pull out some structural bits—walls and floor and the like. Fixing that up is where I come in."

"I see."

"It'll be a good job, nice when it's all done. Took a while to get going on it, but now there's been an influx of money for the project." He rocked back on his heels, looking the place over. "Yep. Looking forward to this one."

A door opened on the top floor and Nathan Dobbs came out.

"Well, there's your man if you have questions about leasing, or . . . ?" Lincoln looked at me with pleasant curiosity, but I only smiled.

"Nate!" he called. "You've got a potential customer here."

Nathan Dobbs came slowly down the stairs, his heavy boots loud on the metal treads. He was just as handsome as I recalled from the signing. Looks don't make the man, but I could see how Dana Dobbs had wanted to hang on to this one. The sun caught the streaks in his chestnut hair, which was longish and delightfully wavy.

He offered me a smile and his hand. "Nate Dobbs. I'm happy for the interest, but you should know it's going to be a while before this place will be ready for renters."

"Hello again. I don't imagine you remember me," I said.

He looked at me then, really looked, and took a step back. "You were there. At the bookstore. The caterer. You brought that damn sweet tea."

Stunned, I blinked. It had never occurred to me that Dr. Dana's family might blame any of us for providing the vehicle that delivered the poison to her. But maybe it should have.

The contractor stared at me, then muttered something about having to go and took off for his truck.

"Mr. Dobbs, th . . . the sweet tea was fine," I stammered. "Surely the police told you that. Lots of people drank it." I could hear the defensiveness creeping into my voice.

Nate took a deep breath. "Yeah," he acquiesced, then looked down at the asphalt rubble at our feet. "Sorry. This has been hard."

"Of course it has!" Sympathy washed through me.

He looked up at the building with an expression I couldn't read. "This place. God. I thought it would give me something to do, be a way to make some real money and not be so . . . Well, it turned out to have some problems, and the money for the project dried up."

"And now?" I asked, cringing as I heard the bluntness of my tone.

Nate met my eyes. "And now it's something to keep me busy so I don't spend every single second thinking about my dead wife."

My swallow was audible. "Sorry."

His expression had hardened, but all he said was,

"So am I." A couple of beats, then: "So are you looking to move from your current location?"

Confused, I scrambled to catch up. "Oh, the Honeybee? No, we love where we're at."

He frowned. "Then . . . ?"

I pasted a big smile on my face. "My aunt and uncle—they own the bakery with me—live down the road there." I gestured. "And we were talking about whether the area could support a second Honeybee bakery."

He fished in his pocket and handed me a rumpled business card. "Another six months or so, and these spaces should be ready. Give me a call if you're still interested."

I thanked him and hightailed it back to my car. He was still standing in the parking lot, watching, as I pulled away.

Declan was waiting when Mungo and I got home around five. I'd texted him to let him know the spellbook club was meeting and that I'd be a little late. He hadn't seemed too disturbed, since he was already planning to watch the Falcons game on the TV up in the loft. I found him sprawled on the futon in front of the screen, a litter of potato chips, onion dip, and an empty beer bottle on the floor. Even though I wasn't personally a fan, I couldn't begrudge him his football Sundays.

He jumped to his feet when he saw me, but after a kiss hello I waved him back to his makeshift lair. "Relax. I'll whip up something easy for dinner."

"You sure?"

"Absolutely. I'm a little on edge, and cooking soothes me."

He frowned. "Something happened at the meeting?"

"Looks like you were right about me trying to find out

who killed Dr. Dana. But at least I've got the help of the other ladies."

One side of his mouth pulled back in a combination grin and grimace. "Ah. Promise me you won't get hurt?"

"Believe me—I'll do my best."

"And you've got my help if you need or want it. You know that."

I nodded.

He gave me another kiss and settled back in front of the television. "Let me know if you change your mind and want some help in the kitchen."

I assured him I would and went back downstairs. Honestly, I was glad he was occupied. We spent a lot of time together during his time off—which was all but the forty-eight-hour shift he worked at the firehouse each week—and the carriage house was small. As much as I loved the guy, sometimes I felt a little crowded. We could have spent more time at his place, an apartment in the historic district. But the furniture was uncomfortable, and that wouldn't really have solved my occasional problem of getting enough alone time.

And right now I needed to think about everything that had happened in the last twenty-four hours. So I mulled things over as I chopped potatoes, shallots, and peppers, tossed them with olive oil, chopped garlic, rosemary, and lemon zest, and dumped the whole shebang into my favorite old cast-iron skillet. Then I took out a couple of bone-in chicken breasts and plopped them on top, doused them with more lemon juice, oil, and salt and pepper, and placed the whole thing into the oven to roast into a melt-in-your-mouth one-dish meal.

Soon the scents of roasting chicken, garlic, and rosemary filled the little house. I decided it was a bit chilly to eat on the patio that night and set the tiny table in the kitchen. Then I slipped on a fleece jacket, grabbed a lantern, notebook, and pen, and went out to the backyard gazebo. Mungo trotted along at my heel, pausing once to roll on his back in the grass.

Most of the backyard was cut into garden beds. Declan had helped me with a lot of the work, and now there were different spaces devoted to flowers and medicinal and culinary herbs, and a separate section by the back corner where the plants were specifically chosen for their magical properties. A small stream ran across that corner, live water that benefited the plants that surrounded it and the spells in which they were used. The gardens were tired this time of year, their growth slowing in the cooler temperatures and shorter days, but there hadn't been a frost yet.

I climbed the steps to the gazebo and sat in one of the mismatched thrift-store chairs. Mungo settled under the table, right in the middle of the five-pointed star in the center of the round floor. It was only ten inches in diameter, painted white with a purple border. A besom, a handmade broom traditional in some old spells, leaned against the railing. It was one of my favorite places to cast, especially garden spells, but I hadn't spent much time out there in the last month or so. The sun had set, though tangerine fingers streaked the low sky to the west. I could hear the stream and smell night-blooming jasmine.

Before lighting the lantern in the gloaming, I focused on a little tree that I'd planted a few feet away from the stream. It was a mountain ash, which is also known as a rowan tree. The Tree of the Goddess. I'd brought it home and planted it in late September. Tangled in its roots was a voodoo talisman that had once belonged to a mentor of mine. Franklin Taite had used it to hunt out evil magic, though he did not think he had any magical gifts of his own. He did, of course, as well as a fervent desire to support the Light. But he was gone now, and I'd been given the talisman.

At first I thought I could just start using it like he had. However, it turned out that's not the way talismans work. It had gone through transformations from light to dark and then back to light again. Unlike a simple charm for luck, or an amulet for protection, it had been created for a specific purpose and a specific person. Once that purpose had been adulterated by evil intent and then actually used to kill, I didn't feel like I could, well, *trust* the talisman anymore. I'd consulted with the spellbook club, who had all been there when the talisman had come back to the light, and they had agreed to a woman that it would be best to deactivate its powers.

So I'd thanked it for its service and reverently buried it beneath the baby rowan. There it would remain as the tree matured. As I reflected on the crazy week I associated with the talisman, I found myself fingering the hair-thin silver circle that hung on a chain around my neck. It was an amulet of protection that I'd worn all year—given to me by Steve Dawes. I'd considered removing it, but it wasn't like I wore it because of him. I wore it because of the power it possessed. After all, who couldn't use a little extra protection?

I lit the oil lamp. It illuminated the interior of the gazebo, squeezing down my pupils and shutting out the dark that surrounded us. I opened the notebook and began to make a list.

Angie Kissel: motive, opportunity, former hedgewitch who possibly could decoct cyanide. Also innocent.

Earl King: motive, possible opportunity. Access to cyanide?

I tapped the pen against my teeth, then wrote, *Nate Dobbs: motive? Alibied by witnesses. Access to cyanide?*

Phoebe Miller: motive? Also alibied by witnesses. Access to cyanide?

Frustrated, I put the pen down and stared at the list. It was awfully short, and the only one who fit the bill was Angie.

Which was why she needed my help.

Earl and Sophie King had left right after Dr. Dana had finished her reading. Could he have come back down the alley later? With or without his wife? And if he/they had, the same argument I'd given Quinn applied. How could he have convinced Dr. Dana to take the poison? As for Phoebe and Nate, they had alibis for the actual time of death, but it was possible that either of them could have slipped the poison into the sweet tea without her seeing. But why? My heart had gone out to Phoebe that morning. Even if I was reading her wrong, monetarily she had benefited much more from her sister being alive than from her being dead. Or had she? Was there life insurance of some sort? And how was Nate affected by the death of his wife?

I sighed and rubbed my eyes. Tomorrow Mimsey would call the manager of the radio station, and I'd see if I could find out anything more there. And since Quinn seemed determined to make the case against Angie without looking at other possibilities, I was going to have to find out more about Earl King—and hopefully have a chat. Too bad I hadn't been telling the truth about Mr. King wanting to hire the Honeybee.

"Katie?" The voice came drifting over the back fence. "Is that you?"

I blew out the lamp and rose. "Margie. Of course it's me."

"It could be Declan," she said, sounding a little defensive.

My eyes adjusted to the darkness as I went down the steps and over to the side of the yard. "Are you doing what I think you're doing?"

Her head popped up. In her back porch light I saw a wisp of creamy frosting on her lip. She licked it off with a sheepish expression.

"Really, Margie?"

"Shh. You're the only one who knows about my Twinkie habit."

One of these days I'll have to make some real sponge cakes and fill them with real vanilla cream for her.

"I've never told a soul," I said. "How're you feeling today?"

"Oh, golly! I had a few bad dreams last night, but I guess things are mostly back to normal around here. Redding is getting ready for a four-day run over to Oklahoma City."

"You okay with that?"

She took a big bite of yellow cake and closed her eyes as she chewed. Then they popped open, and she nodded. "Sure. We've gotten pretty good at figuring out how to make it work." She snapped her fingers. "Speaking of that—I started Dr. Dana's book."

I leaned my arms on the top of the fence. "What do you think?"

She looked troubled. "Well . . . some of the things she says to do seem a little . . ."

"Draconian?"

She blinked. "Um, I was thinking they were kind of severe, you know? Over-the-top."

"Radical Trust, huh."

"Oh, don't get me wrong. I'm not criticizing. The poor woman is dead, after all. I'm definitely going to finish the book."

"Let me know what you think," I said, turning toward the carriage house. "And give a call if you feel nervous with Redding gone. I've got to run in and check on supper right now, though."

"Okeydokey. Thanks, Katie!"

Chapter 11

I fell asleep reading on the couch after supper and then never managed to get back to proper sleep that night. Hours passed in that strange twilight between waking and sleeping, my mind swirling with images of Dr. Dana, sweet tea, Twinkies, and Angie Kissel scratching my familiar under his furry chin.

The dark hour of four thirty the next morning saw me downtown again. I parked in the nearly empty lot around the corner, and Mungo and I walked down Broughton toward the Honeybee. The street was abandoned at that hour on a Monday morning, and the sound of the key in the dead bolt seemed to echo down the sidewalk. I paused to eye the Fox and Hound before going inside the bakery and locking the door behind me. Hopefully, Croft would be able to open his store today.

I wove through the tables and chairs in the customer area, aided only by the quiet light we always left on in the corner of the kitchen. Back in the office, Mungo jumped up on his club chair and immediately fell back asleep. Unlike me, he was not in the least a lark. He wasn't an owl, either, though. My familiar was fond of sleep whatever the hour. Sleep and food.

After shucking my tote, I selected a yellow-and-green-striped chef's apron from the row of hooks on the wall and tied it on. Making my way through the calm of the pre-bustle kitchen, I started one of the ovens to preheat and then headed to the big refrigerator.

As I carefully removed pan after pan of sourdough loaves risen overnight to puffy goodness, my mind kept going back to Steve driving by the day before. A part of me had expected to hear from him sometime in the afternoon, and then later it had been in the back of my mind that he might call during the evening. He hadn't, though. Which was good. Declan was not going to be happy to hear that Steve had returned to Savannah.

They had a past. Part of it included me—there had been a time when I'd been attracted to both of them, but it hadn't taken long for me to choose Declan. Steve was sort of a bad boy, and I had to admit that had been part of his appeal. Heck, it still was, if I was being honest. Plus, he'd figured out I was a witch nearly as quickly as I'd learned of it, because Steve himself was a druid. I couldn't deny the *zing* between us, but then he'd decided to join a druidic clan with questionable ethics, and I had wanted nothing to do with it.

So there was that. But Declan had known Steve long before I'd moved to town. Steve's brother, Arnie, had been Declan's best friend and a fellow firefighter. A tragedy during a fire call had cost Arnie's life, and Steve had always blamed Declan for letting it happen. It hadn't been his fault, of course. Declan would never put anyone's life in danger. Arnie, like his brother, had tended to be rash and had made a decision with fatal repercussions. Steve refused to believe that.

The enmity between Steve and Declan was fierce and difficult. They had done their best to tame it when

I was around. That hadn't been easy, since Steve and I had tried to remain friends. For the most part it had worked out fine, until the events last August.

Where had Steve gone? What had he been doing? In the brief moment I'd seen him, he'd looked as healthy and fit as ever. More so, maybe. His tan had been deeper than I'd ever seen it, and his hair blonder than ever.

Sunshine, and lots of it.

Should I call him? I shook my head, all alone there in the kitchen. No. If he wanted to talk to me, he knew my number. And if he didn't, then that was that.

I turned to check the oven temperature and saw the overflowing garbage by the back door. *Dang it.* Lucy and I had been so anxious to close down and chat with the spellbook club the afternoon before that we'd forgotten to take it out. Though to be fair, Ben usually schlepped the garbage out to the Dumpster in the alley—except on Sundays.

In the half-light of the kitchen, I slid the loaf pans onto the oven racks, inhaling the sour tang of the raw dough. I'd brought the starter from Akron when I'd moved, and in the year and a half since I'd been in Savannah it had taken on the flavors of the local yeasts, the South deepening and ripening it much as it had me in such a short time.

Timer set, I began to bundle up the garbage. Hauling the bag out of the bin, I opened the alley door and went outside. I paused to inhale the cool, humid air. I loved to run this time of morning, and I vowed to start again after Thanksgiving. The Savannah River, only a few blocks to the east, filled the air with its distinctive energy—mysterious and oddly thrilling, as if it had recorded the deep and unique history of the place in its ever-changing current.

One advantage to being an über-early riser was the opportunity to experience silence. It wasn't blackout quiet—birds were beginning to call to one another, the thrum of some kind of compressor vibrated down the alleyway, and my cotton skirt rustled against my canvas apron. The lack of engines, conversations, and the ubiquitous tour bus guides was notable, though.

So I heard the new sound quite clearly, though it was barely above a whisper. A scraping, surface against surface. I paused with the bag of garbage suspended over the Dumpster. My breath stilled as my ears twitched like Mungo's, and I tried to unravel what it might be. Cat? The wind moving a branch? But there were no branches back here. Only brick and metal, asphalt, fuse boxes, and back doors.

A flash of light to my left caught my eye. It lasted only a microsecond, but I recognized it anyway. Head high, sweeping quickly across brick. Someone was standing in the alley mere yards away, close to the building and wearing a bicycle headlamp like the one I sometimes used to garden in the middle of the night when I couldn't sleep.

A shiver ran down my back, and my muscles froze.

The light flickered again, faint, as if shielded. Then I realized the person was standing in the alcove surrounding the back door of the Fox and Hound.

The scraping grew louder.

Someone is trying to break in to Croft's store.

"Hey!" I yelled before I had the good sense to think about it.

The figure backed out of the doorway, and I hesitated, hoping to see what the culprit looked like before he—she?—ran away.

Bulky. Shapeless. Tallish. Hat.

But whoever it was didn't run away. The interloper ran *toward* me.

Reason flooded back, and I dropped the garbage in the container. I turned on my heel and sprinted toward the open door of the Honeybee.

A rattle split the night, clanging and urgent. I spun around in time to see that the figure was pushing one of the big eight-yard Dumpsters toward me faster than I would have thought possible. The lumbering behemoth bore down on me like a freakish Mack truck. As I turned back to run into the bakery, my toe caught on the edge of a pothole in the alley, and I went down to my knees.

Terrified, I looked up to see the metal container blocking out the stars above. A scream rose in my throat as it crashed and bumped across the rough pavement straight for me. Instinctively, I swallowed my voice into my chest, squeezing the silent shriek into something hard and powerful.

The Dumpster suddenly stopped, one of its wheels also caught in a pothole, but its momentum tipped it up, up, up, until it teetered over my head. Falling . . .

"Nooo," I mouthed, still on my knees with one hand on the ground. Time slowed as I drew strength from the earth below. My mind coiled out to the river flowing nearby and the air all around me. Finally, I accessed the fourth element, fire, in my own chest—my scream tucked away and hardened to a red ember of fear. My other hand came up, glowing with white light as I *pushed* the Dumpster away.

The heavy metal container flipped back onto its wheels, spinning halfway around with its own force.

Or maybe *my* force.

Hard to tell. All I knew was that I was more or less okay, and mighty glad about it.

The light faded quickly from my fingertips, and footsteps sounded down the alley. I peered around the Dumpster in time to see a figure turning the corner.

I tried to push myself to my feet but fell back, shaking all over. Taking a deep breath, I reminded myself to calm down.

You're safe. They're gone.

Wincing, I brushed gravel out of a cut on my knee.

Mungo came flying out of the bakery, barking like a crazy dog.

"Nice of you to show up," I gasped, even though a part of me knew it had all happened in mere seconds.

He ran down the alley like a shot.

"Mungo!" I shouted. "Come back here."

He spun like a top and hightailed it back to launch himself at me. I barely managed to keep my balance but finally got to my feet with him in my arms. He licked my neck and chin and cheeks and nose, stopping long enough to look into my eyes as if checking to see that I was really okay, then starting in all over again.

I was still shaking, but I had to giggle. "Stop it. You're making me all soggy."

"Katie? Honey, where are . . . what are you doing out here?" Lucy asked from the doorway.

"I thought I was taking the garbage out," I said. "Turns out I might have foiled a burglar."

Her hand went to her throat. "Oh, dear."

"Would you mind calling 911? I need to get cleaned up."

"Well, good heavens, of course. Get in here. Let me look at you. What happened?"

I was glad to hear her lock the door behind me as I began to tell her.

*   *   *

A pair of patrol officers came and took my statement. Then they drove down the alley and lit up the area behind the bakery with the floodlight on their patrol car. I described what had happened as they took notes. One policeman gave the Dumpster a push, and it rumbled a few feet.

"You said it came at you pretty fast before you tripped?"

"It seemed like it was going sixty miles an hour," I said.

He smiled. "I doubt that. But it's empty and rolls easily. You couldn't see anything about them? Tall, short? Anything about how they moved that seemed distinctive?"

I shook my head. "I'm sorry. The figure seemed a little taller than me, but other than that, I didn't see much. It all happened so fast."

They called Croft, who showed up about half an hour later looking grizzled and disheveled and grumbling about being dragged out of bed before dawn. After Lucy gave him a couple of cups of coffee, his grumbles turned into a bitter diatribe about bad luck. Lucy offered him a slice of spice cake with the next cup of coffee, and I knew she was hoping the copious amounts of allspice in it would help with that luck problem of his.

After the police had gone, Lucy and I began taking loaves of sourdough out to cool on racks as quickly as possible, knowing we had to play a bit of catch-up with the morning baking despite my intentions to get an early start.

As we worked, I asked, "Do you think it was really bad luck that someone tried to break into the Fox and Hound this morning?"

She frowned and reached for the ingredients for the special we'd decided on for the day: chocolate croissants. "You mean you think it's related to the murder?"

I shrugged. "Seems kind of a weird coincidence otherwise."

My aunt looked speculative.

I pointed to the butter she held. "I don't think we have time to make the croissants now."

Lucy nodded. "You're right. Let's figure something else out."

Ben came in a little after six thirty to open up. When Lucy had filled him in on what had happened, he turned and gave me a hard look. "What were you thinking, Katie?"

"Uncle Ben! All I did was take the garbage out. You can't possibly think what happened was my fault."

"In the dark—," he began, but I held up my hand.

"I run in the early hours all the time," I said.

My aunt and uncle exchanged a significant look.

I shook my head emphatically. "No. I'm not going to live my life in fear." My fists found their way to my hips. "Besides, I can take care of myself—and did. Now, I'm going to get cleaned up and get back to work. We're behind with the baking, if you hadn't noticed." I stalked into the restroom and shut the door.

As I finally got around to picking the bits of asphalt out of my scraped knee, I knew I was lucky that I hadn't suffered a more severe injury. The incident in the alley hadn't been my first brush with danger. If I continued along the path of being a lightwitch, then it likely wouldn't be my last. I didn't relish the idea, believe me, but it didn't frighten me as much as it could have. As much as perhaps it should have.

A knock at the door. "Katie?" It was Lucy.

I opened it. Mungo stood beside her, worry creasing his furry face.

"I'm sorry," we said at the same time, and then laughed.

Ben was watching from across the room. Relief eased onto his face when he heard us.

"He's just worried about you," Lucy said.

"I know."

"Let's take a look at that knee."

"Lucy, I don't need—"

"Nonsense." She pushed past me and grabbed the first-aid kit from under the sink. "Come out here where the light is better."

I followed her out to the still-closed bakery and sat down in a bistro chair. With cheery thoroughness, my aunt bandaged my knee as if I were a little girl.

Which was kind of nice, actually.

Mungo supervised as she insisted on slathering my knee with antibiotic ointment and used up all the gauze in the kit. When she had finished, it felt like I had a cast around my knee, but I didn't dare complain. Besides, the ointment quickly numbed the stinging pain, and my skirt was almost long enough to cover the bandage. Soon I was back in the kitchen, and Ben was opening the door to a waiting customer.

As I measured and mixed, I tried to ignore the slightly spacey feeling that flooded my brain. It was a little like the endorphin high I got from running, but I knew from experience that this time it was a result of the supernatural "push" I'd given the Dumpster. It would wear off in an hour or so, and other than a scraped knee and feeling a bit disconnected, I was none the worse for wear.

Or so I thought.

Chapter 12

I was in the kitchen, washing down the main worktable and wishing Iris didn't have her metalsmithing class on Monday mornings. On this Monday, at least, we could have really used her help. Still, we'd made a few adjustments—switching simple molasses cookies in for the daily special instead of the more labor- and time-intensive chocolate croissants. Ben had stepped in to do some KP when he wasn't needed at the register. Plus, the spacey feeling I got after practicing big magic came with a boost of extra energy.

But that was wearing thin as I wiped my hands on a towel and quickly ran through my mental task list, checking things off.

We're in good shape.

My stomach chose that moment to grumble loudly, and my thoughts shot to the fresh loaves of sourdough cooling on racks. Maybe just a nice, plain piece of buttered toast . . .

A small noise drew my attention to Mungo, who was sitting patiently in the half-open door of the office. Waiting for his own seriously late breakfast.

"Oh, gosh, little guy. I'm sorry!"

I quickly scrambled an egg and toasted three slices of still-warm bread. One of them I split with my familiar, along with the egg. It didn't take either of us very long to plow through the makeshift meal. The other two pieces of toast I slathered with spicy peach jam made by a local farmer and took out to Lucy and Ben.

As I handed over their snacks, Lucy handed me a cup of steaming liquid. I inhaled the strong herbal aroma.

"Rosemary?"

She nodded. "And peppermint and turmeric. Good for the nerves and grounding." She looked at me knowingly. "Which I bet you could still use."

I smiled gratefully and took a healthy swig.

"I talked to Mimsey a few minutes ago," Lucy said. "She said you have an appointment with Bing Hawkins at WMBK at eleven o'clock."

"Wow. That was fast."

My aunt smiled. "You know how much influence Mimsey Carmichael has in this town."

"Lucky us," I said. "I'll call Jaida and see if she's free to go with me."

She was, and agreed to drive. I hung up as the bell over the front door sounded.

Declan came in with two of his buddies from Five House, Scott and Randy. Scott was older and certainly the wiser of the two. Randy was a habitual flirt, though he kept it low-key with me, presumably because of Declan. The chiseled planes of his face always made me think of my father, and I felt sure he boasted Native American blood.

"Hey, guys," I said. My heart warmed to see Declan's eyes light up as soon as he saw me. At the same time, I felt a crack in my tough-girl act—an act I had apparently even fooled myself with.

"Hey, Katie," Scott said, heading straight for the pastry case with Randy right behind him. "You still have those Parmesan scones I like?"

Ben hurried over and got the guys their regular treats and poured them some coffee. Soon the three men were chatting about all things firefighter at a table in the corner.

I pasted on a cheerful smile as Declan strode behind the register where I stood. "Missed you this morning." His muscular arms wrapped around me, and instantly I felt that depth of safety I knew nowhere else. In his enthusiasm, he lifted me right off the ground.

"Deck, I'm at work," I mumbled halfheartedly into his shoulder.

He set me down. "Sorry," he began but stopped when he saw me wince. "What's the matter?"

"Nothing," I said.

Lucy chimed in. "If chasing off a burglar in the dark and nearly getting taken out by a giant Dumpster is nothing."

"What?" Affection turned to alarm on Declan's face.

I sighed and looked around the bakery. Ben was still occupying the other firemen, though Randy was watching Declan and me while trying to look like he wasn't. Then Scott caught my eye by accident and looked away quickly, but not before I saw the beginning of a grin tug at his lips.

What's that all about?

"Katie?" Declan was impatiently waiting for more information.

I gave Lucy a thanks-a-lot look, even though she didn't really deserve it. It wasn't like I wouldn't have told my boyfriend about what had happened that morning.

She knew that, of course, and merely gave me a cheerful grin in return.

"Come over here." I grabbed Declan's hand and led him over to the empty reading area. Other than his friends and a couple with their teenage son by the front window, the only other customer was our resident writer, Arthur, lost in his own fictional world fueled by dark-roast coffee and protected by noise-blocking headphones.

Mungo surreptitiously padded out of the kitchen behind us, a small black wraith that none of the customers seemed to notice. He settled into his bed on the bottom bookshelf as we sat down on the sofa, where I filled Declan in on the details of my earlier adventure.

When I was done, he frowned. "You promised you wouldn't get hurt."

"I promised to try." I poked at the bundle of gauze on my knee, undecided about whether I should tell him magic had saved me from being crushed by the Dumpster.

He started to say something, then hesitated, looking away. "Oh, Katie," he finally said, and met my eyes. He gave a little nod and squared his shoulders.

As if he just made a decision of some kind.

"What?" I asked, feeling my eyes narrow.

But he only smiled. "I'm just glad you're okay." He eyed the elaborate bandage. "You *are* okay?"

I bit my lip and nodded. "It looks worse than it really is."

"Hmm. Okay, so someone was trying to break into Croft's," he said. "Does it have something to do with the murder?"

I shrugged. "Could be a regular ol' attempted burglary."

He gave me a look. "Right. Everyone knows what cash cows bookstores are."

"He did have a very good night on Saturday." I grimaced. "As far as sales go, I mean."

"I don't suppose you'd reconsider letting Quinn handle this one on his own, would you?"

Down at floor level, Mungo made a noise in the back of his throat.

I looked at him, then back at my boyfriend. Declan had my best interests in mind. I knew that. But it still kind of surprised me that he didn't know me better than that.

Or maybe he did.

"In about an hour, Jaida and I are going to the radio station where Dr. Dana recorded her call-in program. We're going to have a little chat with the station manager."

He took a deep breath, then: "I see."

"Deck, please don't worry."

"Sure. No problem." A bit of sarcasm leaked through, though. "Listen, the reason I stopped by was to ask you not to make any plans for tonight. I have a very special supper planned for us."

"'Very special,' huh." I grinned.

"Seriously. Don't go hying off after some clue tonight. This is impor—" He stopped himself. "I just want to know I can count on you being there."

"Of course," I said, surprised. "I'll be home right after work. And I'll grab something for dessert."

A single nod. "Okay. Good." And then a smile, almost as an afterthought. "I can't wait, darlin'." His intensity fell away as he leaned in and gave me a big smack on the lips. "I'll see you then."

"What are you up to?" I asked.

"You'll see." He rose and walked back to his friends.

I raised my eyebrows at Mungo, but if a dog could shrug, he did.

The three firefighters left together. As they went out the door, Scott gave me a conspiratorial look over his shoulder.

Baffled, I returned to where Ben and Lucy stood behind the espresso counter.

"Did you see that?" I asked.

"See what?" Ben responded.

"Never mind." *Probably just my imagination.*

Jaida showed up at the bakery a few minutes before eleven. Her blazer over a long-sleeved white T-shirt made me think it wasn't a court day for her, and her brightly painted toenails peeking out of open-toed shoes beneath her dark slacks confirmed it.

"Thanks for making time to go with me," I said.

"Sure. Gregory can handle things at the office for a couple of hours." She was referring to her partner—both in love and in lawyering. He was also a witch, but he preferred to practice solitary.

In the office, Mungo hunkered down in my tote bag to stay out of sight as I carried him through the kitchen. On the way, I paused.

"Are you sure you and Ben will be all right? I could see if Jaida can go with me after Iris comes in this afternoon."

My aunt gave me a gentle smile. "We'll be fine, honey. You go ahead and see what you can find out from that radio station manager."

"Sure we will!" Ben chimed in from behind the register. "Just be careful not to let that Bing Hawkins talk you into buying airtime. He's a wily salesman."

"You know him?" I asked.

He nodded. "From the Rotary Club."

I grinned. "I'll try to resist."

"Hope you do more than try," he muttered as I walked away.

Jaida and I went out to Broughton Street. Mungo peeked his head out, eager for his next adventure. The sun felt warm on my shoulders. Lucy had planted sweet William, nicotiana, and autumn clematis in the yard-square wooden box on the sidewalk in front of the Honeybee, and their heady fragrances curled together in the crisp fall air.

As we passed by the Fox and Hound, I saw the sign in the window said OPEN, and the interior lights were on. Flames in the gas fireplace flickered. Breathing a sigh of relief, I said, "Good to see things are getting back to normal."

Jaida nodded. "Poor Croft. All he wanted was for a celebrity to sign her book in his store, and he ends up in the news and out of business for a day. At least it was *only* for a day."

"Not to mention that someone tried to break into his store this morning," I said, and went on to tell her the rest of what had happened.

"You did that thing where you glow?" she asked when I'd finished.

"Uh-huh. Just for a few seconds."

She laughed. "I bet you scared the pants off that burglar."

I snorted. "I hadn't even thought of that."

Halfway down the block, we reached her dark blue minivan. Given Jaida's tendency for inserting a bit of underlying rebel into her lawyerly ensembles, whether a dash of color or a piece of unexpected jewelry, most people would have expected her to drive something more exciting. But then again, when you have little ones . . .

Not that Anubis was little in any literal sense. The

Great Dane leaned his giant square head out of the back window and gave a low-throated woof. Mungo yipped in response.

Old-home week for the familiars.

Once inside, Mungo scrambled out of my tote and joined the big brindle beast in the backseat. I looked around to see them touching noses, both descended from wolves though one weighed a hundred and fifty pounds and the other a tenth of that. Anubis settled onto the seat and Mungo tucked in between his front paws. I couldn't help smiling.

Jaida steered the minivan down Broad Street and turned onto Victory Drive. Blake Shelton crooned on the radio, and the breeze that winged through the open windows smelled faintly of burning leaves and ripe apples.

"I had no idea you liked country music," I said.

"I don't, but Anubis won't listen to anything else."

Surprised, I looked back to see him grinning his agreement. Mungo seemed to be enjoying himself as well.

"Yeah, well, mine thinks heaven is spending the day surrounded by snacks and binge watching *Days of Our Lives.*"

Yip!

I suddenly wondered whether he'd watched soap operas when he lived with Angie.

Stop it.

But apparently I wasn't the only one thinking along those lines. When we were stopped at a red light, Jaida turned to me. "I've been thinking. About how I'd feel if I were in your same situation." Her eyes flicked to the backseat, and I understood she was referring to having my familiar's ex-witch show up out of the blue.

A quick glance over my shoulder assured me she

wasn't fooling either of the pups, who were watching us with wise wolf eyes.

One side of my mouth pulled up. "And?"

She glanced in the rearview mirror and saw what I had. "Oh. Well, I'd be torn about helping her. Like you, I guess."

"Do you think witches have a special responsibility to be moral?" I asked.

She pursed her lips and flipped on her turn signal. "Because we have power, you mean?"

I nodded.

"Well, yes. Of course. But then again, everyone has power—more than most people realize. Don't you think?"

I nodded again.

"So, of course witches need to wield their power with an eye to morality. Or, in the parlance of a lightwitch like you, with an eye to the good. But so does everyone else. So while witches certainly have a responsibility, I don't think it's exactly special." She glanced over at me. "Not that I don't think *you're* special."

That made me laugh. "Actually, I like the idea of being just like everyone else. It's comforting." Especially for someone who had spent her first twenty-eight years feeling like she didn't fit in anywhere.

Chapter 13

The building that housed WMBK-AM radio was so nondescript we drove right by it the first time. The big satellite dish would have given it away, but it was on the back side. Jaida made a U-turn and pulled into the nearly empty parking lot on one side of the long, one-story expanse of brick. We left the windows down for the dogs and headed toward the front door.

It opened before we could push inside, and a man exited. My jaw slackened in surprise when I saw who it was.

His precision-cut hair was the color of heavily salted caramel. The fine lines etched into his face further indicated his age. Irises so light gray they seemed to have no color at all were ringed with deep charcoal. And there was that curve to his upper lip, which exactly mirrored his son's.

Heinrich Dawes. Steve's father. One of the richest businessmen in Savannah—heck, in Georgia, if not the United States. And leader of the Dragohs, the exclusive druid clan that had existed in the area since before Savannah had even been established as a city.

Not, I might add, the most ethical druid clan. The

spellbook club had worked with them once, but I had serious questions about how their magical men's club did business.

He paused for a split second when he saw us, quickly schooling his face into a bland smile. "Katie Lightfoot. It's been a while." A slight bow that would have looked corny if anyone else had done it. "And Ms. French. A delight, as always."

"Mr. Dawes," she said.

He tipped his head to the side and regarded me. "Let me guess. You're up to your old tricks."

I bristled. "Meaning?"

"It's big news in town that Dana Dobbs died in the Fox and Hound on Saturday night. Right next to your little bakery. Since she taped her shows here, I assume you're here in some kind of connection with that."

"For your information, I'm here to talk about advertising with the station manager."

One eyebrow slowly lifted. "Not the ad manager?"

"Bing Hawkins happens to be a friend of Mimsey's," Jaida said. "She referred us to him directly."

"And you?" I asked. After all, if he was going to be rude, so could I.

Little bakery. Ergh.

"Business," he said curtly.

Fine. "I saw Steve yesterday. When did he get back into town?"

Jaida's gaze slid sideways to me.

A stony expression settled on Heinrich's face. "My son and I are not currently speaking to each other. I certainly am not inclined to speak *about* him, either. Good day, ladies."

I frowned as he walked by, watching as he climbed into a dark Mercedes and drove away.

"What was that all about?" Jaida asked.

"No idea," I said, and pushed through the door.

"But Steve's back?"

"Well, he was driving down Broughton Street yesterday. That's all I know."

Inside the station, the air smelled of burnt coffee and Pine-Sol. Somewhere, speakers broadcasted someone talking about politics, the volume low enough that I couldn't make out most of what he was saying. The small entry was decorated with fake ferns that needed a good dusting, a few Scandinavian-style chairs, and a low table strewn with magazines. Industrial carpeting led down a hallway studded with doors on the left side and a big glass window on the right. We glanced at each other and started down the hall.

The first door was open, showing an empty office. The next was closed, and the sign on the door said PRODUCTION STUDIO. Across the hall, the window revealed the working studio. Two desks were packed with computer consoles, a board with all sorts of little levers, and a series of boxes and consoles covered with buttons and lights that performed who knew what functions. A woman sat behind one of the desks, a huge microphone arching over her head on an articulated arm. It didn't look like she was on the air, but she was doing something on the computer and didn't look up. The talking head droned on in the background, evidently a recorded show rather than a live one. The place felt empty and weirdly quiet.

Movement at the end of the building caught my attention, and I looked just in time to see none other than Phoebe Miller walk around the corner and go through one of the doors.

"You must be Katie Lightfoot."

I turned to see a man coming out of an office one door down from where we stood. In his late thirties, he was about my height. His dark hair was pulled back from a receding hairline and twisted into a hipster man bun. As he came near, the smell of wet dog wafted from his flannel shirt.

"Guilty as charged. And you must be Bing." I smiled and shook his hand. "This is Jaida French. She's another friend of Mimsey's, and, er, helps with our marketing."

"Nice to meet you both," he said. "Come into my office so we can chat."

We followed him inside and perched on the guest chairs. He plopped into his desk chair, already speaking a mile a minute.

"So you want to buy some airtime. Excellent! It's really the best way to spend your advertising dollar, especially for a business like yours. Mims said you have a bakery? Perfect!"

"Well, we're just exploring—"

"Oh, believe me, you're going to want to do more than explore. Radio is immediate, it's intimate, and it reaches the audience in every aspect of their lives— work, play, in their cars, when they wake up in the morning, as they go to sleep at night. It's cost-effective and reaches the customer over and over. After all, the more someone hears about your business, the more they'll remember it, and the more likely they'll frequent it. And I haven't even talked about the theater of the mind yet!" He beamed at us.

"Wow. That all sounds very interesting," I said. "And I know Mimsey is quite pleased with how your station has helped her flower shop."

Bing opened his mouth, and I hurried on before he could get going again. "So can you choose when your ad will play? I was thinking of *The Dr. Dana Show*, because she was so popular, but then, well . . ." I trailed off.

He sighed. "Right. You heard about what happened. Horrible. Just horrible. And yes, you can certainly choose. Different slots cost different amounts, of course. Ad slots in her show were our most expensive for the very reason you just mentioned—she had a huge audience. But I'm afraid there's no *Dr. Dana Show* without Dr. Dana."

"I'm very sorry," I said, feeling like a heel.

"We heard there was a movement to shut down the show," Jaida said.

"Oh, I wouldn't go that far. I mean, sure—there were a few letters suggesting that we take Dana off the air. But there are always nuts out there who write in. You think Rush Limbaugh doesn't get hate mail as well as fan mail?" He made a rude noise. "But we'd never have fired Dana. Sheesh."

"Because of the ad income?" she asked.

Bing frowned. "That, but WMBK made a lot more from syndication." He brightened. "But let's talk about which shows would work for you! I'd advise hitting the airways in the morning before people leave for work, again at noon, and then when people are driving home. In fact—"

"Excuse me," I cut in. "Do you happen to have a restroom I could use?"

He blinked. "Oh. Sure. There's one at the end of the hall."

Jaida gave me a slightly puzzled glance, but she stepped in like a trouper. As I left Bing's office, I heard her say, "Perhaps you could tell me a little more about how syndication works."

I hurried down the hall, slowing as I neared the door

I'd seen Phoebe go into. It was open. I stopped in front of it.

"Excuse me, is the restroom . . . Oh, hi."

She looked up, and surprise crossed her tired face. "Katie, right?"

"Right."

The space looked like it was used primarily for storage, with file cabinets along one wall, banks of cupboards on both sides, and a table stacked with all manner of equipment in the middle of the room. One of the cabinet doors was open behind Phoebe, and a cardboard carton sat open on the table. She put the stack of notebooks she was holding into the box.

"Are you looking for someone?" she asked. I could tell she was wondering why the heck I was there, and I saw her eye the bandage peeking out from under my skirt.

"I was just chatting with Bing about buying some radio time and needed to use the restroom."

I stepped into the room, casually looking in the box. It was mostly paperwork and a couple of hardback books. Then I saw one of them was simply titled *Tarot Spells.* A shiver ran down my spine. Nestled next to it were several red candles with burned wicks, and a purple velvet bag that reminded me of the one Jaida used to store her tarot deck.

All that from a single, quick glance, but Phoebe saw me looking. Her face turned pink, and she quickly shut the cardboard flaps.

"I'm just clearing out some of Dana's things. She recorded her show here, you know. Then she distributed it all over the country." Her gaze flicked to the now-closed box. "My sister had some . . . unusual interests."

Lots of people are interested in tarot. But those candles. Good heavens, was Dana Dobbs a witch? The thought made me a little dizzy, but I managed a noncommittal smile.

"I know some people didn't care for her methods. For the kind of old-school, traditional-value advice she dispensed," Phoebe said.

"Radical Trust."

She snorted. "More like Radical Control." Her eyes widened, and her next words sounded defensive. "But it worked for her and Nate. She helped a lot of people, you know."

I nodded.

Phoebe ran one hand over her face. "God, she could be a royal pain in the patootie sometimes. She went through four assistants before I took the job. Heck, we were late to the signing the other night because she was firing her literary agent."

My ears perked up at that nugget of information.

"I knew how to manage her, though," Phoebe said. "She was my sister, and I knew her better than anyone. She was a good person at heart." Her eyes welled.

"I'm really sorry," I said, feeling helpless.

She reached into the cupboard and drew out a couple of envelopes. Shook them at me. "Do you know what these are?"

I shook my head.

"The letters I told you about. The ones that Kissel woman sent." She shook her head. "But this was just the tip of the iceberg. She sent e-mails to all the other stations around the country that carry the show."

Great. I wondered whether Detective Quinn knew that. My bet was that Bing Hawkins was right—most radio personalities received both good and bad audience feedback—but it didn't make Angie look good at all.

Phoebe waved her hand. "Listen to me going on and on. I guess packing up this stuff is more difficult than I expected." Her laugh had a bitter edge to it. "And here you just wanted to find the restroom. It's right around the corner there."

"Thanks." I was sorry I'd interrupted the painful process of clearing her sister's things. But I stopped in the doorway. "Did you find your wallet?"

She blinked. "Oh! Yes. On the floor of my car. Thanks for asking."

"And you mentioned a memorial for your sister. I'd like to come if there is one."

"Yes, I managed to put something together on the day after tomorrow. I tried to get Bryson Hall, but they were booked for a wedding. So we're having it outside, in Chippewa Square. The station will announce it a few times over the next couple of days, and I'm hoping her local fans will attend."

"I'm sure there will be a big turnout for your sister."

"It's at two in the afternoon."

"I'll try to make it." I backed into the hallway, remembering at the last second to turn toward the restroom.

A few minutes later I was back in Bing's office. Jaida was on her feet and thanking him for answering all of her questions.

"No problem!" he said. "Not very many people are interested in how syndication works. And I'm looking forward to working with you in the future." He nodded to include me in the *you.*

My smile tightened. "Working with us?"

Jaida gave me an apologetic smile. "Bing really thinks

we need to try out a few ads for the Honeybee during the holiday season."

I opened my mouth to speak, then closed it. "You can fill me in on the details in the car," I finally managed.

"I'll call you to follow up," Bing said, his tone triumphant. "I guarantee you'll see the difference in business in no time."

Smiling weakly, I said good-bye. We went back out to the familiars waiting in the minivan, who greeted us with wagging tails and slurping kisses.

"Now, don't get mad," Jaida said once we were buckled in. "I didn't sign anything. I didn't even say yes."

"He seems to think you did. You know Uncle Ben will blow a gasket." I groaned. "Especially after all his warnings about what a good salesman that guy is."

She grimaced and started the vehicle. "You can tell the guy you changed your mind. Say I didn't have the authority to even say we'd consider it—which is totally true, of course. But he did make a lot of good points, and he offered a steep discount."

"Because of Mimsey?"

"Partly. But the station is in dire straits and needs the business. They had a lot of eggs in the Dr. Dana basket."

I looked sideways at her. "Sounds like you drew Mr. Hawkins out quite a bit after I left."

She grinned and pulled into traffic. "You're not the only one who can find things out, you know."

I held up my hands. "Boy, do I ever. You've helped me so many times I've lost count. So what did you learn?"

"A lot of boring stuff about how syndication works. In a nutshell, most talk shows are syndicated through a radio network. Dana Dobbs' show was self-syndicated, however. So rather than a network acting as a go-between with other stations around the country, WMBK produced and recorded all her shows and then distributed them via FTP download directly to the other stations they'd sold rebroadcasting rights to. Turns out, that's what Bing really concentrated his sales abilities on. They partnered directly with Dana Dobbs and one other investor. International syndication was next."

"That sounds like a lot of work for a small station like that."

She nodded. "From what I understand, once everything is in place, it's not too hard to maintain. But when they started out, they needed more staff and a pile of money."

"The third investor?"

Our eyes met briefly before Jaida looked back at the road.

"Heinrich Dawes," I guessed. It made sense. Dawes Corp. was a venture capital firm. Investing was what he did.

"Bing didn't mention a name," she said. "But it would explain why he was leaving the station. He might be out a lot of money."

"I wonder if Steve would know," I mused. It was a perfectly reasonable excuse to call him.

"But his father said they weren't speaking."

Steve, who had a column in the *Savannah Morning News*, had begun working for Dawes Corp. soon after he'd joined the Dragoh clan.

"How could they not be speaking?" I made a face. "Something weird is going on there."

Jaida was quiet for a few beats. Then: "Does Declan know Steve's back in town?"

I shrugged. "I didn't mention it. He says he's okay with our friendship. I wish it were true. After all, it's been . . . oh, my God."

"What is it?"

"I'm an idiot."

She laughed. "How so?"

"I was wondering why Deck came in this morning and made such a big deal about supper tonight. *I totally forgot that tomorrow is our one-year anniversary.* And he's on shift starting tomorrow morning, so we're celebrating *tonight*."

Chapter 14

"Oh, man," Jaida said. "You are in trouble."

I buried my face in my hands. "He's making some special menu, and who knows what else, and I didn't get him anything at all."

"Yep. Trouble."

The minivan hit a bump, and I looked up to see she'd pulled into the Dairy Queen.

"Ice cream time," she sang.

"I don't want any." My mind was still scrambling for what I could get Declan on such short notice.

"It's not for you," she said.

Yip!

While the dogs slurped their vanilla cones, I told Jaida about talking to Phoebe.

"Dr. Dana fired her literary agent right before she was killed? That's an interesting coincidence. Was it someone local?"

"No idea. She was pretty upset, and I didn't want to ask for more details."

"Of course not. Maybe Quinn would know."

"Not that he'd care," I grumbled. "Maybe Croft can help." Then I told her about the tarot book and candles.

"Wait—was the book about tarot reading or tarot spells?"

"It was called *Tarot Spells*," I said, "so I assume the latter."

"How many candles?"

"I didn't count them."

"More than five?"

"Definitely."

"More than ten?"

"I think so."

"Could there be thirteen?"

"Maybe. Why?"

She sat back with a bemused expression. "Well, I'll be darned."

"What?"

"Thirteen red candles are used in a classic tarot love spell, along with the Lovers card and the significator cards on either side."

I knew from what she'd taught me over the last year that a significator card was simply one that the spell caster felt best represented a person—the Empress as a powerful female figure, for example, or the Hierophant as a teacher. Sometimes it was a card that represented the best version of a person, and sometimes it was more realistic.

She looked rueful. "Maybe that whole thing about Radical Trust wasn't working so well for Dr. Dana after all."

Jaida dropped me off in front of the Honeybee, saying she had to get back to the office. I knew darn well it was because she didn't want to have to tell Ben she'd succumbed to Bing Hawkins' sales skills. My uncle waved from the reading area, where a mix of mothers and fathers and their children clustered around the big coffee table, which was covered with a thick layer of newspaper. It looked like they were making turkeys out of paper cups with the bottoms cut out, pom-poms, googly eyes, brightly colored craft paper for feathers—and plenty of glue. Iris was with them, too, bent over her own craft project so that I could see only her flamingo pink ponytail sprouting from the top of her head. I returned my uncle's wave and veered toward the kitchen.

Lucy had just taken a pan of cranberry coconut cookies out of the oven, and they smelled heavenly. I grabbed one and asked, "What's going on out there?"

"It's a homeschooling group. They were going to meet at Croft's, but then the parents heard what happened."

I made a face. "That's too bad. But at least he's open."

She nodded. "Things will get back to normal soon. Did you find out anything interesting?"

I motioned her into the office and closed the door. "A few things—though I don't know how interesting they are." I ticked off the high points on my fingers. "*The Dr. Dana Show* was the lifeblood of the radio station, and they might be in real trouble without it. Heinrich Dawes may or may not have been a primary investor in the syndication of the show. Dana fired her agent right before she died." I tapped my pinkie. "And if Dr. Dana wasn't a witch, she at least dabbled in tarot magic. Jaida says it might have been love magic."

Lucy whistled. "No kidding. That's kind of sad, really. Considering that her whole reputation was built on relationship advice. Still, it's another possible magical connection to the murder."

And one Detective Quinn would just call "woo-woo nonsense" and ignore.

I nodded. "And on a completely unrelated note, I have to leave again. Just for a little bit."

She raised her eyebrows.

"I'm so sorry, but tomorrow is Declan's and my anniversary. That's what tonight's supper is all about. I'm sure of it."

"Oh, honey! I didn't realize! Congratulations!"

"Lucy, I'm such a lame girlfriend," I wailed softly. "I totally forgot. At the very least I have to go get a card. Say," I said with sudden hope, "I don't suppose you have any clever ideas about what I could get him in the next"—I looked at my watch—"three hours?"

"Gosh, Katie. I'll think about it. But I'm sure if you don't get him a gift, he'll understand."

I wasn't so sure.

She made a shooing gesture with both hands. "Go get that card. Cardiologie will have something, and it's just down the street."

"It looks pretty busy out there with all the kids. I'll hurry!" I winced. "And I told him I'd grab something for dessert. I'd better come up with something impressive."

"Don't be silly. Iris and Ben can stop playing with paste and come help me if we get a rush, and I can whip up a flourless chocolate torte while you're gone. That should be a match for any fancy dishes he has planned."

"Thanks, Lucy. You're a lifesaver." I gave her a quick hug.

Mungo and I left through the back door, so we could check out the alley in the daylight. The big Dumpster the potential burglar had shoved at me that morning looked just as huge, but utterly harmless in the sunshine. The patch of pavement where it had tipped toward me looked a little scuffed, but not as scuffed as my knee. The memory of the power that had rushed through me when I'd pushed it away made my skin goose-bump.

Mungo wanted down, so I leashed him for our short walk. We headed west down the alley, then cut through to Broughton at the next cross street. As we strode down the busy sidewalk, I racked my brain for what I could get Declan.

A gift card to his favorite restaurant? Lame. *Clothes? Jewelry? Watch?* Lame, lame, and he always wore his late father's timepiece. It needed to be something romantic for the first anniversary. Something special. I felt panic arrow through me, but instead of the adrenaline sparking a great idea, my mind went utterly, stupidly blank.

Think!

Experiences were good gifts, right? Often far better than stuff. *A hot-air balloon ride?* I shuddered. Heights were not my cup of tea, and it wouldn't be very romantic to send him up alone. He'd mentioned taking our relationship to the next level a few times lately, casually saying it would be less expensive to combine households, especially since we already spent most of our off-hours together. But I hadn't even gotten around to making the trip to Boston to meet his mother and sisters yet—another thing he'd been trying to get me to do . . .

I came to a dead stop. "Mungo! I've got it. I know exactly what to get Declan! And all I have to do is write it in the card."

A passing couple stared at me standing smack-dab in the middle of the sidewalk and talking to my dog. I offered a feeble smile and started walking again. In front of the card shop, I looped my familiar's leash around a light standard so he could spend a little more time outside, and went in. He could easily get loose, but I knew he wouldn't take off.

Unless Angie Kissel was to walk by.

I pushed the uncharitable thought out of my mind as I pushed the door open. A clerk greeted me as I wound through the displays of gag gifts, candles, bath products, toys, and decor items to the card racks.

There were so many cards to choose from: funny, serious, romantic, silly, flowery, and sappy poetic ones. None were quite right. Finally, I went to the blank cards and found one that spoke to my heart. It was a black-and-white close-up photo of clasped hands, a man's and a woman's, from behind.

"Katie?"

My heart stuttered as I turned to find Steve Dawes standing right behind me. Blond hair flopped over his forehead, and the tan I'd noticed the day before was even richer than I'd realized. His dark green T-shirt accented a few more muscles than I remembered him having.

His lips curved into a smile. "Of course it's you." He eyed the card in my hand.

Annoyed as well as relieved, I said, "I saw you driving by yesterday morning. Nice car."

"It's good to see you."

I put my hands on my hips. "Where the heck have you been for the last three months? You didn't answer my texts, and I e-mailed, and . . . and . . ." I trailed off. "Why are you smiling like that?"

His teeth flashed. "And here I was afraid you'd be mad at me."

"I am!"

"But still worried. So you still care about me."

"I'm not *worried*. Just . . . curious. Plus, I saw your father earlier today, and he said you two aren't speaking. Does he even know you're back in town?"

He looked around to see if anyone had heard me. We were the only customers.

"Ah, Father. Yes, well. Listen, I saw Mungo outside, so I assume you're on foot. Are you heading back to the Honeybee?"

"So if you saw Mungo, what was with the 'Katie, is that you?'" I shook my head. "Yes, I'm walking. And I need to get back."

"Mind if I walk with you?"

Now that I knew he was okay, I wanted to strangle him. "Suit yourself."

I bought the card from the friendly clerk and went out to untie Mungo. We started down the street in the direction of the Honeybee.

Steve hurried to catch up. "I saw in the *Savannah Morning News* that someone was killed in the Fox and Hound Saturday night."

"Dr. Dana Dobbs."

"You were there, of course."

I looked at him sideways.

"Don't bother denying it. I'm back working at the *News*, doing my column again and working part-time on the crime beat, as well."

"Were you the one who called Croft for an interview?"

He shook his head. "That wasn't me."

"But that's the sort of thing you're doing now."

"Yes."

My steps slowed. "What about Dawes Corp.?"

We walked in silence for a few moments. "I quit."

I stopped short. "Just . . . quit?"

"The last three months I've been living in the Bahamas and working on a charter fishing boat."

That explained how tan and fit he was. *The Bahamas. Sheesh.* I couldn't believe I'd been concerned. We started walking again.

"I needed time to think after what happened with Samantha."

I grimaced, remembering the fiasco with the woman he'd been dating in August.

He cleared his throat. "And I came to a conclusion, Katie."

Something about his tone made me look over at him again.

"When you chose Declan over me, I tried to let it go. To let you go. But after what happened with Sam, it became obvious that there's simply no one else for me."

"Oh, for heaven's sake, Steve. We've talked about this—"

He barreled on. "I truly believe we're supposed to be together, Katie. I know you and Declan have been together for a year."

Darn it—even Steve remembered that.

"But the truth is, if I can't have you, I won't have anyone."

At our feet, Mungo made a low, growling noise. He'd never liked Steve as much as he liked Declan.

"Now, come on," I said, feeling a little desperate. "Stop being so dramatic. You'll find someone."

He shrugged. "I don't want anyone else. I love you."
Ack!

"Which means I want you to be happy, more than anything. If that means you stay with Declan, then so be it. But I thought you should know how I feel."

"Steve," I tried again.

"And I think you should also know that I understand why you turned away from me in the first place. So I've not only quit working for Father, but I resigned my membership in the Dragohs."

I stopped and gaped at him.

"I know you disapprove of how we—those—druids conduct their business in Savannah. At least now I'm not one of them."

I realized my mouth was still hanging open and snapped it shut. "Is that why you and Heinrich aren't speaking?"

He nodded. "In fact, I'm pretty sure he's going to disown me. I moved out of the guesthouse on my parents' estate and rented a basement apartment in Midtown. I've cut all those ties."

For me? The thought made me feel sick with guilt. Good heavens—he was *pining* for me. But I truly loved Declan. Sure, there had been a *zing* of energy between Steve and me since the first time I'd seen him sitting across the Honeybee, and Lord knew he'd been a good friend to me. But that wasn't anything like what I had with Declan. *I have to fix this somehow.* Steve was giving up an enormous fortune and familial ties to the community . . .

No. Wait.

Is that my fault?

I'd given him no encouragement after I'd started dating Declan. I hadn't asked him to go to the Bahamas or to give up anything for me. I'd only saved him from what would have been a truly horrible marriage—and I'd done it as a friend.

We reached the Honeybee, and as we stopped in front I found myself growing angry. He had no right to pressure me like that. If he wanted to give up everything, then that was his business.

"I'm sorry you feel that way," I said, slowly. "And while I don't think you're deliberately trying to manip-ulate me, it still kind of feels like it." I held up the bag I'd been carrying. "This is the anniversary card I got for Declan. And there are going to be more of them."

Yip! Mungo added his two cents.

Steve's face clouded. "Katie."

"I'm sure I'll see you around," I said with as much dignity as I could muster, and escaped into the bakery.

He didn't follow.

My hands were trembling, and my insides felt like jelly. I'd forgotten to put Mungo in my tote, but no one seemed to care. The homeschoolers were oblivious, but Ben, Lucy, and Iris were all watching me as I hustled behind the reg-ister. Mungo beelined through to his chair in the office.

"So Steve's back," Ben said. Obviously we'd had an audience. My uncle's disapproval was clear. Declan had been his protégé in the fire department long before I'd come to town, and he viewed him as the son he'd never had. He'd never cared that much for Steve and had been over the moon when Declan and I got together.

"He is." I kept my tone neutral.

"Ohmagod," Iris breathed. "He is so *hot*. I would just die if he asked me out."

"He's twice your age," I said wryly.

"The chocolate torte is in the oven," Lucy said diplo-matically. "I see you found a card."

"You didn't forget your own anniversary, did you?" Ben asked.

I managed a bright "Of course not!"

Lucy frowned at the lie, but I crossed my fingers that I could count on her not to give me away.

"A whole year!" Ben grinned. "From what I understand you can expect filet mignon tonight."

"Ben!" Lucy admonished. "Declan may have wanted to surprise her."

"I promise I won't let on," I said, hustling to drop my tote in the office and get back to work.

Chapter 15

As I went about my work, I kept an eye on Arthur, the writer who came in to work at the corner table several days a week. When he sat back, removed his noise-canceling earphones, and looked around, I sidled over. He looked up with surprise.

"Hey, Arthur. I hope I'm not breaking your concentration."

"Not at all. I needed to take a little break. What's up?"

I sat down across from him. "I was hoping you might be able to tell me how to find the name of an author's literary agent."

He leaned his elbows on the table and grinned. "Why, Katie. Are you writing a book?"

"Heavens no!" I mentally scrambled and settled on the usual: "It's for a friend."

He looked puzzled but shrugged. "Some authors list them on their Web site."

Dr. Dana hadn't. I'd just checked in the office.

"And most agencies list their authors. But that's not what you're asking. You could ask the author directly."

I wrinkled my nose. "Not in this case."

Understanding dawned. "Your 'friend' wants to know who repped Dana Dobbs?"

I nodded.

"Well, I don't know why, but you could always check the back of her books. Most writers that I know thank their agents in the acknowledgments."

I brightened and stood. "Thanks. I'll try that. Can I get you more tea?"

He held out his mug. "Sure." As I walked away, he said, "For a friend, huh."

I pretended I didn't hear him.

Even though I'd ducked out twice already, I couldn't help running next door about half an hour before we closed. Croft was perched on his usual stool behind the register when I came in, and he looked up hopefully. When he saw it was me, his face fell.

"Gee, thanks," I said.

"Sorry, Katie. I was hoping you were a real customer. I can see there's traffic out on the street, but no one's coming in except reporters and looky-loos who want to know the gory details." He looked disgusted.

I didn't blame him one bit. "Did they at least buy Dr. Dana's books?"

With a rueful twist to his lips, he said, "A couple, but there aren't many left." His shoulders slumped. "I just couldn't bring myself to bring the ones she was signing in the back room out to sell."

"Oh, man. I hadn't thought of that."

"And Mrs. Potter was so upset by what happened that she didn't come in to work today. Since she's the story lady, story time was canceled."

"Yeah, I'm pretty sure some of the kids came over

to the Honeybee this afternoon," I said. "I'm sure they'll be back over here in no time."

"If Mrs. Potter is." He sighed. "I don't suppose you're here to actually buy anything."

"Sorry. But I'll sure be in after Thanksgiving to do some Christmas shopping. Today I just wanted to take a look at one of Dr. Dana's books."

He waved his hand. "Knock yourself out. There are some left over there on the table."

Dr. Dana's earnest and slightly judgmental eyes gazed up at me from the cover.

Who hated you enough to slip cyanide in your drink? At least Angie had been up-front and honest about her feelings regarding the psychologist. Whoever had killed the woman was as sneaky as they came.

I flipped through to the acknowledgments. It was a short paragraph. The author had listed her husband first, then her fans, and then her sister. There was no mention of anyone else. Closing the book, I sighed. "Well, so much for that."

"What are you looking for?" Croft asked.

"The name of Dr. Dana's agent."

"Well, that's easy. Ronnie Lake."

I whirled. "How did you know that?"

He slipped off the stool and came around to the front of the counter. "She was here the night of the signing. Long blond braid, wore some crazy Mexican poncho? Only showed for a couple of minutes. I didn't talk with her, but Phoebe told me that's who she was."

A small whistle escaped my lips. "That was her agent? Golly. No wonder she looked so unhappy."

His forehead wrinkled. "I don't remember that."

"You had a few other things on your mind, Croft.

But she was definitely unhappy. And since I heard Dr. Dana had just fired her, I can see why."

Croft looked thoughtful. "Phoebe didn't mention that part. All I know is that Ms. Lake lives in New York and came down for her client's event."

So she was long gone. My shoulders slumped.

Shuffling back toward the office, he said, "Apparently she's spending the holiday in Savannah with family. I've got her card if you want it. Phoebe gave it to me as backup when she was arranging the signing."

I tried to keep the glee out of my voice. "Yes, I'll take it. Thanks."

He returned with a business card and held it out to me. "I get the feeling you're doing that investigative thing you've done before. I don't get why you feel like you have to snoop around when the police are already on the job."

"Croft—"

He raised his hand like a traffic cop. "But you got your uncle Ben off the hook last year, and that makes you golden in my book. Seems to me that Kissel woman probably did it, but I want the right person to be prosecuted for what happened in my store. So you let me know if there's anything I can do to help."

"Oh, Croft." I gave him a hug. He stiffened at first, then awkwardly patted me on the back. "Thank you."

"Sure thing," he said in a gruff voice and turned away.

I grinned. *Old softie.*

I couldn't follow up with Ronnie Lake personally that night, and it would be difficult to get away the next day. Perhaps I could convince her to come into the Honeybee for a cup of coffee. How, though? I was a complete stranger, and she'd likely already been inundated with calls from reporters wanting to know more about her deceased client.

What if I used my Voice? A little shudder went down my back. *No. Bad things happen when you do that.* Like that time I'd almost killed Declan. Or when I'd told the kids in the schoolyard to leave me alone—and none of them had spoken to me for years.

But you didn't even know you had that power back then. You have better control now.

Slowly, I punched in the number Croft had given me, running over in my mind what to say. If I compelled Ms. Lake to come to the bakery, would I have to use my Voice to get her to talk to me? What if other people heard? That seemed like a recipe for disaster.

I was almost relieved when the call went to voice mail. I left a simple message asking her to call me back.

And yes, I might have infused the words with the tiniest smidgeon of Voice.

Before leaving for the day, I carefully wrote in Declan's card:

> *Happy Anniversary, Sweetheart! I decided the best gift would be a getaway together to Boston. You can show me around, and I can finally meet your mom and sisters. We could go for Christmas, or New Year's! Love you!*

I sketched a quick heart but stopped myself from adding a smiley face. That plus the heart and exclamation points would definitely alert him that I'd almost forgotten our anniversary.

After a quick text to let Deck know I was on my way, I loaded Mungo into the tote, grabbed the yummy torte

Lucy had made, and headed home. The ambrosial scent of dark chocolate filled the interior of the Bug, and by the time I got to the carriage house my mouth was watering.

Declan met me at the door. The aromas of baking meat, caramelized onions, and tarragon boiled out to the porch, piquing my appetite still further. He wore jeans, a crisp collared shirt—and one of my vintage ruffled gingham aprons.

I grinned. "Something smells delicious. And you have no idea how sexy you look in that apron." I raised my face to his.

But instead of kissing me, he took the torte out of my hand with a grimace and stepped aside to reveal Margie sitting on the couch, her face streaked with tears.

"Welcome home, honey," he said with the faintest trace of sarcasm.

"What on earth happened?" I asked, rushing in and throwing the tote on a chair.

"Oh, Katie! I don't know what to do!" Margie wailed.

Looking uncomfortable and bewildered, Declan called the dog in from the yard and returned to the kitchen. Mungo settled in the corner by the bookshelf, out of the way but watching intently.

"Now, honey." I took Margie's hands in my own. They were trembling. "Tell me."

"I did what she said, and now he hates me."

"What . . . who . . . oh. You mean Dr. Dana?"

She nodded, her red-rimmed eyes welling again.

I retrieved a tissue and sat down next to my friend.

Margie blew her nose. Hiccuped. "I'm sorry, Katie. I can tell you guys had a special night planned."

"Now, don't you worry."

A snorting noise came from the kitchen. I hoped Margie hadn't heard it.

"What did you do?" I asked.

She took a shaky breath. "I installed a GPS tracker on Redding's phone. He leaves for Oklahoma tomorrow. I'm not very tech savvy, though, and he found it right away."

Ugh. "But isn't part of Radical Trust for people to know they're being, er, monitored? Isn't that where the trust part is supposed to come in?"

"I guess so," she said in a small voice. "But I thought he might get mad, so I didn't tell him."

"How did he take it?"

"Oh, God. He's furious!"

I would be, too. "Honey, did you explain about the book?"

"I tried. He was too mad at me to really listen, though. Katie, do you think he's hiding something from me? I mean, he could have a whole other life I don't even know about!"

"Oh, now, come on. You know better than that! You two have been married for what? Seven years?"

Her head bobbed an affirmative. "Almost eight. And we dated for three years before that."

Declan dropped something in the kitchen, and I heard him swear under his breath.

"So you're trying to tell me that your husband of almost eight years, the father of your three children who calls them on the computer *every* night he's on the road so he can read them a bedtime story, is leading a double life?"

She looked at the floor. "I guess not."

"No. I guess not. How would you feel if he hired

someone to follow you around when he was gone to make sure you weren't doing anything he didn't like?"

"He'd never—! Oh. No, I wouldn't like that at all." She gave me a pleading look. "But that's not what I was trying to do."

"First off—how was he to know that? It looks like you're suspicious. Are you?"

Her ponytail swished back and forth. "Of course not. At least I wasn't."

"Then why did you do it?"

"Because Dr. Dana—"

I stood. "Radical Trust might have worked for Dana Dobbs and her husband, but I just can't see how it would work for most people." And remembering Nate Dobbs' face when his wife had been regaling the public with private details about their marriage, I didn't think it had really worked for them, either.

Margie let out a big sigh. "You're right. Like I said the other night, the whole thing seemed a little heavy-handed. But since she's gone now, I thought I could at least give it a try."

"Out of respect?" I ventured.

"Uh-huh."

That was a first: follow bad advice as a way to honor the dead.

"You are a sweet thing, Margie Coopersmith. But you know darn well that Redding loves you and those kids like crazy."

She sniffled. "Yeah."

"He's a proud man, though. And now he thinks you don't trust him. You need to go back over to your house and let him know that you do."

One last honk on the tissue, and she stood. "You're

right." Her shoulders straightened. "I'll fix this if it's the last thing I do."

I smiled at the dramatic statement, but I didn't stop her as she marched out the door. When it closed behind her, I turned to see Declan had ventured out of the kitchen.

"Is it safe?"

Nodding, I moved toward him. "Now, where were we?"

Chapter 16

Ben had been both right and wrong about the filet mignon on the menu. Declan had made beef Wellington—simple enough, but decadent as all get-out.

"I'm impressed," I said, peering into the oven at the small tenderloin roast smothered in duxelles and wrapped neatly in puff pastry. "And hungry!"

He looked relieved. "Good. I was afraid that whole business with Margie's marriage falling apart might have affected your appetite."

I looked at the ceiling and shook my head. "Not a chance, darlin'. And for the record, I don't think she and Redding are in any serious trouble. Just a little misunderstanding. It happens."

He gave me a wry look. "Yes, I seem to recall that."

"Now, is that any way to talk tonight?" I gave him a playful grin. "Since you're all buttoned-down this evening, and in honor of the magnificent meal you've made, I really think I'd better put on something a little better than my usual garb. Maybe cover up this knee, while I'm at it."

Concern entered his eyes. "How are you feeling?"

"Bah. It's nothing. Be back with you in a jiff."

"Don't cover up too much," he called as I went into the bedroom.

At least I'd given a bit of thought to what to wear as I'd driven home. Twin armoires served as my closet, and one was entirely taken up with the clothes I liked to wear to work. The other offered a sparser selection, but there were a few surprises Declan hadn't seen. Mungo sat on the bed and watched as I donned a skirt inspired by a swirly chiffon number Bianca had worn to a spellbook club meeting. A short skirt was covered with a longer sheer handkerchief skirt in shades of purple and blue. The combination managed to subtly show off my legs at the same time the bandage on my knee was nearly hidden. I topped it with a silky spaghetti-strap tank in rich violet and turned to look in the mirror.

"Not bad with this crazy hair, huh?"

Mungo made an approving noise.

I ran my fingers through my short dark red locks and tucked them behind my ears. The small pearl earrings I had worn that day would do, but the chain with the amulet Steve had given me caught my attention. I'd worn it for most of the year without even thinking about it. Tonight, however, it somehow seemed wrong.

Slowly, I unclasped it and let the chain dribble through my fingers into my jewelry box.

Mungo made another noise of approval.

My neck felt naked, though, and more important, I felt suddenly unprotected. But thinking back, how much good had it really done me? I'd almost been killed more than once while wearing it. And really, what could possibly happen tonight?

Slipping my feet into open-toed sandals with higher heels than I usually wore, I spared a thought for the idea that I really ought to invest in a fancy pedicure one of these days. In the bathroom, I applied a bit of plum eyeliner to accent the green in my eyes and added a quick swipe of pink lip gloss. I switched out the bulky gauze bandage on my knee for a small Band-Aid, gave myself a nominal nod of approval in the mirror over the sink, and went back out to see what Declan was up to.

I stopped dead in my tracks when I saw what he'd done in the short time I'd been getting dressed. The two wingback chairs had been moved to one side, and the Civil War–era trunk I used as a coffee table in the living room was pulled away from the couch and set for dinner. A rough woven tablecloth set off my simple old Fiesta-ware dishes. A small vase of red roses sat in the middle. And there were candles, a mixture of white and red, on the trunk, on the shelves, set on the floor around the periphery of the room, and on all the windowsills. I even saw a few flickering in the kitchen. Miles Davis' "All Blues" played low on the stereo.

"You look amazing." Declan moved from where he'd been standing by the French doors to where I stood gaping.

"Th . . . thank you," I stammered.

He slowly ran his fingertip along my throat and jaw, then tipped my chin up for a kiss.

A really long kiss.

Finally, he said, "Sit down, and I'll bring you a glass of wine to sip while I finish up."

"Can't I do anything to help?" I protested.

"Shh. No, you can't. Sit." He indicated a plush cushion on the floor.

Obediently, I sat.

He grabbed our supper plates off the table and went back into the kitchen. The rich scent of roasted meat became stronger. The oven door rattled, and I heard the clink of the plates. Mungo sat in the doorway, watching with covetous eyes. Suddenly he took off for the corner where his place mat sat, and I knew Declan had served the little dog his own feast.

I love that man.

Which reminded me of the card. Quickly, I scrambled up to retrieve it from the tote, which I'd taken into the bedroom. I regained my seat just before he carried our plates in and set them on the table.

"Madam," he said, trying for a British accent but unable to hide the smooth lilt of his Savannah upbringing. "Dinner is served."

"Thank you, Jeeves," I said, leaning forward and closing my eyes to inhale deeply. My stomach growled, and I cleared my throat to cover the sound.

He settled on a cushion across from me. "On the menu tonight is beef Wellington with béarnaise sauce, potato and celery puree, and roasted broccoli with pecans."

"Ohmagod. That is stunning, Deck."

"And for dessert . . . some kind of chocolate cake made by the woman of my dreams."

I smiled and didn't correct him as to the provenance of the cake. Instead, I lifted my glass. The reflection of candle flames danced on the curved surface of the glass.

"To the chef."

He lifted his own. "To *us.*"

I nodded and smiled. "To us."

We each had a sip, and turned to the delectable goodness in front of us.

As I cut into the tenderloin and crunchy puff pastry, I marveled. "I had no idea you knew how to make béarnaise sauce."

"Scott taught me on our last shift together."

"Aha. That's why he looked at me so funny this morning. There's been a conspiracy behind my back." I shook my finger at him. "Very sneaky."

He'd obviously been planning this for a long time. Declan was a bit of a romantic, but this was over-the-top even for him. Then again, we'd never had an anniversary before, so maybe this was something I should expect every year.

"It's hard to keep a secret from a witch."

"Apparently not that hard." I took my first bite, closed my eyes, and couldn't keep from moaning. "Oh, Lord. That is *good*."

When I opened my eyes, he was grinning at me. "I love it when you do that."

Feeling my face redden, I turned my attention back to my plate.

"You're not wearing your necklace," he said after a while.

My hand flew to my neck. "No, not tonight." I'd never told him where it came from, or the purpose it served.

His lips curved. "Maybe you need a new piece of jewelry."

I shrugged. "I'm not much of . . ." I trailed off, realizing it was a hint. "Yeah, maybe I do."

Pushing aside thoughts of Dr. Dana and Angie and murder suspects, I immersed myself in the exquisite meal, the fairyland of flickering lights, and the small talk and long looks between us.

When we were finished, we donned jackets and went out to the patio to finish off the meal with coffee laced with Baileys Irish Cream. Mungo, who had discreetly stayed in the kitchen during supper, trotted out with us and curled up in his bed. Within seconds, he was snoring like the contented pup he was.

Declan reached over and took my hand. "Did you find out anything at the radio station this morning?"

"I . . . do you really want to talk about this right now?"

"Maybe later."

"Yeah."

"Ben said Steve Dawes is back in town."

Thanks, Ben. I shrugged and looked over at him. "I ran into him when I was, er, running an errand."

Declan was silent, for which I was grateful. I definitely didn't want to talk about Steve tonight.

"I start my forty-eight tomorrow," he said.

"Which is why we're celebrating our anniversary tonight." I circled the back of his hand with my fingertip. "I figured that out."

He opened his mouth, then shut it again, searching my eyes.

"What is it?" I asked, feeling like I could stay submersed in that blue gaze forever.

"I have something for you." He dropped my hand and stood.

"Oh. Right—I have something—"

"Stay there," he demanded, then took a breath. "Sorry. Please stay."

I sank back from my half-standing position. "Okay."

I'd thought he was going inside to get my gift, but instead he pushed his chair to the side and took something out of his pocket. Then he dropped to one knee in front of me.

"Katie, you are funny and fascinating, beautiful and smart, talented and just crazy enough. You're the woman I've been waiting for my whole life, and I want to be with you the rest of my life."

"Declan," I gasped in shock.

He opened the box he held in his hand and removed

a ring from it. The silvery metal filigree caught the moonshine, seeming to absorb it into its own glow, and the royal blue sapphire set deeply into the middle of it echoed celestial magic.

"Katie Lightfoot, will you marry me?" He held out the ring with a nervous smile.

"Oh. Oh, gosh. Deck, I . . . Oh."

Mungo went crazy then, yipping and bouncing and running in circles. Then he did it again.

All the while Declan kneeled in front of me with the ring in his outstretched palm.

I wanted to offer my left hand, to let him slip it on my finger. I wanted to see him smile, and my heart ached with the thought of how much thought and love he'd put into his proposal.

I wanted to, but I couldn't. I just couldn't.

"Deck," I whispered. "Can we talk about this?"

His smile had become more and more tentative, and now it dropped altogether. Awkwardly, he came to his feet and brushed off his jeans. "I guess I shouldn't have expected a tearful yes out of some romantic comedy."

"Can't we just—"

"I jumped the gun." He gently put the ring back into the velvet-lined box and placed it on the table. "You wanted to take it slow, and we have been. But I know this is what I want. You are what I want. Forever."

"Deck, this is just such a surprise. I mean, we hadn't talked about getting married at all. I have to—"

"Think about it," he finished for me. "Okay. I'm going to leave you alone to do just that." He began walking into the house.

"You're *leaving*?"

He paused in front of the French doors and nodded. "The rest of the evening is going to be pretty weird after this. Sorry. I knew there was a possibility you'd say no, but I didn't really think through what would happen after that." He smiled, but it was tinged with sadness. "I had a *very* good idea about what would happen after you said yes, though."

I leaped to my feet. "I'm not saying no," I protested. "I need time, though. You know what happened with Andrew."

"I'm not Andrew," he said sharply. "I'm not going to back out on you."

"Of course you're not." I walked up and put my hands on his chest, snagging his gaze, trying to make him understand. "My life was much different then. I didn't know my true nature—as a witch, but also as a person. I got engaged thinking that being married would fix things in my life. It wasn't until I moved here that I realized it never would have. Never *could* have."

His hands came up to my shoulders, and the look he gave me was full of so much tenderness it almost brought me to my knees. "You're right. You don't need to be fixed. I don't want to fix you, and I don't expect you to fix me. I want to build our lives together. And that's a different thing altogether. Don't you see?"

I stared at him, wide-eyed.

He turned and walked inside.

I hurried after him. "Wait. I got you a . . . card."

Lame. I felt tears welling. I swallowed them back and retrieved the envelope from where I'd slipped it under the cushion by the coffee table, ready to give to him over dinner. I handed it to him and looked away.

He opened it, then nodded. "Thank you. I'd like to take you to meet my family." He kissed me, sweetly and yet with a trace of bitterness.

"Please don't go," I whispered.

He laughed. "It's okay, Katie. Really. But if I stay, what are we going to talk about?"

I tried a sly smile. "Maybe we don't have to talk."

He acknowledged my attempt to flirt with an appreciative look, but he turned to go anyway. "I know you think better when you're by yourself. And I really want you to think about saying yes." He opened the front door and turned back. "I want to marry you. I know there are always complications, but that is the simple truth, and we can figure all the other stuff out. If you decide you want to marry me, that is."

"Deck," I tried one last time.

"I'll call you tomorrow."

The door closed behind him and a few seconds later I heard the engine in his truck roar to life. I was left with a sink full of dishes, a roomful of half-burned candles, and a ring sitting in its box on the patio table. My feet hurt, my knee hurt, and my familiar was glaring at me from the corner.

I sat down on the edge of the couch, grabbed the bottle of wine still sitting amid the plates on the coffee table, and poured myself a dose of comfort. Mungo stopped glaring at me when I started to cry.

Chapter 17

It wasn't that I never wanted to get married. I wasn't afraid of commitment. Once before I'd been engaged, but I hadn't been the one who'd backed out at the last minute. Declan was right—he wasn't anything like Andrew. I knew I could trust him. That wasn't the problem.

The problem was that I loved my life so much. It was a nice problem to have. I loved my job, even if it meant long, sometimes crazy hours. I loved practicing hedge-witchery with Lucy at the Honeybee. I loved my friends, and the city, and the somewhat new knowledge of just who the heck I was. More important, the knowledge that I was doing what I was supposed to be doing. It felt like a gift I'd been given less than two years ago, and I honestly wanted to revel in it for a while longer.

I looked around the room, now lit only by the fringed floor lamp next to the couch. Declan had helped me pick up both of them from an ad on Craigslist. Brought them over in his pickup. Gave me the patio set and the little hibachi that was still my only grill. He'd helped me cut the garden beds out of the expanse of back lawn, rototilled, and helped me plant.

All that only made me love the tidy carriage house

more. But if I married Declan, I'd have to give it up. The thought brought tears to my eyes all over again. I reached for the wine bottle, then stopped.

Wine with dinner. Baileys with coffee, even if I only finished half of it. Wine again.

Not a good idea.

With a sigh, I wiped my eyes, gave Mungo a kiss on the forehead, and stood. I changed into yoga pants and a tank top and got to work storing leftovers, loading the dishwasher, moving the furniture back into place, and gathering the candles. The last I took up to the loft. After consolidating two bookshelves into one, I piled the candles into the empty space. The whole time I worked, my mind had gnawed on Declan's marriage proposal. Now I was feeling jittery and not a little afraid. What if I'd ruined everything? Was I going to lose the man I loved?

My altar stood nearby. It was housed inside a secretary's desk that Lucy had given me, closed against casual attention but easily accessible. Lowering the cover, I sat down and took a deep breath.

My nonna had knitted the lace shawl that served as my altar cloth. She'd been a witch, too, and since I'd learned of my heritage, her spirit had even stepped in a few times to help me from the other side of the veil. The items placed upon the cloth were variations on magical tools and reflections of the four elements. My chalice was a small swirly glass bowl I'd found at the flea market. A worn, antique kitchen knife was my idea of a ritual athame. There was a collection of smooth stones that I'd gathered over the years, and an Indian arrowhead my dad had given me. A small amethyst geode nestled beside a brilliant blue jay's feather that had drifted into the gazebo.

Of course. I need to calm myself. Luckily, I had a way to do that.

I retrieved two of the white candles from the bookshelf and put them at the front of the altar. Between them I placed a small ceramic disc designed to diffuse scents, and placed a drop each of lavender and ylang-ylang oils from my small stock. Closing my eyes, I sat and breathed.

I am peaceful.
I am calm.
I am protected from all harm.
All will be well.

I picked up the amethyst and traced its contours with my fingers, allowing myself to absorb its inherent tranquility while I continued the calming incantation under my breath.

Soon a peace settled over me, and I came to know in my core that indeed, all would be well.

I don't know what it will look like, but things will work out.

Licking my finger and thumb, I carefully pinched out each candle, thanked the Goddess, and closed the altar.

As I came down the stairs from the loft, I heard the text tone on my phone in the bedroom. When I dug it out of my tote, I found a message from Declan.

Just realized I left you with a big mess. What a heel. I'm sorry. Hope that doesn't affect your decision. The text ended with a smiley face.

I texted back. *No worries. It gave me something to do while I think. Going to sleep now. Love you.*

A few seconds later he replied. *Love you, too.*

But of course, I wouldn't be able to sleep for hours yet. Maybe a book would . . . my eyes fell on the list of suspects I'd made the night before, sitting where I'd left it on the bedside table. I grabbed it and went into the kitchen. There I cut myself another piece of chocolate torte and sat down at the table with my laptop.

First, I searched for Earl King. There were three listed in Savannah. Pulling up images on the search engine solved that problem. The one I was looking for owned a bar that was only a few blocks away from the Honeybee. I'd been in King's Castle once or twice but didn't remember seeing the portly gentleman from Saturday night.

Maybe another visit was in order.

Next, I looked up Nate Dobbs. The first page of results showed him linked to his wife or referred to by his wife, or led to excerpts from the book his wife had written. Next were links to his presence on social media, but he hadn't posted any updates for at least six months. Not his cup of tea, I guessed. The only other link I found was an agenda from a conference in Atlanta. It was centered on food processing, and, at least last year, Nate Dobbs had worked for an agricultural fumigation company. It sounded pretty boring, and I had to wonder if he still worked there after his wife had achieved national stardom.

I shut the laptop, considering. Of all the suspects on my list, I knew the least about Nate Dobbs. Somehow, I didn't think he'd appreciate me showing up on his doorstep with a pile of personal questions. Detective Quinn could probably fill me in on a few details, but it was unlikely he would unless I could give him a good reason to. I needed someone else who knew details about Nate Dobbs.

Like someone who had been following his wife.

Angie.

I looked at my watch. Too late to call anyone with a normal sleep schedule. But I could at least text Bianca and ask if she would go with me to talk with Angie, even if she wouldn't get back to me until morning.

Not only would I welcome Bianca's moral support, but I figured she and Angie might be able to connect because they'd had similar experiences with their husbands. Bianca had discovered an affinity for Wiccan beliefs and began studying on her own long before she'd joined the spellbook club. The more she'd learned, the more excited she'd become, until finally she'd shared that excitement with her husband.

He'd blown a gasket and left Bianca and their daughter, Colette. From what she'd said, he hadn't wanted to listen to any explanations, either. All else aside, she'd realized that she was better off without a man who would leave his family over something like that. However, Bianca had started practicing the Craft after she'd gotten married. According to Angie, she'd stopped practicing before her marriage.

At least Declan really knew who and what I was. I didn't have to keep secrets from him, and I was pretty sure he felt the same way.

To my surprise, Bianca texted back a little after midnight that she would be happy to go with me. Then I realized she might have been out on a date. Huh. Declan and I preferred to stay home most of the time, rather than hitting the town.

Just like an old married couple.

The Tuesday and Wednesday before Thanksgiving were considered "high pie" days at the Honeybee Bakery. We'd been taking orders for holiday pies for weeks, but of course we wanted them to be as fresh as possible. We already had racks of extra fruit and pecan pies in the big freezer for those who wanted to bake them up on Thanksgiving Day, and today we'd prep for the slew of pies we'd bake the next day for afternoon pickup.

A part of me was grateful to be so unusually busy. Images of Declan's face the night before—when he'd asked me to marry him, and then when he'd realized I wasn't going to say yes to his proposal right away—had haunted my dreams and continued to rise in my mind as I worked. However, baking soothed me, distracted me, and allowed me to sink into a deep sense of self-assurance that I rarely felt, at least to such a degree, in most other parts of my life. Since I couldn't help second-guessing every thought I had about getting married, pro *and* con, the confidence and pure joy that came with measuring and mixing, scooping, and kneading was more than welcome this particular morning.

Suddenly, I remembered Nate Dobbs at the commercial building in Ardsley Park, trying to stay busy the day after his wife died. Maybe he'd been telling the awful truth.

As for the pies, there were the standard apple, cherry, and peach, as well as gooseberry, apple cranberry walnut, salted caramel apple, and a dark chocolate bourbon pecan pie that made my mouth water every time I thought of it. All the pumpkin pies would be baked the next day, as they didn't freeze well.

Ben took care of the everyday customer business of dispensing pastries and making coffee drinks. Lucy helped him between helping pie customers. Cookie, who had worked at the Honeybee for a few months before she decided the hours weren't for her, had come in to help after the regular day's baking was done.

She and Iris were standing at the main worktable, preparing fillings to bake up the next day. Across from them, I mixed up flaky piecrust and buttery pâte brisée.

I added a bit of rum to each bulk batch, then quickly measured out precise amounts for top and bottom crusts and put them in oversized zip-close bags before the alcohol could evaporate. The dough would then be rolled into circles inside the bags, saving mess and enabling us to stack them in the fridge for quick pie construction the next day. The alcohol would all burn out during baking, leaving behind extra pockets of flakiness, and the rum flavor lent a subtle piquancy to the sweet pies.

Since our production needed to be efficient, we couldn't take the time to practice a lot of kitchen magic. However, the rum that went into each crust inherently attracted good luck, and we gave that a boost for each and every person who took a bite of Honeybee holiday pie. When we could, we added intentions for gratitude, good luck, and love into the various fillings.

"Mr. Clovis is still being a pain," Iris said as she chopped a pile of walnuts. "That teacher I told you about? He yelled at a friend of mine for coming in thirty seconds late. I mean, really *yelled*."

"That's a bummer," I said, distracted by the mental list of what would need to happen the next morning.

"Did you try giving him the cookie like I suggested?" Lucy asked, passing through to grab a frozen pie for a customer.

Iris shook her head. "Nah. It wouldn't work, anyway. I feel terrible for my friend, though. She was almost in tears. After we get back from Thanksgiving break, I'm thinking of casting a spell against him. Like a curse."

Lucy stopped dead in her tracks. "Iris!"

Cookie waved my aunt's admonition away. "What did you have in mind?"

Lucy took the frozen pie out to the woman waiting

by the register, tossing a worried look over her shoulder as she went.

Iris grinned. "I was thinking a nasty rash."

I started to protest, but Cookie spoke first. "How would that help?"

"Well, it would make me feel better." She laughed.

Cookie snorted. "It might."

I paused in my work and turned to them both. "What about karma?"

"There is that, of course." Cookie shot me a glance, then looked back at Iris. "But I want to know how that would solve the problem."

"Well . . ."

"It wouldn't, would it?" Cookie asked.

Iris stopped chopping. "Maybe not, but—"

"But nothing. It's revenge. And revenge, like guilt and regret, is useless. None solve any problems whatsoever."

I stared at Cookie.

"You're training in the Craft, yes?" she went on.

Iris nodded, wide-eyed.

"And Katie and Lucy are your primary teachers."

Another nod.

"I know neither of them would suggest anything like a curse. Therefore, you've been reading, investigating on your own. I understand." Cookie whacked an apple in two, and Iris jumped. "I was raised in a tradition of magic that embraces curses. Voodoo."

Iris blinked.

Cookie gave her a hard look. "Curses are part of that belief system's lifeblood. I turned my back on it for a long, long time. But recently I became, shall we say, reacquainted with my native religion. Thanks to Katie here."

I smiled uncertainly, unsure of where she was going.

"I will tell you this—curses are not to be trifled with. Not for stupid revenge."

"Uh, and there's the Rule of Three, too," I said as I dropped cubes of cold butter into the big food processor. "You wouldn't want a curse to come back to you threefold, would you?"

Cookie looked at me. I knew she had a complicated relationship with the Rule of Three, but she didn't contradict me.

"Golly, no," Iris said. Then she smiled. "I guess giving him a cookie isn't such a bad idea. Maybe it would come back to me as a good grade."

"Good idea," I said, and changed the subject. "So how are your other classes going?"

Iris scraped the walnuts into a bowl and started sorting through cranberries, looking for any that were soft or underripe. "I finished the short story. It's about a girl who's bitten by a vampire at a football game."

"Sounds . . . interesting," I said.

Cookie smiled.

"And yesterday a professional goldsmith spoke to our metalsmithing class. He did an electroplating demonstration. Did you know pennies aren't really copper? They're made out of zinc, and the copper coating is electroplated onto the outside."

I paused. "Really?"

She nodded. "Uh-huh. They dissolve metal in a bath using cyanide, and then use an electrical current to get it to deposit back on whatever is being plated." She frowned. "I think I got that right. There was a lot of chemistry stuff."

But I'd stopped listening at the word *cyanide*.

"What kind of cyanide?" I asked.

Iris' eyes grew wide. "Oh. Gosh. That lady who was killed next door . . ."

I exchanged a look with Cookie. "Detective Quinn said it's highly regulated and really hard to get ahold of."

Our teen helper shook her head. "It might be for some people, but I can tell you it's used in at least two of the classes I'm taking."

"Which ones?" I asked, stunned.

"Metalsmithing, like I said. And it's in some photographic chemicals, too." She rolled her eyes. "Not that normal people actually develop film anymore. I read about it in a textbook. They used to use it in printmaking, too. Something about blue dye."

"Wait a second. You can get cyanide at *school*?" I was having a hard time wrapping my mind around the idea.

"Well, I can't just go in and pick it up. I wouldn't even know where to look. Maybe I could find out, though." She looked eager at the prospect.

But I shook my head. "That's okay, hon. I don't want you to get in any trouble." Besides, classes wouldn't be resuming until the next week.

She looked disappointed, but it was short-lived. Soon she and Cookie were exchanging fashion tips, and Iris was back to her cheery self.

Quinn had made it sound like cyanide was some kind of biohazard, under lock and key by the powers that be. But it was starting to sound like it wasn't that hard to find after all.

Chapter 18

I finished rolling out the piecrusts for the next day, and we wiped down the kitchen. Cookie left to meet with a client, and Lucy set Iris to tidying the library area. I took Mungo a snack of leftover quiche for his elevenses. I'd called Angie Kissel, and she'd agreed to meet with Bianca and me at noon. The morning's work had gone swiftly with Cookie's help, so I had an hour to fill before then. I was heading over to the coffee counter to brew up some peppermint tea when my cell buzzed in my apron pocket.

I recognized the number as Ronnie Lake's.

Whirling around, I went back into the office and shut the door. "Hello?"

"Ms. Lightfoot? I have a message to call you?" Her voice was deep for a woman's, but it fit the image of the woman I remembered from Dr. Dana's signing.

"Yes," I said. "Thank you for returning my call."

Mungo blinked at me with sleepy eyes, tummy full and ready for his second nap of the day.

"Do I know you?"

"No, we haven't met. At least not formally. I was at Dana Dobbs' signing on Saturday night."

"Oh . . . I'm sorry, but I can't comment—"

I broke in. "Actually, I'm calling for Croft Barrow, the owner of the Fox and Hound."

He *had* said he'd do what he could to help me investigate Dr. Dana's murder, so I hoped Croft wouldn't mind my little prevarication in his name. "Since you were Dr. Dobbs' agent, he was wondering whether . . ."

"No, I wasn't, actually. Dana fired me right before that signing." Ms. Lake didn't sound all that sorry about her former client's demise.

"I see." I really didn't want to have to use my Voice if I didn't have to. Treading with caution, I said, "I'd heard Dr. Dana could be difficult to work with."

Ronnie blew out a breath. "She started out great, but then she hit the big time and became a total prima donna."

I made a sympathetic noise.

"But you didn't call to hear about all that."

Darn. She wasn't a gossipy sort. Come to think of it, gossip about clients, current or former, was likely frowned upon in her business. Unfortunately, that left me no choice. I carefully feathered a little Voice into my next words.

"Tell me more."

Yip! Yip!

Mungo was on his feet and looked at me expectantly. With alarm, I realized he was responding to what I'd said. My own familiar!

Oh, no! This is exactly why I shouldn't use my Voice. It never turns out the way I think it will.

I held the phone away and patted the chair. "Shh. Sorry, little guy."

He looked bewildered but lay back down.

Ronnie Lake was talking when I put the phone to

my ear again. "It was pretty simple. She wanted to rene-
gotiate my commission. I said no, we had a contract. So
she terminated it."

Motive?

"I'm very sorry," I said.

"Meh. Good riddance, I thought at the time. Then she
was killed, of course. That's no good." Her words came
out in a tumble, as if she'd had one too many margaritas.

But since she was under my influence anyway . . .
"Why did you go to the signing, then?" *And did you
have any cyanide on you?*

"I'm fairly good friends with her sister. Phoebe. She
felt terrible about what Dana had done. I wanted her to
know there were no hard feelings between us. Poor thing.
She's devastated." Another long pause. "Why did you
say you were calling?" Her tone was frightened now.

I plunged on. "What did you say to Dana before you
left?"

A laugh. "I wished her good luck in finding another
agent who could do as much for her as I had." Sarcasm
dripped from her voice.

"I don't suppose you have any ideas about who killed
her," I said.

"Probably one of her readers or listeners. That whole
thing about Radical Trust was complete bunk. Especially
since her own marriage was such a shambles. Her husband had been trying to get a divorce for months. Dana
had convinced him to wait until after she was done with
her marriage-advice book, then until after it was published, and then again until after her promotional tour
was over." Her speech was slowing. "I don't know why I
just told you that." She sounded really scared, almost
panicky.

I felt terrible. Should I try to fix what I'd done? *No.*

You'll make it worse. The effect will wear off in a few more minutes. No more Voice!

"I'm so sorry," I said softly.

"What?"

"Croft and I wanted to extend our condolences to you and to her family," I said in a normal tone, as if she hadn't said anything unusual. "Do you know about the memorial?"

"Yes, Phoebe told me. I imagine it will be quite crowded."

"We'll send flowers."

"I believe they are asking for donations to a scholarship fund in lieu of flowers."

"That's a good idea. Perhaps I'll see you there on Wednesday?"

"Definitely. Even if she was difficult, Dana was a valuable client of mine."

We said good-bye, and I hung up.

A valuable client indeed. Her books would continue to sell, perhaps at an accelerated rate for a while. Did that mean Ronnie Lake would continue to make money off them, even thought she'd been fired? Probably, if she'd negotiated the original publishing deal. Was that also a motive?

But under the influence of my Voice, she hadn't told me that she'd killed Dr. Dana, even though I'd asked if she had any ideas about who had. I slumped in my chair. Voice was such a slippery thing. Could she have lied? Lied by omission? I hadn't told her not to.

The image of Declan with his heart and breathing stopped because of one word I'd said with my Voice came flooding up from memory.

No. Even though I think I can control it, no more Voice. Ever.

*   *   *

Lucy and Iris were in the kitchen, and I was making my tea and chatting with Mrs. Standish, when Steve came in. Ben looked up from where he sat checking our inventory lists behind the register. He frowned but quickly recovered as Steve approached.

"Ben. Good to see you."

My uncle nodded. "Steve."

Steve's lips twitched. He hadn't missed the subtle snub and directed a questioning look at me.

I kept my face neutral. Let him think I'd blabbed about all the things he'd told me the day before.

"Those jalapeño corn pones sure look good," Steve said.

Ben put one on a plate and handed it to him. "Anything to drink?"

"Dry cappuccino," I said.

Steve smiled as I turned to fill the order.

"Why, Steven Dawes, as I live and breathe," brayed Mrs. Standish. She wore a leopard-print caftan with a burnt orange scarf wrapped about a dozen times around her broad shoulders. "I heard you'd left town for a while. Glad to see you're back, my boy."

He opened his mouth to speak, but she kept right on going. "I spoke with your father last month, and he said you were living the life of a beach bum." She grinned. "Must suit you, because you look healthy as a horse. Honestly, you were looking a little peaked the last time I saw you."

"Thanks, Edna. I feel great," he said. "I wasn't exactly being a beach bum, though." He brought his corn pone over and leaned against the counter. "I've sure missed the Honeybee pastries, though. And I brought Katie a trinket from the Bahamas."

The steamer shrieked, drowning out his next words. He waited me out and tried again when I turned it off.

"It's just a kitschy souvenir I thought you might like. Nothing fancy." He handed me a little statue about three inches long. It was heavy, perhaps bronze, and had the body of a large dog, the face of a cat, and a beak like a bird. My hand closed over it automatically, and I savored how perfectly it fit in my palm.

"It's just a little keepsake. I hope you'll think of me when you see it—and I hope you put it someplace where you'll see it a lot."

This was getting ridiculous. I put the figurine down on the counter. "I can't accept this."

He looked surprised. So did Mrs. Standish. Lucy came around the corner and stopped when she saw us.

"Gosh, Katie," he said.

"You have to stop this," I said, unable to keep my frustration out of my voice. "Declan asked me to marry him last night!" As soon as the words came out, I wanted to shove them right back. I knew what was coming.

"Oh, Katie!" Lucy squealed.

"Holy smokes!" Ben said.

Mrs. Standish reached around and clapped me on the back, nearly sending me sprawling into a rack of mugs. "Congratulations!" she all but shouted. Heads all over the bakery turned our way.

I felt heat in my face, and it was suddenly hard to breathe. The pressure of their approval felt suffocating.

Steve was watching me through all the exclamations. Now his eyes narrowed, and he smiled. "You didn't say yes, though. Did you?"

I was silent.

"Uh-huh." He pushed the figurine toward me, took

the cappuccino I'd set on the counter, and walked toward the door. "See you later, Katie-girl."

"Don't—" I stopped myself. I'd had a knee-jerk reaction from the very first time he'd called me that. Now he was making a point.

He was still smiling when he left.

"Is that true?" Ben demanded. "You said no?" He sounded incredulous.

I took a deep breath, my eyes scanning the bakery. The customers had gone back to chatting, working, or reading. "I don't think we need to talk about it right now."

Mrs. Standish started to say something, but a curt shake of my head stopped her. I adored the woman, but she could disseminate news more efficiently than any media outlet in existence.

"Bianca and I have an appointment," I said. "I need to get going."

Ben looked surprised, but Lucy's face was placid as she followed me through the kitchen to the office. Of course, I'd already told her of our plans to visit Angie over the lunch hour.

"Honey, are you all right?" she asked as I quickly texted Bianca to see if she was on her way.

"I'm fine." I stopped and put the phone down. "No, wait. You know what? I'm not okay. Steve has resigned from the Dragohs and stopped working for Dawes Corp. in an attempt to convince me I made the wrong choice when I started dating Declan."

Her mouth formed an O of surprise.

"The very same day, Declan asks me to marry him when he knows darn well I'm not even sure about moving in together. And now everyone is upset that I haven't made a decision yet! I get to make my own choices, and not just when it comes to magic."

"Of course you do, Katie," Lucy said gently. "And not everyone is upset with you." She wrinkled her nose. "Ben, yes. And no doubt Declan himself is feeling a bit on edge. I don't even know what to say about Steve. But you stick to your guns, honey, and know I'll support you in whatever you decide."

My shoulders slumped, and I felt tears prick my eyes. "Thanks, Lucy. I didn't mean to go off on you there."

She patted my arm. "I'm glad you can talk to me."

"You're the best."

My phone buzzed. It was Bianca. She was out front.

I squared my shoulders. "Okay. I'm off to see a witch who is on the verge of being arrested for murder. Let's hope she can shed some light on the victim—and the victim's husband."

Bianca's red Jaguar was sitting at the curb out front. I got in and we roared away. She had the top down, and the wind made it hard to talk. Nonetheless, I managed to remind her about Angie's experience with her ex-husband.

"Sounds a lot like what happened to me," Bianca said as she slowed for a turn. "Except my husband might not have been such a jerk if I wasn't practicing the Craft anymore. It was my growing interest in magic that made him decide I wasn't good enough to be his wife. He was such a social climber and was terrified I'd embarrass him." She snorted. "Good riddance."

She pushed down on the accelerator, and the force pushed me back into the plush leather of my seat.

"Well, maybe Angie would appreciate hearing your story," I shouted over the rushing air.

Bianca nodded as she pulled into the parking area in front of Angie Kissel's small apartment building. "I'm happy to commiserate if it comes up."

We got out of the car and stood looking at the building. It didn't take long to identify the upper unit that was Angie's. The balconies were all surrounded by wrought iron, but hers was lined with planter boxes filled with trailing geraniums and creeping Jennie that spilled over the sides in such profusion that the greenery nearly hid the sturdy metal of the railing.

We walked up the exterior stairway to the entryway, our footsteps loud on the hollow wooden steps. At the top we discovered more pots planted with herbs and flowers, many with magical properties. That didn't mean anything, though. They were also simply pretty— jasmine, verbena, alyssum, and corkscrew reeds, among other things. Anyone could have chosen them for decoration, whether a former green witch or not.

The door flew open before we could knock. Surprised, I stepped back. Then I saw Angie's tear-streaked face.

"Oh, Katie. Thank heavens you're here." She glanced at Bianca and wiped at her eyes with her fingertips. "Hi."

"Hi," Bianca said with a mix of curiosity and kindness.

Angie looked fearfully over our shoulders, scanning the parking lot and street as if they held a threat. Alarm bells went off in my brain, and I hurried to introduce the two women.

"Angie, this is Bianca. Bianca, this is Angie. Can we come in?" I moved toward her as I was speaking, and Angie stepped back and opened the door wider.

We stepped into an herbal oasis. There were potted plants on every surface, tucked into corners, lining the windowsills, and even clustered on the counter that separated the living room from the kitchen. They all boasted verdant health. A skylight above poured indirect light into the space. The air smelled green, and I could sense the live energy thrumming through the atmosphere.

"Wow," I said.

"Katie." Bianca pointed to where Angie was holding out a piece of folded paper to me. It trembled in her hand.

I took it. Inside was a simple, typed note.

We all know you killed our Dr. Dana. If the police don't punish you, we will.

Wide-eyed, I handed it to Bianca. "When did you get this?"

"I came home from work and found it slipped under my door." Angie's voice quavered. "I'm really scared." She swallowed, hard. "Maybe I'm overreacting, though." She sounded hopeful, like I'd assure her the note was utter bunk.

Bianca handed it back to her. "Better safe than sorry. I really don't like how they used the word *punish*."

Angie blanched.

"She's right," I said. "Have you called the police?"

"The police? Right. Because they're on my side. If I called them about this, that Detective Quinn would probably arrest me on the spot."

I didn't think that was true, but I understood why she didn't exactly see the police as reliable allies. "I can't force you to call them."

She shook her head. "It would only make it worse." She buried her face in her hands.

I put my arm around Angie, and a small sob escaped her. She took several deep breaths, struggling to get control of herself again.

When she had, she said, "I don't want to stay here by myself. I'm off work until Friday, too."

"Is there a friend you can stay with?" Bianca asked.

Angie sniffed. "I thought about that. My good friend is hosting a big Thanksgiving dinner, though. Her house is full of family from out of town." She turned a pleading gaze on me. "Maybe I could, you know, if you have room . . . ?"

I'm sure my face showed surprise, but I managed to hide the suspicion that rose with it. Why would she want to stay with me? Because I was helping her? Because of Mungo?

Mungo. He wanted me to help her. If he'd been standing there, I knew darn well he would have wanted me to invite her to stay at the carriage house. It also occurred to me that having a little company while Declan was on his forty-eight-hour shift at the firehouse might be nice.

More than nice. It might keep me from obsessing about his proposal.

But I wasn't willing to go so far as to just give her the keys to my home. "Is there someplace you can stay until I get off work?"

Angie looked doubtful.

"I have to get back to the Honeybee." I looked at my watch. "And soon. We have a gazillion pumpkin pies to make tomorrow, as well as the usual prep for tomorrow morning."

"Maybe I could come with you?"

My eyebrow rose. "You bake?"

"Not so much, but I can still help clean up or whatever manual labor you might need."

Cookie had said she'd come back after her client appointment, but Iris was leaving with her family for

Hilton Head that afternoon. Maybe Lucy would welcome a little extra help. I looked at Bianca.

She smiled and inclined her head. "You've hired day help before."

"Oh! You don't have to pay me," Angie said.

"Nonsense," I said. "Bianca, do you mind if I ride back with Angie?"

"Not at all. I have to get back to Moon Grapes soon, anyway."

Angie looked surprised, then nodded. "Okay. Just let me take care of a couple of things here and pack a bag."

"We'll help," I said.

Chapter 19

Angie asked me to water some plants, while Bianca offered to help her pack her overnight bag. I could feel the power wafting from the delicate star-shaped flowers of the borage, protecting the apartment with peace and cheer. A trio of amaryllises held fat buds on their long stems, promising to bloom in time for Christmas, and potent with something I couldn't identify. Since they were poisonous, Lucy and I never used them in the kitchen. But no doubt Angie knew what the amaryllis' properties were; she might claim to have stopped practicing the Craft, but the fertile greenness in her home demonstrated an innate gift she couldn't escape.

I heard my coven mate's soothing voice in the bedroom, and then Angie responded in a low tone. From the few words I caught as I tended the garden, they were talking about their ex-husbands. The meeting with Mungo's former witch hadn't gone at all as I'd intended, but at least she and Bianca had discovered their common ground.

And I'd have a chance to talk to Angie about Nate Dobbs on the trip back to the Honeybee.

Bianca took off for Moon Grapes, which she said

was doing a booming business for the holiday. "Good thing I stocked up on Pinot Noir."

Angie locked up, and soon we were on our way back to the Honeybee in her Toyota. She seemed to become more relaxed by the mile.

"Feeling better?" I asked.

She nodded. Then she glanced over at me. "You said on the phone that you wanted to talk to me about Dana Dobbs."

Glad that she'd brought the subject up herself, I said, "Actually, I thought you might be able to tell me some things about her husband."

"Really? Why?"

I shrugged, trying for casual. "Well, they were talking about getting a restraining order against you. So I figured if you were following Dr. Dana around, you might have seen some things about her husband as well. Or their marriage." After what Ronnie Lake had told me, I was curious about whether the Dobbs' relationship problems had been evident.

However, Angie glared at me with her red-rimmed eyes. I suppressed a sigh. Maybe I should have been a bit more tactful, but we were getting close to the Honeybee, and I didn't want to ask her these questions where others could hear. It also seemed slightly precious to think I had to tread on eggshells around a stalker.

"I wasn't following her," she said.

"Oh, now. She saw you . . ."

"No! I went to two signings—one in Port Royal, and the one the other night. That's all." She slowed to a stop at a red light and turned to me.

"Really?" I said. "Why would she say you were following her?"

Angie's lips pressed together. "Dana and Nate happened to live about five blocks away from my apartment. We belong to the same gym, we shop at the same grocery store, and she was a jogger. Naturally, we ran into each other every once in a while." She made a face. "She ran by my apartment and then accused me of following *her*. Though I do admit—I tried to approach her when I saw her at the gym. I wanted her to understand how literally people took her advice and how ruinous it could be." She sighed. "Not that she'd listen. I thought I'd try one last time on Saturday night." She fell into silence.

"And the letter-writing campaign aimed at taking *The Dr. Dana Show* off the radio?"

She nodded vigorously. "Yep. I did that. Absolutely."

"All because you blame her for your divorce?" I couldn't help it. It just didn't add up.

Angie shook her head. "Not just that. I mean, I made the decision to tell my husband I used to be a witch. I own that. In fact, maybe I wanted him to know all along. But what happened to me made me pay more attention to her show, and I realized that she was doing real damage to her listeners. Katie, have you ever heard her?"

"Once. She told a woman to stop talking to her father because he didn't get along with her new husband."

"Yes! I remember that one. What if the woman followed her advice because she assumed Dr. Dana knew more than she did? And believe me—Dana Dobbs made sure that people thought she was smarter than them."

I thought of Margie crying on my sofa because she'd fallen for the psychologist's concept of Radical Trust.

"Was all of her advice bad?" I asked.

Angie shook her head. "No. But enough of it was." She made a left-hand turn onto Broughton.

"Okay. I get it." I frowned. "So you don't know anything about Nate Dobbs."

Angie shook her head. "I don't even know where he worked." She pulled into the parking lot around the corner from the bakery.

"I looked that up. Some kind of agricultural fumigation."

She parked and shut off the engine. I opened my door, but she didn't move. "Fumigation? Like grain silos and the like?"

"I think so. Why?"

"Sometimes big nurseries get insect infestations in their stock. The one where I work never had that happen, thank goodness, but there's a method they borrow from big agriculture to solve the problem." She turned to me with wide eyes. "They tent the affected plants and dose them with hydrogen cyanide. They use the same method to kill insects in grain silos, weevils in cotton, and the like."

"Agricultural fumigation uses cyanide," I said thoughtfully. "Good Lord."

Things were hopping in the Honeybee. Lucy was working the register, Ben was making one coffee drink after another, and Cookie was in the kitchen mixing up the sourdough levain for the next day's baking. They all looked surprised when I brought Angie in, but after she greeted Mungo briefly in the office, I set her to work measuring out spices for the pie filling. Soon we'd made real headway into prepping for the four dozen pumpkin pies we had orders for the next day.

Once the rich custard had been mixed and poured into large lidded containers to sit in the fridge overnight, Angie started in on the cleanup. True to her word, she was a hard worker. I brought her a rosemary Parmesan scone and a cup of tea, then headed out to the main seating area and began wiping down tables. I had just finished with the one nearest the door when Detective Quinn walked in.

"Hi, Katie. Boy, you guys are busy today."

"And loving it. Are you here for a Thanksgiving pie?"

He sat at the table I'd just cleaned and shook his head. "My wife insists on making her grandmother's banana toffee pie every Thanksgiving."

"Sounds delish. Maybe I can convince her to share the recipe."

"I'll ask her. For now I was hoping for a slice of lemon pound . . ." He trailed off as something behind me caught his attention. "Who is that working in your kitchen?"

I deliberately didn't turn around, as if that would magically remove Angie from his view. "Cookie still comes in to help sometimes when we're swamped."

"I'm not talking about Cookie Rios," he said through gritted teeth.

My smile slid off my face like warm butter.

"Why is the prime suspect in Dana Dobbs' murder doing dishes in the Honeybee Bakery?"

Glancing at the nearest customer, I sat down across from him and summoned my courage. What I ended up with felt a lot more like stubbornness than courage. My jaw set. "Angie's staying at my carriage house tonight, too."

"What? Why on God's green earth would you put yourself in that kind of danger?" he hissed. "And here I'd thought you'd given up on messing around in that murder. I should have known better."

"Angie Kissel is innocent."

He made a rude noise. "And you know this how?"

My dog told me. Oh, and he also acted as a conduit

*between Angie and me so I could sense her innocence
for myself. Because he's her ex-familiar.*

"You remember when we've talked about intuition?"
I asked. "I just know."

"Oh, come on." He shook his head emphatically.
"You know that's not good enough."

Knowing I should check with Angie first, I said,
"Someone left her a threatening note. Shoved it under
her door. Someone who sounds like a crazed fan—or
fans—of Dr. Dana. So she's scared and doesn't want to
be by herself."

"Oh, really." He still didn't look convinced. "Did she
call us?"

"Of course not. She's frightened of you, too. And I
don't blame her."

A flash of surprise crossed his face.

"There are plenty of other suspects in this case, and
from what I can tell, you haven't followed up with any
of them," I said.

He sighed. "Like who?"

"Like Earl King and/or his wife, Sophie."

"Who are they?"

"A couple who Dr. Dana nearly broke up with her
Radical Trust nonsense. They were at the signing and
had just as much opportunity to slip poison in her drink
as anyone. Furthermore, Mr. King heckled Dr. Dana just
like Angie did, and before that he and his wife were
happy to tell Ben and the rest of us about Dana Dobbs'
lack of professional credentials. They didn't like her at
all and were definitely not at her signing to purchase a
book."

Quinn still looked doubtful.

"I was actually there and saw them," I said. "And I
told you about them in my statement."

"Yes. I remember. You didn't give me their names, though." His face creased in thought. "Bring me some lemon pound cake and tell me more."

With a sense of gleeful hope, I hurried over and put the biggest slice of cake on a plate and poured him a cup of freshly brewed dark roast. Back at the table, I started back in, keeping my voice low so passing customers couldn't hear.

"A big problem is finding out how the killer got access to the cyanide. Right? As you said, it's not something you can just walk in and buy at the hardware store."

He nodded.

"And I don't know enough about the Kings—they own that bar King's Castle, down the street, by the way—to figure out how they could get it. But there is one suspect that might very well have had access to the poison."

Quinn took a big bite of cake and chewed slowly, watching me.

"Nate Dobbs."

Now a sip of coffee. "Do tell."

"He works for an agricultural fumigation company. Or used to."

He held up a finger. "Not anymore. He quit a year ago."

"So he had access to cyanide. Or at least it's a possibility. I haven't gotten that far."

"Mmm-hmm. Did you know that Ms. Kissel's ex-husband is an industrial scientist? It turns out there is cyanide in his lab."

I felt the hope slipping away. "But they aren't married anymore."

"They were in contact during the breakup. She came by his lab a few times after the divorce proceedings had started." He glanced up at Angie, who was standing in

the kitchen watching us with wide eyes. When she saw
us looking at her, she quickly moved out of view.

"Maybe she was thinking ahead," he said.

I couldn't very well tell him that Angie wouldn't have
stolen cyanide from her husband since she could likely
extract it from the pits of stone fruit herself.

"Anyone else?" He wore an amused expression that
I didn't appreciate.

"Dr. Dana fired her agent," I said.

"Ronnie Lake. Yes, I spoke with her."

"So you already know about the Dobbs' failing
marriage."

His forehead wrinkled. "No . . ."

I nodded. "Yep. The relationship guru was heading
for divorce, at least according to her former agent."

"Huh. Well, I have to admit that people sometimes
tell you things they don't tell me, Katie."

I smiled weakly, then went on. "Plus, Nate Dobbs
has a piece of commercial real estate that's been sitting
empty and useless ever since he bought it. Money problems, apparently. Now that his wife is dead he's suddenly back in business."

"Is that so? Well, I guess I'd better look into that."
He reached in his wallet and handed me a bill, then
wrapped the rest of his pound cake in a napkin.

"It's on me, Detective."

"I prefer to pay up. Keep the change."

"Okay. Thanks." I suppressed a grimace. His unwill-
ingness to let me treat him to the cake told me he was
more upset about my involvement in his investigation
than he was letting on.

Standing, he shot a look toward the kitchen and
leaned toward me. "Stay on your toes around her. Okay,
Katie? You drive me nuts, but I like you."

I nodded. "I will. And, Quinn? Will you follow up on the Kings and Nate Dobbs?"

"Sure," he said. "Or I'll have someone else make inquiries. Turns out that other case I told you about is more complicated than I'd anticipated."

Great. Quinn made me nuts, too, but I didn't want anyone else working on the Dr. Dana case.

"I'll be in touch," he said, and gave my shoulder a light squeeze before he left.

Angie was waiting in the office. "What did he want?"

"He just stopped in for a pastry," I said. "He saw you, though. I'm afraid I told him about your note."

"Did he ask to see it?"

I grimaced. "Now that you mention it, he didn't."

Her face fell. "He's still sure I'm the one who killed Dana Dobbs."

I didn't deny it.

A little before five there was a line four deep at the register, all there to pick up their frozen pies. Cookie had stuck around, and now she and Angie were fetching pies for customers, while Ben rang them up. Lucy was closing the window blinds, and I tidied the reading area. A book club had met there that afternoon, and the ladies had felt free to rearrange all the furniture. As I put the chairs and tables back in place by the floor-to-ceiling shelves, I reflected that it was actually kind of nice that people felt so free to make themselves at home in the Honeybee.

The last customer left, and I walked by Ben on my way back to the kitchen. "You were right about Bing Hawkins being a good salesman," I said casually. "In fact, I need to tell you about something that happened at the radio station yesterday."

"Maybe later," he said. The coldness in his voice gave me pause.

"Ben?"

"Come on, Luce. We can stop by Zunzi's for takeout on the way home." He loaded cash into the bank bag and brushed by me on his way to the office.

"What the . . ." I turned to Lucy, who gave me an apologetic smile. "Does he already know Jaida half agreed to a radio spot?"

She shook her head. "I don't think that's it."

Realization dawned. "He's giving me the cold shoulder because I'm still deciding how to handle Declan's proposal?"

That smile again. "Don't mind him, Katie. He'll get over it."

My aunt and uncle left. Lucy called her good-byes over her shoulder, but Ben just vaguely waved his hand.

"What's wrong with your uncle?" Cookie asked as I flipped off the overhead lights. Angie was in the office with Mungo. Again.

Sighing, I told Cookie that Declan had asked me to marry him, and waited for her response. True to form, it wasn't like anyone else's had been. Instead, she tipped her head to the side and considered me.

"Do you want to marry him?"

"I don't know."

"Do you not want to be married at all?"

"No, it's not that."

"All right. Do you want to be with Declan McCarthy, forever and ever, so mote it be?"

I hesitated. "I think so. I really do."

"You need to know so. And if the answer is yes, then you need to know whether that would be possible without marriage."

"Not for Declan, it wouldn't."

She took off her apron and hung it on one of the pegs on the back wall. "Whatever you decide, Katie, stand your ground. Do what you know is right for you."

I walked up and gave her a hug. "Thanks, Cookie. I needed to hear that."

Angie came out of the office, Mungo on her heels now that he knew the bakery was closed. "I really enjoyed myself," she said. "Thanks for letting me hang out with you guys this afternoon."

Cookie snorted. "Hang out? You worked your tail off."

"Well, I'm still grateful. Katie, I'm ready to go whenever you are."

I considered her. "I don't suppose I could talk you into having a drink with me before we head home."

Cookie grinned. "Can I come along? Oscar isn't off work yet, and he has the car."

"The more the merrier," I said.

Angie tipped her head. "What did you have in mind?"

"The King's Castle, down the street," I said. "I'll buy."

Chapter 20

The King's Castle was narrow and dark. A massive mahogany bar on the right side reached into vague shadows at the back of the establishment. A row of red Naugahyde barstools offered seating in front of the bar, and small booths with high-backed, scarred wooden benches marched down the wall to the left. The eight-foot ceilings felt oppressive after all the time I spent under the high ceilings of the Honeybee and my carriage house, but the air smelled so delicious I immediately decided to have a snack with my drink.

As we made our way down to the center of the bar, I noted the plethora of framed photos arranged on the wall over the booths. They were of birds—in flight, at rest, nesting, eating, perching—and quite stunning. Good-enough-to-be-in-a-gallery stunning.

Cookie slid onto a stool, and I took the one beside her. Angie climbed up next to me, and I noticed her shoes didn't quite reach the brass footrest. Half a dozen people were sitting in pairs, recently off work like us or maybe getting an early start on the holiday.

Sophie King came bustling down and leaned her elbows on the top of the bar. "Ladies, what can I get you?"

"I'll have a Sazerac," Cookie said.

The bartender did a double take. "What's in that again?"

"Cognac, absinthe, and bitters. A little sugar."

Sophie bobbed her head. "Of course. Coming right up." She looked at me. Puzzlement pinched the corners of her eyes as she tried to place me.

I pulled the bar menu over and saw we'd arrived in time for happy hour. "I'll have a Guinness."

Angie nodded. "Sounds good. I'll have one, too."

"And some boiled peanuts and Tupelo hot wings," I added, visually checking with my two companions.

They nodded their agreement.

When Sophie came back with our drinks, I smiled. "Hey, I remember you from the other night at the Fox and Hound."

Recognition dawned. "Right! I knew I'd seen you before." Her face clouded. "What a crazy thing to happen to that radio host. Lordy, I can hardly believe it."

"No kidding," I said.

Beside me, Cookie took a sip of her Sazerac and winced.

Suddenly Sophie pointed at Angie. "Heck, you're the one who got Earl all het up about that silly stuff Dr. Dana told him to do, calling her on the carpet like you did." Sophie crossed herself. "God rest her soul."

Angie looked uncomfortable for a moment, then sat up straighter. "It's nice to know I wasn't the only one who thought Dr. Dana dispensed poor counsel to her listeners."

"Oh, my. Earl looked up all sorts of things about her. There are a whole bunch of people online who didn't like her." She looked torn between dishing on Dr. Dana and feeling bad about it. "You know she didn't even have any kids, but that woman still felt like she could tell other people how to raise theirs." She shook her head and tsked.

"I think your husband mentioned that," I said, and took a sip of Guinness. The creamy foam coated my upper lip, and I licked it off.

"She was misguided in many ways," Angie said. "Not that I wished her any harm," she hastened to add.

The bartender waved her hand. "Oh, heavens no!" She looked both ways at the other customers, then leaned toward us. "Were you still there when it happened?"

Cookie tried another sip of her drink. After a few moments, she took another. It appeared to be growing on her.

Angie and I exchanged glances. I nodded. "We were."

"Is it true that she was poisoned?"

We all nodded.

"Well, goodness, how could they tell? Did she look funny?" Sophie's eyes widened. "Oh, gosh. Did you see her, you know, *after*?"

Angie blanched, and I felt sure she was remembering exactly how Dr. Dana had looked when she found her.

"Is your husband here, too?" I asked.

"Earl's in the back. Our cook called in late."

"You left pretty early that night, didn't you?" I asked.

"Pretty much right after Dr. Dana stopped talking." She tsked again. "Who knew?"

Now I leaned toward her. "I'm curious. Why did you go to see her if you didn't like her?"

She laughed. "Oh, Lord, honey. We didn't mean to go to see her at all. Earl just had to get the latest book by that Western mystery writer he likes so much, so we stopped in on our way home from here. We had no idea she'd be there."

That took the wind right out of my sails.

"But boy howdy," she continued. "When he saw she was gonna be there, he couldn't resist staying to see what she'd say." Sophie reddened. "I didn't expect him to shoot his mouth off like that, though. Or to drag me into it."

A door down at the end of the bar opened, and a rectangle of bright light briefly illuminated the dark atmosphere. Earl himself came lumbering down with a bowl of peanuts and a platter heaped with chicken wings still sizzling from the fryer. He set them down on the bar and distributed napkins and moist towelettes.

"Hon, you remember these two from the bookstore the other day, don't you?" his wife asked.

"You betcha," he boomed. "Hell of a thing that happened."

We all murmured agreement.

The Kings moved away to check in with their other customers, and we dug in.

"How's your drink?" I asked Cookie around a bite of sweet and fiery chicken.

"Terrible," she said, and raised her empty glass. Sophie saw her and nodded. Within moments my friend had another in front of her. "I think she's using as much absinthe as cognac—only the cognac is actually cheap brandy. But I'm developing a fondness for the combination."

I laughed. "I'm glad you're not driving."

She grinned. "Thank goodness Oscar's going to pick me up in half an hour or so."

My phone rang in my pocket. Quickly, I wiped hot sauce off my fingers, slipped off the stool, and went to an empty corner.

It was Declan.

"Hey," I said.

"Hey. Are you home from work yet?"

"Nope. Out partying at the bar," I joked.

"Seriously."

"I am serious," I said.

"Who are you with?" And suddenly it wasn't funny anymore, because I heard actual suspicion in his voice.

He doesn't think . . . he couldn't think . . . Steve? Nah.

"I'm with Cookie and Angie. Listen, can I call you later? Angie's going to come home and stay the night with me."

A pause, then: "Are you sure that's a good idea?"

"I am."

"Okay . . ." He cleared his throat. "I'll pick up if I can. The holiday crazies are starting up already. We had to go fetch a guy who'd had too much eggnog out of a tree earlier."

I laughed.

"Oops. Just got a call. Talk to you later." And he hung up.

Unsettled, I returned to the others. We chatted and ate until there was nothing but empty peanut shells and a few ribs of celery left. Angie and I finished our stouts, and I asked for the check. Earl brought it over. I waved away the others' attempts to pay and put a couple of bills on the bar.

As we started to leave, Earl came over again. "Need change?"

I shook my head. "Nope. That's for you. Those wings were fantastic."

"My own special recipe," he said with a grin.

"Say," I said, shrugging into my jacket. "Who took all the bird photos? They're awfully good."

Pride infused his face. "Those are mine." He walked down to the end of the bar and came around to where we stood. Pointing at the first picture in the array, a beautiful hawk perching on a piece of driftwood, he said, "This was my first one. Red-tailed hawk at my father's hunting cabin. Saw it and just happened to have my camera with me. Took that photo, and I was hooked." He looked fondly down the line of images. "I've been taking pictures of birds ever since."

"On film?" Cookie asked.

He laughed. "Yep. Old-school."

My head came up from buttoning my jacket. "Do you develop them yourself?"

"Absolutely. Learned how to do it years ago, and built myself a little darkroom at home."

"Earl?" Sophie called.

"Thanks for stopping in," he said as he turned away. "Come again soon."

Out on the sidewalk, Cookie and I stopped. Looked at each other.

Angie frowned. "What's going on?"

"Maybe Sophie King didn't know Dr. Dana was going to be at the Fox and Hound, but her husband might have," I speculated slowly.

"And if Iris was right," Cookie said, "the chemicals he uses to develop his photos contain cyanide."

Angie's jaw slackened. "Do you think he killed Dana Dobbs?"

I shrugged. "I don't know. But he sure didn't like her, and if he had access to the poison . . ." I pulled my phone out. "I'm going to call Quinn. He said he'd have someone follow up with the Kings, but this information might light a fire under him."

I had just finished leaving a message when Oscar Ruiz, Cookie's handsome husband, pulled his SUV to the curb.

As they pulled away, Angie and I started back to the Honeybee to pick up Mungo and head to my house.

"Oh," Angie breathed when I got out of the Bug. She'd followed me home in her Toyota and stood on the front walk. "You live here?"

I smiled. "Mmm-hmm." How could I leave it behind if Declan and I got married? It was too small for two people day in and day out. I pushed the thought away and got out of the car.

Yellow light streamed from Margie's front window, and I saw the JJs jumping off the sofa into a pile of pillows. Somehow, I didn't think Dr. Dana would have approved. Their shrieks and giggles drifted out to us, a sound so contagious I couldn't help laughing. Angie grinned, too, and even Mungo's eyes danced with humor.

I lowered him down, and he ran out to the lawn. "Has he always attracted fireflies?" I asked as I watched him.

Angie nodded. "When they're in season."

The lightning bugs were long gone by late November, of course, but during the months when they were plentiful—and sometimes when they weren't supposed to be around at all—their little winking lights congregated around my familiar in droves. They were his totem, like dragonflies were mine.

And apparently they always had been.

I led her inside, which she found just as charming as the outside.

"There's a futon in the loft upstairs. And I'll clear a shelf in the bathroom for you."

She gave me a grateful look. "This is really nice of you."

"It'll be fun to have the company. And maybe we can get to know each other a little better."

"I'd like that."

We made up the futon, and she unpacked a few of her things. Then she went back down the narrow stairs with a bag of toiletries. When she was out of sight, I quickly retrieved the key to the secretary's desk from behind a stack of books. I twisted it in the lock and put it in my pocket. Angie might be innocent of murder, but I didn't know her that well, and altars were very personal.

She was looking up at me from the bottom of the stairs when I turned back but didn't comment.

I made tea and gave Mungo a bit of leftover beef Wellington sans béarnaise sauce, and we went into the living room. Grabbing my tote, I took out my phone and was about to put it in the bedroom when my hand encountered something unfamiliar. I drew it out.

The figurine Steve had given me. How had it gotten in there? I'd left it on the coffee counter at the bakery, and then later it had been gone. Perhaps Lucy had decided to tuck it in my tote?

"Where did you get that?" Angie asked from her wingback chair. Steam drifted up from the tea and curled around her face. However, her bow mouth was pursed with concern.

I hefted the little statue. "A friend gave it to me. At least I thought he was a friend."

She leaned forward and put her tea on the coffee table. "What do you mean?"

"We dated—almost dated—a while ago. Then Declan—the fireman from the other night? That's my boyfriend. Anyway, we got together, and Steve—that's who gave this to me—Steve and I agreed we'd be friends."

She frowned. "This Steve character wants to be a lot more than friends, believe me."

My eyebrows rose. "How do you know that?"

"Because that"—she pointed at the dog/cat/bird figure in my hand—"is a furata."

My face went blank. "A what?"

"Furata. It's like a poppet, or a voodoo doll, but it doesn't represent you. It represents the giver. And it's used exclusively to force the love of another."

A chill ran down my back. "How do you know that?"

"Just because I don't practice anymore doesn't mean I don't remember my training." Her face reddened, and she looked away. "And I considered using a furata spell on my husband."

The bronze cat's eyes laughed up at me from my shaking hand.

"But I didn't," Angie continued. "It's gray magic at best, and dark at its worst. I'd already tempted the Rule of Three once, and I knew better than to do it again."

"Is that why you don't practice anymore?" I asked, oddly unwilling to talk about the furata in my hand even though now it wasn't just my hand shaking. My whole body quivered with revulsion and disbelief.

And hurt that Steve would violate our friendship in such a horrible way.

Yip! Mungo had finished his supper and now jumped up on the couch next to me. One look at my face and he scooted into my lap. He sniffed at the figure in my hand and his lips pulled back to expose his teeth.

Slowly, Angie's chin dipped. "Mungo remembers why I stopped. It was a spell that went terribly wrong." She nodded at the furata. "Does the man who gave you this have any knowledge of magic?"

Only the kind handed down from generations of the blatantly unscrupulous Dragoh clan.

With an effort, I tipped my palm over, but the little

figure didn't seem to want to leave my hand. I felt my eyes go wide, and my voice wavered. "He's a druid."

"A druid! Not one to believe in the Rule, then. And he's trying to come between you and Declan."

My eyes met hers. "I didn't think so, but it seems obvious now. He seems pretty determined, too."

"Katie, you have to get rid of that thing!" Angie said.

I couldn't keep the panic out of my voice. "How do I do that?"

Angie leaped to her feet. Mungo barked. "Water. Do you have any bottled spring water?"

I rose as well, still clutching the furata in my unwilling fist. "Better yet, I have natural live water. Come with me."

She followed me out to the patio and across the backyard to the corner where the stream crossed my property. "Perfect!"

"Shh," I warned with a glance at the Coopersmiths' house. "My neighbor has a crazy instinct for showing up when I'm casting out here."

"Okay, submerse the figurine in the water." Angie looked skyward. Light clouds skidded across the face of the moon. "Luna is waning gibbous tonight. That will do. Place the furata in the stream and allow the natural water to wash away the spell. Leave it there until the new moon. As the light decreases, it will also take the power of the spell with it."

I stared at her and said between chattering teeth, "You really know your stuff."

She smiled. "When it comes to this, I do. Now, go ahead."

Kneeling by the stream, I put my whole hand into the water. It instantly grew cold, but at the same time I was finally able to open my fingers. The spell figure drifted out. I pushed it down into the mud, sending a request to the elements of earth and water to strip all power away from it. Mungo leaned against my leg, peering into the stream. I let the mud rinse away from my fingers, then stood, feeling a clarity I hadn't known was missing.

"That *creep*," I said. "When I get my hands on him—"

A crash out front cut me off. My head whipped around. "What was that?" Dread ran down my spine.

Angie looked suddenly scared, the confidence she'd shown when telling me how to get rid of the furata instantly evaporating. "I don't know."

Mungo took off for the front of the house. I heard a voice yell and recognized it as Margie's.

Chapter 21

I began to run, wiping my cold, wet hand on my shirt.
Angie hesitated, then followed. The front gate latch
stuck at first. Frantically, I rattled it back and forth. An
eternity later, it slipped open. Pushing through, I
rounded the corner of the house and skidded to a stop.

Someone had set a fire smack dab in the middle of
my yard.

It was so out of place that I was stunned into inertia.
Smaller than a bonfire but larger than a campfire, it
crackled cheerily, as if inviting the neighbors to come
over and make s'mores. The smell of patchouli swirled
up in the smoke, so strong it made my eyes water. It was
a scent I always associated with Lucy, but I was instantly
certain she had nothing to do with this. Another odor
joined it then, sour and rank.

Mungo circled the blaze, keeping his distance, the
worry that was etched on his furry little face visible in
the flickering light.

"I'll call the fire department," Margie called from
her front walk.

Her voice broke my trance. "No, wait!" I said. "I
have a hose right here."

The last thing I needed was a full-fledged visit with ladder trucks and all the rest, especially when Declan was on shift. I ran to the spigot on the side of the house, grabbed the hose, and unreeled it out to the yard.

Angie rushed over and grabbed the nozzle out of my hand. "I've got this! Turn on the water!"

Soon the spray was hitting the flames, knocking them back and eventually defeating them. It seemed to take a long time. When the fire had been reduced to a few puffs of smoke, Margie approached with Baby Bart on her hip and a flashlight in her other hand. I saw the twins watching out the window.

Margie kept looking at them over her shoulder. "I told Jonathan and Julia to stay inside. There's someone out there, Katie."

"Out where?" Angie asked.

My neighbor did a double take when she recognized my companion. "What are you doing here?"

"It's a long story," I broke in before she could get her back up. "Did you see who set this?"

Margie shook her head and glanced back at the JJs again. "No. I heard something knock over my garbage can out by the street. I thought it was probably a dog or a raccoon or something and came out to shoo it away. But I saw someone running away. And that was when I saw the fire."

"You saw them? What did they look like?"

"Oh, gosh. I couldn't see them that well."

"Man or woman?"

She shook her head. "I just got a quick look before they cut around the corner. Dark clothes, some kind of hat." Her brow wrinkled. "Why would someone set a fire in your yard, for heaven's sake?"

My shoulders rose and fell. "I have no idea." I was

baffled more than frightened. The fire had been out in the open, away from the house, and there was no wind. It probably would have burned itself out if no one had noticed it. There hadn't been any real danger, though I'd certainly have to do something about the ring of charred grass the fire had left behind.

Angie, though, looked quite shaken. Her eyes searched the shadows, then returned to the still-smoldering pile of . . . what?

"Margie, could you direct your flashlight over here?" I asked.

Instead, she handed it to me. "Take it. I need to get back to the twins. Be sure to lock your door tonight, Katie." Her gaze raked the street in front. "Whoever it was might come back."

Well, that was a cheery thought.

"Thanks, Margie. You, too."

"I think you should call the police."

"It was probably just teenagers," I said, remembering Declan's earlier reference to how many people misbehaved during holidays.

With one last concerned look at Angie, my neighbor trotted across to her house and went inside.

I turned the beam of the flashlight onto the little pile of wet charcoal. "I wonder if we *should* call the police."

Angie kneeled and pulled out a length of ribbon. It was satin and had started out shiny white. Now it was smudged with ashes. The patchouli scent had lessened, but now a spicy clove scent rose into the air. She continued to pull until the ribbon came free. It was about a yard long.

"What the . . . ?" I bent down beside her as she reached into the ashes again.

This time the ribbon she pulled out had started black and was smudged lighter in some places by the ashes. Only eight inches of the fabric hadn't been consumed by the flames.

And finally, she pulled out the remnants of one more ribbon. Careful inspection revealed it to be dark red.

She looked over at me, her big eyes haunted. "This was burning magic. A binding spell."

Magic? But the only magical connections to this case were Angie and, if she'd been serious about the tarot deck I'd seen in her things, perhaps Dr. Dana herself. Was there another player?

"Binding who?" I wondered out loud. "You or me?"

Angie pointed at the red ribbon. "This ribbon represents the one to be bound. It's likely you."

I blinked.

"It's your house, for one thing. Not many people know I'm here. But I'm also guessing the red represents your hair."

A thought occurred to me. Slowly, I rose to my feet. "Could Steve have done this?"

She stood as well, her mouth set in a grim line.

I felt the blood drain from my face. "Oh, no. You really think this was him?" The twinge of sorrow that had tempered my anger about the furata unfurled into a deep regret for my friend. "Holy smokes. He's really gone to the dark side."

And he directed that darkness against me.

My anger surged back, hot and tinted with fear. "Could the spell have really worked? Am I somehow bound in a way I don't know about?"

Angie came over and gave me a hug. "You're fine, thanks to your observant neighbor. You put the fire out before the spell could be completed."

*   *   *

We decided against calling the police. What were they going to do? Without understanding the fire was a burning spell, they'd put it down to pranksters, shake their heads, and walk away. Also, I could see the idea of dealing with the authorities made Angie nervous.

So we gathered what was left from the fire and put it in a metal bucket, which we then filled to the brim with water from the stream. After one more dousing of the blackened grass in the yard, we went inside.

"The police might not be able to help," I said, "but at least there are a few things I can do to protect this house."

Up in the loft, I edged around the now-open futon and removed a few items from a cupboard. First, a bundle of white sage to give my little abode a thorough smudging. Then I dug out a vial of four thieves vinegar—this batch infused with black pepper, cayenne, rosemary, and thyme. Legend had it that a similar herbal vinegar had protected the four thieves who had been sentenced to bury plague victims in medieval France. Finally, I grabbed a bag of small quartz crystals. They rattled together as I went down the stairs.

Without any discussion, Angie stepped in to help. As we burned the sage and walked the periphery of the house, I could feel her power. It was considerable. Afterward, I opened the French doors to let some of the smoky smell escape. Keeping a sharp eye out for any movement in the shadows, I went out and retrieved the besom from the gazebo. Back inside, I used a stepstool to hang the ceremonial broom over the back door. A decorative woven bag filled with cumin, lemongrass, and dill already protected the front door.

Then we shut the doors and checked the locks on the

windows. At each one, I placed a small crystal on the sill with a request for protection, and Angie placed drops of the four thieves vinegar on the corners of the glass with her fingertips. Finally, she went one more step and sprinkled some kitchen salt on the floor in front of the doors.

"I think that should do it," I said. "If anything can get past all that, we'll have to do battle using other methods."

Angie turned from where she was drying her hands in the kitchen. "What do you mean, 'battle'?"

"Just an expression," I said, not wanting to get into the whole lightwitch thing. "Want some more tea? We never did get to finish."

"Ha. We never even got to start. Is it always so exciting around here?"

Yip!

I gave Mungo a look. "Nah."

"Well, I've got to tell you, I'm beat. Do you mind if I go to bed?"

"Of course not. Feel free to turn the television on up there."

Her lips tugged up in a tired smile. "Thanks."

"I have to go to to work really early, you know. So when you wake up, I won't be here. You can hang out, though."

"I can't think of anything better," she said. "I haven't felt this safe in a long time."

It was only ten o'clock, but I went to bed, too. Curling up with Mungo on the blue patchwork quilt Lucy had given me, I texted Steve.

Discovered what your gift really was. I never would have believed you capable of such a stunning violation of trust. But your little love spell failed, and so did the creepy binding spell. This time you went

*too far. I can't trust you ever again. Our friendship is
OVER.*

Turned out that was a mistake, because seconds later
he was texting me back with a series of denials and apol-
ogies. I thought about confronting him, but I was so
angry that I knew the exchange would deteriorate into
nonsense. Besides, after he crossed the line like that,
there was really nothing left to say.

I blocked his number.

The text tones on my phone stopped. Blissful quiet.
Never mind the pang of loss I felt. Steve had meant a
lot to me.

How could he have done that?

I called Declan. Of course, when I really, really wanted
to hear his voice, he didn't answer. I had to assume he was
out on another call, and first sent a hope for his safety, and
then one that he'd have a chance to get some sleep that
night. I sent a text asking him to call when he could.

The phone rang in my hand. I didn't recognize the
number.

"Hello?"

"Katie, please listen to me," Steve pleaded.

He called from someone else's phone? Holy cow!

"I don't know what you hope to gain from all this,"
I said. Mungo bounded to his feet. "Right now the last
thing I want to do is talk to you."

"Katie—"

I hung up.

Almost instantly, my phone rang again.

"Stop calling me," I almost yelled into it.

"Katie!" The voice that reached my ear was quite
different from Steve's.

"Oops. Sorry, Mama."

"What on earth is going on there?"

Stroking Mungo's ears, I settled back into the cocoon of pillows on the bed. "Another murder," I said. "And Mungo's ex-witch is the prime suspect. She's staying with me right now. Plus Steve is back in town and tried to cast a love spell on me—not to mention a burning spell in my front yard tonight. Oh, and Declan asked me to marry him. Other than that? Not much."

A few beats of silence, then she said, "Well. I guess I'd better get another cup of decaf. This sounds like it might take a while."

I imagined my mother sitting in the living room of the house I'd grown up in. Her red hair, still bright thanks to a bottle of color, would be piled up on her head. She'd be wearing her long flannel nightgown and fuzzy slippers, and her face would be freshly washed. Still, she would have expertly reapplied her lipstick. Even if Fillmore, Ohio, had a population of only 564, not a single one of those citizens would catch my mother without her lipstick, whether she was wearing her bathrobe or not.

I filled her in on what had been going on the last few days. Over the last several months, she and Daddy had become used to my involvement in murder investigations. I didn't always tell them about the dangerous bits, but they probably guessed. Still, being my mother, she was most interested in the news about Declan.

"I can't believe you didn't call me right away. Have you set a date?"

"Hmm. Not exactly."

A pause. "You said yes, didn't you?"

"Actually I didn't."

"What? Katie, I was just starting to hope again, after

what happened with Andrew." She wouldn't come right out and say it, but deep down Mama had blamed me when he'd bailed on our wedding.

"I didn't say no, either. I'm still deciding."

There was a long silence. I heard her take a sip of her coffee, which by now must have been growing tepid. "Do you love him?"

"Yes. But there are a lot of things to work out. Practical matters."

"Of course there are. That's how it works." Surprisingly, her frustration seemed to have abated. "Listen to me, sweetie. You've blossomed and grown so much since you moved down there with my sister. I know I fought it at first, but you've truly come into your own. I know you're a strong and capable woman. You'll make the right decision about whether to marry Declan or not."

My mother was perpetually full of surprises. "Thank you," I breathed, realizing on some level that if Mama had urged me to marry Declan—or anyone else—I might have decided against it just to be contrary.

We said good night, and I set the phone on the nightstand. The velvet box sat next to the lamp, its plush fabric absorbing the light. I opened it and took the ring out. It was heavy—not white gold, but platinum. Declan knew I wasn't a diamond kind of woman, and he also knew I used my hands a lot—kneading bread, doing dishes, rubbing cold butter into flour. The bright sapphire was set deep into the filigree, stunning and utterly practical at the same time.

He knew me.

Do you want to be with Declan McCarthy, forever and ever, so mote it be?

I slipped the ring on my finger. It felt nice. Solid. Right.

Mungo nudged at my arm. I held out my hand, and he nosed the sapphire. Looked up at me with a question in his eyes.

I ruffled his ears, slid the ring off, and returned it to the box. Getting off the bed, I turned out the light and went to the window. The moon was still bright outside, and a swath of its silvery light cut through the glass and into the room. I placed the open box on the sill, in the moonbeam, and muttered a few words over it.

So mote it be.

Taking a deep breath, I turned the light back on and opened my book.

I read for a while but found it hard to concentrate. For one thing, I kept thinking of Margie's description of the fire starter. If, that is, the person she'd seen had been the same one who'd started the blaze in my yard. It could have just been somebody who accidentally knocked over a garbage can and became frightened when Margie came out to yell at them.

But I didn't think so. I'd assumed it was Steve because he'd already tried to hex me with the furata. Who else would have placed a binding spell on me? Such magic wasn't only used to bind someone in love. You could bind an enemy, or it could even be used for protection.

Had I jumped the gun, thinking it was Steve? Still, there was a bronze figure in my backyard where water and moonlight could strip its power—and I had no doubt he was responsible for that sorcery.

Even so, I remembered how I'd described the foiled burglar in the dark alley behind the Honeybee to the police: bulky coat, hat, hard to tell if it was a man or a woman.

Could it have been the same person Margie had seen? If the attempted burglary had been connected to

Dr. Dana's murder—and given the coincidence of someone trying to break into a store the day after a murder
had been committed there, it seemed more than likely
they *were* related—and the same person had cast a binding spell on my lawn . . . what did that mean?

Maybe, just maybe, it meant there was something in
the back room of Croft's store the police had missed.
Something the burglar had wanted to retrieve, and bar-
ring that, wanted to keep me from finding. And why
me? Well, I was the only one looking at suspects other
than Angie, which made me a threat to the real killer.

Tomorrow, between baking eight dozen pies in the
morning and stopping by Dana Dobbs' memorial in the
afternoon, I needed to look in that back room.

Finally, I turned out the light. As I snuggled down
with Mungo, another thought occurred to me, and my
eyes popped back open.

That evening, Angie Kissel had given me magical
information and instructions, both of which I was grateful for. But when we'd been setting protections, she'd
been actually invoking power. She'd been *practicing*
magic. Like a real witch.

Did that mean she was coming back to the Craft
after all?

Yet again, sleep did not come quickly.

Chapter 22

The next morning, I was surprised when Angie came downstairs as I was making coffee. It was four a.m., and I was getting a later start than I wanted, but I hadn't expected her to be awake.

"You mind if I come in to work with you?" she asked. "I know I said I felt safe here, but I really enjoyed myself yesterday."

"We could probably use the help," I admitted. Especially with Iris gone until Monday, and my mission of getting away to look in the storage room of the Fox and Hound. "Sure. But I'm leaving in twenty minutes."

She grinned. "Deal."

Not many women can shower and dress that quickly. Surprisingly, she was ready to go on time, sans makeup and wearing jeans, boots, and a long-sleeved brown T-shirt. It also helped that her pixie hair was even shorter than mine. She rode with me, and it dried in the car on the way.

At the Honeybee, we got right to work. First thing, I set the ovens to preheat. Then lights came on, upbeat music wafted from the speakers, and the loaves of sourdough went in to bake. Soon the heady aroma of browning bread filled the kitchen, and I breathed it in with a sigh of contentment. Magic and murder aside, I loved being a baker as much as anything.

Next, I pulled the crusts I'd mixed and rolled the day before out of the refrigerator and started arranging them in aluminum pans. Angie was ladling pumpkin filling into them when Lucy and Ben came in.

"Ah, you're back," my aunt said to her, taking off her coat and putting a forest green chef's apron over her rust-colored skirt. She smiled. "I'm glad."

By the time we opened, the first batch of still warm pies was ready for pickup. Half were pumpkin; half were a mix of fruit and pecan pies. The first customer showed up a little before eight o'clock, and after that there was a steady stream of pies into the oven, out of the oven, and out the door.

Around ten we'd finished with all the baking. Lucy, Angie, and I grabbed our caffeine of choice and sprawled in the library for a break, while Ben continued to help customers.

"I never knew running a bakery was so much work," Angie said, visibly stifling a yawn.

"Oh, honey," Lucy said. "It's not always like this. High pie days are unusual."

"There's always something, though," I said. "A catering job, wedding cakes, fund-raisers."

"And I thought working in a nursery was hard," Angie said.

I sat up from my half-prone position on the sofa. "Say, would you mind helping Ben out for a bit longer? I want to steal Lucy for a little while."

"Sure," Angie said easily.

My aunt raised her eyebrows in question.

I glanced around to see if there were any customers

close enough to hear. There weren't. "Angie, I don't think you know that someone tried to break into the Fox and Hound."

She shook her head.

"Two mornings after the murder, super early. I scared them off."

Lucy snorted. "After they almost killed you."

Angie's mouth dropped open.

"It wasn't that bad. Lucy, I haven't had a chance to tell you someone set a fire on my lawn last night."

She scooted to the edge of her seat. "What?"

"It was burning magic. A binding spell. Angie and I thought it might have been Steve."

"Steve!" she exclaimed. "Why would you think that?"

Angie and I exchanged a meaningful look. "Because that little 'souvenir' he gave me yesterday turned out to be another kind of binding spell," I said. "A love spell."

Lucy gasped.

"You did put it in my tote bag, didn't you?" I asked.

"Me? Why would I do that?" she asked. "You didn't seem to want it."

I frowned. "So how did it get in there?"

The look of horror on my aunt's face deepened.

"Don't worry," I said quickly. "Angie showed me how remove its power. But when someone set a burning spell in front of my house right after that, we thought of Steve immediately."

"Oh, dear," Lucy said.

"But I was thinking about it overnight," I continued. "And the person who set the fire might have been the same person who tried to break into the Fox and Hound."

My aunt opened her mouth to say something, but I barreled on to explain how similar Margie and my descriptions of the spell caster and the burglar had been.

"What if it was the same person? And what if he or she was trying to get into Croft's store for a reason other than robbery?"

Lucy frowned. "Like what?"

I shook my head. "I don't know. But I'd like to take another look around that back room where Dr. Dana died."

"The police checked it already."

My shoulders rose and fell. "True. It's probably a long shot."

Or maybe not such a long shot.

Lucy must have seen something in my eyes, though, because she nodded as if making a decision. "Let's go next door right now."

I was happy to see there were several customers in the Fox and Hound when Lucy and I went inside. Mrs. Potter was back in the children's section, helping customers select books for the little ones on their Christmas list. Croft bustled out from the mystery section with an actual smile on his face. It broadened when he saw us.

"Hey, you two."

"Hi, Croft," I said, gesturing at the numerous browsers. "Looks like things are getting back to normal."

"Thank God," he said with feeling. "It's not as good as last year yet, but I have high hopes." He put his hands on his hips. "Now, what can I do for you ladies?"

I walked to a secluded corner. Lucy and Croft followed. His smile had dropped once he realized we weren't in shopping mode, but he listened as I said, "Remember when you offered to do whatever you could to help find Dr. Dana's killer?"

"Sure I do. I'm not senile yet, you know."

"Of course not. I'm wondering if you'd let us look in

your back room. The police have released it, haven't they?"

"Yup." One side of his mouth came up. "What are you looking for?"

"No idea. But I got to thinking about why someone might want to break in from the alley. What if it wasn't random?"

"Huh. Well, I don't know what you think you're gonna find, but you're welcome to check it out. I haven't moved much around since, well, you know. Just tidied up a bit." He made a face. "I don't know if I'll ever be able to go back there without thinking about that night."

"Thanks, Croft." I smiled and considered bussing him on the cheek. I was pretty sure he'd die of apoplexy, though.

We went through to the storage room and shut the door behind us. Silence descended. There were no windows, so it was utterly dark. I flipped on the light switch by the door, and fluorescent bulbs flickered to life above us. Lucy's eyes moved over the room and its contents with an expression of sorrow on her face. I knew she was thinking about the loss of life that had occurred there so recently. Witches might profess that death was simply a journey to the next plane, but that didn't mean we handled it better than anyone else.

I'd never been farther into this room than the doorway with Margie, though apparently my aunt had ventured quite near the body before the police had arrived Saturday night. Now we moved inside to assess the situation. Without the scents of mulled cider and—for Lucy, at least—almonds to flavor the air, the distinct smell of ink on paper I always associated with libraries and bookstores filled my nose and tugged at a nostalgia for something I couldn't quite define.

Croft wasn't the tidiest housekeeper, but things were arranged in a fairly logical manner. Industrial wall-mounted shelves were divided into sections. There were a few cartons of books, but most of the extra books were stacked freely, easy to view and restock out front. One shelf was labeled RETURNS. Other shelves held boxes of toys, games, and gift items.

The space on the floor where the victim had fallen was clear now. One small section was cleaner than the rest, and from what I could remember, that was probably where the sweet tea had spilled. The table where Dr. Dana had been signing Croft's extra stock had been moved to one side, but it was still stacked with her books. A rack in the corner held the folding chairs that Croft used for events.

Here and there I saw dark smudges of powder that I recognized from another crime scene. Quinn hadn't mentioned fingerprints, but I supposed the police had to make an attempt. Since Dr. Dana had probably been given the poison before she ever came back here, it seemed unlikely fingerprinting would be helpful, though.

"Let's try to be methodical," Lucy said briskly. "You take the upper shelves since you can reach them better, and I'll take the lower ones. This unit first."

I nodded. "Look for anything that might seem strange, out of place, or in the least bit suspicious."

We got to work, checking each stack of books, looking behind them, and even flipping through a few.

Nada.

Then we checked the bins of nonbook items for sale, taking things out of shipping cartons, lifting boxes, and looking underneath them. I peered behind the shelving units and got down on the floor to check beneath them.

Zilch.

We went to the rack of chairs, taking each one out and looking for anything that could have been tucked between them. Then I got the grand idea of checking under the seat of each one, and Lucy gamely pitched in. That took several minutes.

Except for an old, dried piece of chewing gum: zippo.

As long as I was checking under things for who knows what—hidden envelopes? a note in a bottle? a random Post-it with a scribbled confession?—I crawled under the table where Dana Dobbs had sat to sign the last books she ever would.

Zero.

I slumped into the chair pulled up to the table. "I guess this was a stupid idea."

Lucy sighed. "It was a good idea, honey. But if there was something the killer was looking for, the police must have already found it and taken it away."

Dr. Dana's face looked up at me from the cover of the books still stacked there. Absently, I lifted the stack and checked between each one.

Nothing unusual.

Flipping through, I saw she'd signed several of them but then found one that was blank. The next one I looked at made me stop cold.

"Lucy," I said slowly.

She turned from where she'd been looking at the middle of the floor. When she saw my face, she hurried over. "What is it?"

Silently, I showed her the last book Dr. Dana had signed. I felt sure she'd been signing it when she'd taken a drink of her sweet tea and realized she was going to die.

"Oh, my," Lucy said in a low voice.

The reason I thought it was the one Dana had been writing in before she died was because she hadn't signed her name.

The name scrawled under *How to Do Marriage Right* on the title page was that of her husband.

Nate.

Next to it was another wavy, illegible line that ran off the edge of the page. I peered at it closely. "Lucy? Is this a word?"

She leaned in. "I can't tell. It looks like the mark left by a pen as the user lost consciousness."

"Oh. Yeah, that could be it." *Ugh*.

My aunt began to pace. "Why would she write her husband's name?" She stopped. "Do you think . . . ?"

I gave a tiny shrug. "That she was identifying her killer? I can't think of any other reason she'd write his name immediately before she died. Can you?"

She looked thoughtful. "But how could she know for sure? I mean, if the poison was given to her before she came back here, she'd have to guess about who gave it to her unless she actually saw them do it. And if she saw them, I can't imagine she would have drunk the sweet tea at all."

"There were a few times on Saturday night when Dr. Dana seemed awfully anxious. It's possible that she was worried her husband had his own plans for ending their marriage—with her death."

Lucy frowned. "I don't know . . ."

I pointed at the book. "It supports what I told Quinn yesterday. Maybe he'll take me seriously now. Nate Dobbs' wife told the whole world about their private life, and then kept convincing him not to file for the divorce he wanted."

"How did she do that?" Lucy mused.

"I don't know. Guilt? Or maybe in the course of practicing Radical Trust, her spouse stalking turned up something she could blackmail him with. Either way, he had motive. And if Angie's right about his old job, then he had access to cyanide. Plus, this"—I pointed to the book now open on the table—"looks like Dana herself thought he was her killer. He must have seen that she'd written his name when he rushed to her side."

"Or when he went back in with the police. I wonder why they didn't notice." Lucy pressed her lips together. "Is all that enough to make a murder case against him?"

"It's a good start. Of course, Quinn has a good start on the case against Angie, too. A really good start, and he never called me back after I left the message about Earl King last night. The only thing that would completely convince him would be a full confession."

An idea took root. I jumped up out of the chair.

Lucy tipped her head. "What?"

I grinned. "And I might know how to get one."

"So what do you think?" I asked Croft. Without him, my plan couldn't get off the ground.

He folded his arms across his chest and leaned against the wall of the storage room. "I don't know, Katie. You're talking about more or less inviting someone to break into my store. I just installed a nice big lock on the back door after what happened earlier."

"All you have to do is skip using it tonight. The other lock wasn't broken, was it?"

"Nah. It's still on there, too. But I hadn't realized how flimsy it is."

"Perfect!"

He glared at me.

"Croft," Lucy said in her gentle way. "Even if nothing

comes of this, don't you like the idea of selling off those books for a good cause? That scholarship fund sounds like something Dana believed in." I'd told them about the *in lieu of flowers* option Ronnie Lake had mentioned.

"Well . . . yeah." One side of his mouth pulled back in thought. "Okay. We'll do the auction. You can tell whoever you want, and we'll see what happens tonight."

He saw the look on my face. "Oh, yes, Katie. This is my store, and if Nate Dobbs decides to visit after hours, I'm going to be here to witness it. *And* throw the book at him."

I hesitated.

"He's right," Lucy said. "You'd never leave the Honeybee if you knew someone was going to break in, would you?"

"No. Of course I wouldn't."

Croft gave a decisive nod. "And I want Detective Quinn here, too."

"I'll give him a call," I said. I didn't mention that he might not call me back.

"All right, then," he said. "I'm closing at seven. We'll stay all night if we have to."

Happy Thanksgiving.

But I was as game as he was to see it through to the end.

Chapter 23

Lucy opted to stay at the Honeybee that afternoon while I went to Dr. Dana's memorial service. While there, I hoped to do more than show my respect for the departed; I wanted to make sure Nate Dobbs knew he had one last chance to retrieve the book in which his wife had fingered him as her killer. He was sure to be there. And if I was wrong about Nate? Well, I had every intention of spreading the word to anyone on my list who had a possible motive.

Ben was still giving me the cold shoulder and probably wouldn't have gone with me even if I'd asked. Angie agreed that it would be better to stay at the bakery and help with the Thanksgiving pie pickups than to accompany me. At best she'd be uncomfortable, and at worse a serious disruption.

Especially if Phoebe caught sight of her.

However, Margie had wanted to go, and she'd convinced her sister to take the kids for a few hours. She showed up at the Honeybee a little after one thirty in clothes suitable for the most formal of funerals: black dress and shoes, even a little black hat with a veil that looked like it came from the 1950s. I felt sure Dana would have approved her fashion choice.

"Evelyn let me borrow it," she explained. Evelyn was her mother-in-law.

Since the memorial was outside, I hoped my more casual dress would be acceptable. A light gray blouse topped my dark gray slacks and ballet flats. At least my bandaged knee was hidden.

"How did it work out with Redding?" I asked as we walked to Margie's Subaru.

She rolled her eyes. "He finally settled down enough for me to explain. You know what? The more I talked about what I was trying to do with the GPS thingama-bob, the sillier it sounded. Pretty soon we were giggling like schoolkids."

I grinned. "See. Told you it would work out."

Margie sobered. "I'm not going to mention that we laughed at the idea of Radical Trust when I'm at the memorial, though."

"Good idea."

Parking was scarce around Chippewa Square, which was already full of people milling about when we drove by. We found a space a block away on Bull Street and walked back. Clouds had moved in, and the overcast sky lent a somber tone to the scene as we approached. The temperature hovered around seventy, though, and there was no rain predicted. A light breeze swayed through the Spanish moss that drifted in thick curtains from the live oak branches above. Tangles of azaleas surrounded the exterior of the square, dormant now but still ever-green and substantial.

The brick front of Bryson Hall rose impressively on one side of the square. The venue had once been the exclusive Packard dealer in Savannah but now hosted weddings and other events. Phoebe had said they were booked that afternoon, so I guessed at least some of the parking issues stemmed from that. The Savannah Theater sat in art deco splendor on the corner of Bull and Hull, advertising a comedy show on the red-and-white marquee.

Chippewa Square was sometimes referred to as Forrest Gump Park and was much sought out by visitors. The bench on which Tom Hanks had sat was now in the Savannah History Museum, though, and other than constant references to the movie from tour guides, there was little to commemorate the famous scene about life being like a box of chocolates.

Ironically, the statue of James Oglethorpe wasn't in Oglethorpe Square at all, but in this one. He stood nine feet tall on a pedestal in the center where the paths converged, facing west in his three-cornered hat and guarded by four stone lions.

Near the monument, a long table offered a selection of nonalcoholic drinks. There were no snacks, which I could see the sense of, given how many people had turned out to pay their respects to Dana Dobbs. They gathered in clusters, conversing in low tones. Off to the side, a six-foot-square photo of the deceased stood on an easel. A quick double take confirmed it was the photo on the front of *How to Do Marriage Right*!

Phoebe taking advantage of the situation? Or simply the most recognizable photo that came to hand?

The fans didn't seem to mind. They'd placed flowers, stuffed animals, and candles around the base of the easel. There were handwritten prayers and well wishes tucked in between the other items.   •

To the right of the display, a canopy covered a table littered with brochures. Phoebe stood behind it, next to a sign that read DR. DANA DOBBS SCHOLARSHIP FUND. She spoke animatedly to a man in a dark blue suit who leaned over the table, writing on a piece of paper with a silver pen. When he stood, I saw it was Heinrich Dawes. He handed Phoebe a check and spoke a few words.

I wondered how many zeros were on the check. A lot, I hoped.

Margie and I made our way to the drinks table and helped ourselves to a couple of bottles of water. They were, I noticed, the brand Dr. Dana had insisted on during her signing. I remembered her face as she lay on the floor, and I put the water back. I knew it wasn't poisoned. I knew only the sweet tea had been poisoned. Still, I was suddenly not in the least bit thirsty.

"I'm going to look at the memorial," Margie said. "I wish I'd thought to bring something to leave for her."

"We can donate to the scholarship fund," I said.

She brightened and moved to where Phoebe stood talking to someone else. I saw Heinrich exiting the square on the far side.

A woman wearing a multilayered combination of skirt, tights, tunic, jacket, belt, and scarves took the bottle I'd just returned to the drinks table. I moved back and saw her long blond braid.

"Ronnie Lake?" I asked.

She whirled. "Yes?"

I stuck out my hand. "Katie Lightfoot. We spoke on the phone."

Her eyebrows drew together in puzzlement. Did she not remember talking to me at all because I'd used my Voice? Then her face cleared for a second before a different kind of confusion took root.

"Katie. Right. We spoke about Dana." She shook her

head. "I apologize. I said more than I should have. Her death must have affected me in ways I didn't realize."

"Oh, gosh. No need to apologize." *No need at all.* "I was very glad to learn of the scholarship fund in Dr. Dana's name. The owner of the bookstore came up with a good way to contribute to it." Watching her carefully, I continued. "He's going to sell the last books Dana Dobbs signed in an auction. All the proceeds will go the fund."

Her eyebrows knit together. "You mean he has more signed books?"

Rather than be indelicate about when they'd been signed, I simply nodded. "They're in the back of his store as we speak."

She shrugged. "Well, her fans might just love that. Some of them were quite rabid." Her fingers crept to her lips. "I mean, er, *fervent.* Heavens, the things that seem to come out of my mouth these days. Good luck with the auction. Excuse me." She scurried away, scarves flying out behind her.

I sighed. She might have slipped Dr. Dana a dose of cyanide, or she might not have. Either way, I'd inveigled my way into her brain, and I felt terrible about it.

Phoebe walked by on the other side of the table, stopping to chat with a young couple holding a spray of flowers in a vase. She pointed to the photo easel and moved on. I turned to see Nate Dobbs had taken over for his sister-in-law at the fund-raising table. Margie was sitting on a bench several feet away and talking to a woman I didn't recognize.

Dodging mourners as subtly as possible, I hurried over to talk to Nate Dobbs.

He looked up and over my shoulder, searching for

something or someone. He had broad shoulders under his sports coat, and capable-looking hands. And he was tall.

Tall enough to be the person I'd seen in the alley? Yup. And certainly strong enough to push the Dumpster that had almost done me in.

"Hi," I said.

"Hi." He absently gestured at the pamphlets that listed details about the scholarships, still not really looking at me. "If you're interested in donating, all the information is in there."

I picked one up. It was slick and professional. Phoebe had been busy in the last couple of days.

"We take checks and credit cards." Then he met my eyes. "Oh! It's you."

I folded the pamphlet and slid it into my pocket.

"Hi, Nate. I wanted to let you know that I'm going to help Croft Barrow auction the books he has left that Dana signed. All the proceeds will go to your wife's scholarship fund."

"The books she . . . ?" His forehead creased. "Oh, God. I guess people might want those, huh? Well, that's really nice of you." His lips turned down. "I think."

I stepped carefully. "I understand you had mixed feelings about your wife's take on Radical Trust."

His jaw set, and he looked over my shoulder again. "You heard her yourself. It saved our marriage."

"But you were planning on getting a divorce," I said gently.

Anger blazed in his eyes, then faded. Suddenly, he just seemed tired. More than tired. Completely drained. "Radical Trust is hard to take, honestly. And God knows the whole world knew about our problems. Or most of them. But we were going to get counseling once this promotional tour was over."

"You were?" Phoebe said, coming around the back of the canopy. "I find that hard to believe."

Nate looked surprised. "She didn't tell you?"

Phoebe shook her head. "And I wouldn't have believed her if she had. No way my sister the relationship maven would solicit advice from someone else about her marriage. She fooled you again, Nate." Bitterness infused her voice. "She fooled all of us."

Then she turned to look at me. "Katie, I sure seem to run into you a lot lately."

Nate frowned. "Really?"

"At the bookstore, at the radio station, and now here. Funny, that."

My smile wavered. "I was just telling Nate here about how Croft is going to contribute to the scholarship fund."

"Dana died in his establishment, and he sends you in his place?" Suddenly Phoebe sounded a lot like her imperious sister.

"He's working at the Fox and Hound today, and since I'm going to help him with the auction, he thought . . ." I trailed off.

"What auction?"

"He's going to sell the last books your sister signed and donate all the money to this." I gestured at the booth.

"Last books . . . you mean the books she was signing when . . . good heavens." She took a deep breath. "Well! I think you'd better announce that to everyone so you'll get lots of bidders. Come on, Katie."

"Where?"

"To the microphone. I don't want anyone to miss out."

My fear of public speaking raised its cobralike head. "Perhaps you could tell them," I began.

"Nonsense. I don't know any of the details."

Neither did I, actually. "We're still working some of that out."

She looked askance at me. Of course, if she'd been in charge of the auction, not only would the details be worked out, but she'd have pamphlets to hand out at the memorial and a dedicated Web site.

"We only came up with the idea this morning," I tried again. "The books are still in his back room—at least until tomorrow." I said the last loud enough for Nate to hear. A quick glance his way confirmed he was still paying attention.

Avid attention, actually.

Good.

"I'll help you set it up," Phoebe said, apparently unable to resist. "We can use Croft's Web site, and there are online auction tools available. Now, let's make the announcement. I just set up the microphone so people can share their stories about my sister."

Sure enough, there was a tiny portable stage over by the photo easel now, complete with mic. She grabbed my arm and pulled me over to it. I stopped right in front and watched as she marched up to the mic and turned it on with an expert hand. I wondered how many times she'd done that for her sister.

Someone came up to stand next to me. I looked over to see it was Earl King.

Uh-oh.

"Hello? Hello." Phoebe's voice boomed out.

Conversations all over the square drifted into silence.

"Thanks to everyone for coming here today and celebrating the life of one of the smartest, kindest, and most influential women I know. I'm Phoebe Miller. Dana Dobbs was my sister. I want to invite everyone who has a story they'd like to share to come up here and tell us. Nothing formal, just tell what you want." Her eyes lit on Earl, and her voice hardened. "Though do keep in mind that this is about *celebration*."

Beside me, he nodded his understanding.

Phoebe's shoulders visibly relaxed. "First the owner of the Honeybee restaurant has an announcement to make."

I shook my head and waved at her to go on.

She stepped away from the mic and gestured regally with her arm, inviting me to speak next.

"Go get 'em, tiger," Earl urged. It was nice of him, really, since I was pretty sure he didn't even know my name.

Slowly, I stepped up to the microphone. An amplified scratching noise echoed through the square as I tried to adjust it lower. It balked, and Phoebe started back toward me. Nate stepped up ahead of her, though, and moved it down for me. Smiled. "There you go."

"Thanks," I said in a small voice.

Everyone who had been milling and talking began to converge on the little stage. Panic burbled through my veins. Margie pushed through to the front of the crowd and snagged my gaze. Nodded her encouragement.

Bless her, it worked. Enough at least. I wasn't eloquent in the least. My voice wavered, and I talked a mile a minute, but I managed to say, "The Fox and Hound Bookshop will be auctioning the last dozen signed copies of Dr. Dana Dobbs' book *How to Do Marriage Right* on the store's Web site. Please look for more details there." I started to step away. "Oh! And the profits will all go to the Dr. Dana Dobbs Scholarship Fund." Another step away; then back I went. "Please feel free to donate to the fund yourselves." Two steps away, then back yet again. "And the Honeybee is a bakery, not a restaurant."

Phoebe rolled her eyes.

My face burning bright red, I escaped. Margie led me over to the drinks table and cracked a bottle of water open for me. It could have been pure poison for all I cared. I swigged it back like a sailor.

Sophie King came up. "That's a nice thing the bookstore is doing. I hope those books are locked away someplace safe. Someone might get the idea to take them and try to make money on them on eBay or something. Heck, now I wish we'd bought a copy." She realized what she'd said and ducked her head, embarrassed.

"They're tucked away in the back of the bookstore," I said. "At least until tomorrow." I looked around, but Nate was no place near. "I'm a little surprised to see you here." She was, I noted, quite tall. Not as tall as her husband was, though.

She gave a little shrug. "I felt kind of bad about the other night."

"Katie," Margie broke in apologetically, "I just got a text. Julia ate a bug, and my sister's freaking out."

"I'm ready," I replied. Then to Sophie: "You mean about your husband confronting the author?"

"Yeah. I mean, she wasn't a horrible person or anything. She just had strange ideas. Earl's a big boy, though. He didn't have to take her advice." She shook her head ruefully. "For some reason, when it comes to love, that man doesn't have the sense of a gnat."

We said good-bye to Sophie and began to walk toward Bull Street.

"What kind of bug did she eat?" I asked.

Margie shrugged. "Who knows? I swear that kid eats a bug a day. You'd think my sister would be used to it by now. God knows I am."

"Katie!" A voice shouted behind me.

I turned to see Bing Hawkins trotting down the sidewalk.

Dang it. Of course, I should have expected to see him here.

He stopped, out of breath. Beads of perspiration glistened on his forehead, and a strand of hair had come loose from his man bun. Margie peered at him with frank curiosity.

"Just wanted to follow up with you about that ad," he panted.

"Uh . . ."

"Now, don't tell me you changed your mind." He grinned. "I'll just sell you on it all over again."

Actually, you sold Jaida on the idea.

But instead, I said, "You should call my uncle Ben at the Honeybee Bakery. He makes the final decisions regarding all our advertising. I think you know him from the Rotary Club."

"Ben Eagel? Sure, I know him. But then why did you and Ms. French—"

I cut him off with a cheery smile. "He sent us to get more information."

Bing didn't seem entirely satisfied with my answer, but I turned and started walking again, calling over my shoulder. "You should give him a call this afternoon. He's at the bakery now."

After all, I figured that my uncle was already peeved with me. A phone call from Bing wasn't going to make it that much worse. And it was the quickest way to convince Bing that his efforts were going to be fruitless.

Right?

We stepped out of the square in the direction of Margie's car, and a figure stepped right in front of me.

"Hey," I exclaimed, backpedaling.

Detective Quinn grabbed my arm to steady me. "Fancy meeting you here, Lightfoot."

I glowered at him.

"What? Homicide cops always go to the funeral." Amused.

Margie looked between us.

"And I understand you left me a message," he went on, the humor dropping from his gaze.

"Margie, could I meet you at the car in a couple of minutes?" I asked, keeping my eyes on Quinn. He acted a little too self-satisfied for my taste. What was going on?

"Sure!" she answered almost before I'd finished speaking, and hurried away.

I didn't blame her.

"So now you think Earl King killed the doctor?" Quinn gestured toward the memorial behind me with his chin.

"I actually think it was her husband," I said. "But whether it was him, or King, or someone else, I'm going to lay a trap tonight."

That self-satisfaction slid right off his face. "Tell me you're not going to do something stupid."

"I'm not going to do something stupid."

"Darn it, Katie! I'm serious."

"I won't be alone. Croft is in on it, and I'll see who else I can get to come. Oh, and I'm pretty sure Angie will want to be there."

"No!"

A passerby turned to look at him.

I sighed. "Quinn—"

The muscles in his jaw clenched and unclenched.

Uh-oh. He's really angry.

But when he spoke, there was worry in his tone. "I talked with Ms. Kissel's husband. He told me a lot of really crazy stuff. Please stay away from her. And whatever you do, don't let her stay at your place for one more night. I want you to ditch whatever you have planned tonight and let me convince the district attorney to try her for murder."

My own jaw set. I had a pretty good idea what kind of crazy stuff Angie's husband had told Quinn. Witches on brooms and evils spells and the like.

We stared at each other for a long moment.

I broke first, looking down at the sidewalk. "I have to get back to the bakery."

When I looked back up, he was watching me. "You really think Angie Kissel is innocent."

I nodded. "I don't just think it. I know it. Just like I did with Uncle Ben. And you have to admit I have a pretty good track record with this stuff."

"Sometimes I wish you didn't." He blew out a breath. "Okay. Tell me about this plan of yours."

Chapter 24

Things were slowing down at the Honeybee when I got back. Most of the pies had been picked up, and since we were closed the next day, we could skip the usual kitchen prep. Of course, the morning after Thanksgiving would see me at work earlier than ever to get ready for the Black Friday shoppers.

Mungo watched from the office doorway as I tied a red-checked apron over my gray ensemble.

"I talked to Declan," Ben said.

I whirled around.

My uncle smiled tentatively at me. "He told me to stop being a jerk. That this marriage business was between you two and not my concern."

I couldn't help the grin that spread across my face.

"Don't get cocky," he said. "I still think you need to make a decision. The right decision."

"Ben—"

He held up his hand. "In the meantime, Lucy told me about what you have planned tonight. Count me in."

"Thanks." I gave him a hug.

"Well, since Declan can't be there to have your back, I figure I'd better step in to protect you."

"Ben!" Lucy said from the register, where she'd apparently been listening to us.

He winked at me and moved out front.

"What was that all about?" Angie asked from where she was organizing canned goods in the pantry.

"He's teasing me," I said.

Protect you. Ben knew darn well I could take care of myself, even if he'd thrown a fit when someone tried to run me over with a Dumpster.

Still, it was nice to know he was on my side. I didn't want to tangle with Dr. Dana's murderer by myself.

As the day wound down and the last of the pies went out the door, the subtle current of energy beneath my skin increased bit by bit. I kept telling myself not to count too much on tonight. There were too many variables, too many possibilities, too many ways for it not to work out.

The most likely outcome would be a night spent in the back room of the Fox and Hound with Ben, Croft, and Angie. None of them would thank me when nothing came of my grand plan except an exhausted Thanksgiving and a murderer still free.

At eight o'clock, the main area of the Fox and Hound was dark, and the CLOSED sign hung in the window. We were all in the back room with the door tightly shut. Croft had even laid a piece of cardboard under the jamb to ensure no light would escape. Anyone who peered through the window facing Broughton would never know someone was still in the store.

"How long do you think we'll need to wait?" Lucy asked.

"I wish you hadn't insisted on coming along on this escapade," Ben said. It came out gruffly, but I knew he would rather keep his beloved out of harm's way.

"I was just wondering whether we planned on staying here until dawn." She marched over and sat down on the folding chair next to Mimsey. The older witch was ensconced on one of the sliding rockers that usually sat in front of the fireplace. Croft and Ben had carried it into the storage room when she had entered the store at closing time and announced that she would be joining us for the duration.

Lucy had told Mimsey what we'd planned. She'd wanted to call all the spellbook club members, but I'd dissuaded her. There was no reason for nine of us to spend the night before Thanksgiving in the Fox and Hound. She'd agreed, but there was still more of a crowd than I'd expected.

Croft was there, of course. And Ben. I hadn't been surprised when Mimsey decided to partake; heaven knew what her husband thought of his seventy-nine-year-old wife taking off like that. Perhaps he was used to it by now. And I certainly wasn't going to tell Mimsey Carmichael no. Once she was in, Lucy had to come, too. Mungo sat by my feet, and Angie—nervous but unwilling to stay by herself in either her apartment or the carriage house—perched on the edge of a stool on the other side of him.

Already tensions were riding a little high. Other than Mimsey, we were sitting around on hard metal seats, and the room was chilly. Ben had grabbed pizza from Screamin' Mimi's, so we'd eaten. Still, the smell of garlic in the air had soon become oppressive in the closed space.

"I don't think we'll have to wait until dawn," I told my aunt. "If the person who tried to break in before decides to try it again, they'll know they could get caught by early bakers if they don't show up before four a.m."

"Four in the morning," Croft said, weariness already threading his tone.

Ben came over to pat his wife on the shoulder. "Of course, the intruder might not worry too much about getting caught on Thanksgiving morning. Most businesses up and down the street won't be opening at all." He gave me a pointed look. "Including the Honeybee."

I passed my hand over my face. Hadn't thought of that.

"Now, don't worry," my uncle said. "All we can do is settle in as comfortably as possible and hope this works."

No pressure.

A banging on the front door made me jump.

"What the heck?" Croft bolted to his feet.

We looked around at one another. The banging stopped. Croft reached over and turned out the light, plunging us into total darkness. He opened the door a fraction to look out.

"Whoever it was left. Good Lord, you'd think customers would understand the concept of a store being closed."

"Maybe it wasn't a customer," I said. "Maybe it was someone checking to see if the store is empty."

Angie sucked in her breath.

A fist pounded on the back door, and my heart jerked against my rib cage.

"Croft! Katie!" A deep voice, not loud, but insistent.

I hurried over and cracked the door. Detective Quinn stood in the dark alley. He wore faded blue jeans, a rag-wool sweater that had seen better days, and a worn bomber jacket. Opening the door farther, I grabbed him by the sleeve and dragged him inside. Quickly cranking the lock closed again, I turned to him.

"Listen, Quinn. Just because you don't like this idea doesn't mean you need to sabotage it. I mean, what harm can it do? We either catch the bad guy or we don't. There's no downside for you. I can't believe you're so—"

He grabbed my shoulders. "Settle down. I'm not sabotaging you."

My arm waved wildly. "But you just announced our presence."

"Will you relax? There's no one out there. Believe me—I checked."

"I assume that was you at the front door? How could you know no one was watching?"

"It's too early—"

I shrugged off his hands and went to stand by Lucy and Ben.

He sighed and turned to the others. "Croft. Ms. Carmichael."

From her rocker, Mimsey twinkled her blue eyes at him. "Detective. Welcome to our little party. I assume you're here to help?"

He shot a glance at me. "Certainly. It's not like I have anything else to do tonight." Sarcastic. And then he turned to Angie. "And I want to keep an eye on things."

She reddened and looked away.

Quinn ate a couple of pieces of pizza, then settled onto a chair and took out his phone. Soon he was tapping away, still working even on stakeout. Mimsey found a bodice-ripper romance on the storage shelves and dove in. Ben, Lucy, and Angie all followed suit, whiling the time away with their own selections from Croft's stock. Croft himself sat with his feet up on another chair, arms crossed, and appeared to nod off.

Hours ticked by. Hushed conversation would flare for a few minutes and then quickly fade. They were all getting tired, and I was beginning to really regret the whole stupid idea. I couldn't stay still and paced the short distance between the rack of chairs and the returns shelf over and over. Mungo trotted along beside me for a while but eventually went to lie in the corner and watch me.

As I paced, my brain replayed the events over the last few days. Our introduction to the concept of Radical Trust. Angie confronting Dr. Dana during her talk. Earl King denying the psychologist's medical bona fides. A drained Phoebe Miller packing up her sister's things. Using my Voice on Ronnie Lake. A book of tarot spells and partially burned candles. The burning spell on my lawn. Three satin ribbons.

I stopped pacing.

Ribbons.

Did druids use burning spells? I didn't know, but the more I thought about it, it was hard to imagine Steve performing any kind of magic that required ribbons. So it had to be the same person I'd scared away in the alley. Right?

Except it was pretty hard imagining Nate performing a burning spell—or any kind of magic for that matter. I'd been fooled before, though.

I resumed my steps.

Cyanide. Who used cyanide to kill in the twenty-first century? Nate and Earl King had access, one via business and the other from his hobby. But something kept bothering me about that, too.

Cyanide. *Study in Scarlet.* Sherlock Holmes.

Poison is a woman's weapon.

A bit sexist, that. But still, Holmes had been pretty smart for a fictional character.

Dr. Dana had written *Nate* as she died. Her killer, I'd assumed. But maybe Lucy was right. Maybe Dana

Dobbs had no idea who had poisoned her sweet tea. So why *Nate*?

Because he was the last thing she thought of when she was dying? Because she loved her husband?

Something twisted inside of me at the thought.

So if not Nate, who? Earl? Maybe. Sophie? Possible, but my gut told me no. Ronnie Lake? Another possibility, but I couldn't help but think that if she was the killer, she would have given some hint of that under the influence of my Voice.

"Hey, Katie. Keep a lookout for Phoebe Miller's wallet," Croft said in a sleepy voice.

Startled out of my train of thought, I paused before resuming my steps. "You can stop worrying about that. She told me she found it."

"Oh, good. I'd wondered." Croft stood and stretched. Lucy looked up at him absently, then went back to her book. "On Sunday she thought it might have fallen out of her pocket back here the night before, when the police brought her back to see . . . you know. Her sister."

Quinn was watching us now.

"I couldn't let her look for it then, though." Croft looked pointedly at Quinn. "Since this area was all cordoned off with police tape. I'm glad she didn't have to deal with the DMV and canceling her credit cards after all."

But I was staring at him. Yellow tape or not, Phoebe had been back by the storage room door when I'd walked into the Fox and Hound bearing sympathy and restorative pumpkin spice cookies. Croft had been in the office. Had my sudden arrival stopped her from going farther?

And come to think of it, she'd seemed slightly flummoxed when I'd asked her about her wallet at the radio station.

The image of Phoebe standing in the Fox and Hound the morning after her sister died filled my mental movie screen. She'd been wearing a peacoat. A very *bulky* peacoat. Add a hat and the darkness of a predawn alley or the darkness of the street outside Margie's house . . .

I hadn't thought of Phoebe as particularly tall, but I was five-eight, and I'd had to adjust the mic at the memorial down a good three inches after she'd spoken into it. And the burning spell? Well, the only proof I had that the book of tarot spells and half-burned candles she'd been packing up at the radio station had been Dana's had come from Phoebe herself.

Jaida said thirteen red candles were part of a classic tarot love spell. To force someone's love.

Ugh.

"Quinn," I said in a low voice. "I think I might have been all wrong about the identity of the murderer."

Croft whirled toward me. "What?"

The others regarded me with frank curiosity, and not a little frustration.

Quinn put down his phone in such a deliberate, careful manner that I got the impression he was trying to control himself. His attention flicked to Angie, who was watching me with a narrowed gaze, then back to me.

"I think the killer is—"

"Shh!" Ben hissed.

In the instant silence, we all heard it. A scratching at the back door, metal on metal.

Quinn faded to the side of the entrance, and I leaped to the light switch. The room descended into darkness just as there was a snapping sound and the door opened to reveal a figure outlined by the lighter shade of night out in the alley.

Tall. Bulky. Hat.

A headlamp switched on, blinding me to everything but the narrow beam of light. I shrank against the wall, holding my breath, as the person took a step inside. Sniffed the air. Would our visitor flee at the scent of garlic from the pizza? I hadn't thought of that, but Lucy had told me that garlic was more than pungent. There was a reason for the belief that it could repel vampires, because the odiferous bulbs actually did contain the potential magic to repel evil.

The figure took another step, then another. The headlamp swished back and forth across the room. Suddenly, it stopped.

Focused on Mimsey, still sitting in her rocking chair, beaming up at the newcomer.

"Hello!" she sang.

The figure turned to run, but the door to the alley slammed shut. I flipped the light switch.

Phoebe Miller stood squinting into the sudden illumination of the overhead light, eyes darting right and left as she tried to assess her situation. She whirled to find Quinn standing with his back to the door, preventing her escape. I obstructed the way into the bookstore. Other than Mimsey, the others had faded to the sidelines.

Phoebe wore the peacoat I remembered from her visit to the Fox and Hound, and a knit hat pulled down over her ears. Slowly, she reached up and turned off the headlamp.

"Do you know this woman, Katie?" Mimsey asked, still rocking slowly. Her feet didn't quite touch the floor.

"That's Dr. Dana's sister," I said. "Phoebe Miller."

"Dear," Mimsey said gently. "I believe what they say is, 'The game is up.'"

Phoebe stared at the older woman, then at me. "What is this?"

"Well," I said in an almost apologetic tone. "It's a trap really. And you fell into it. Though, honestly, I don't know for certain why you came."

Quinn's eyes narrowed.

"I mean, I understand that you killed your sister. That I figured out. You slipped the cyanide in her sweet tea and waited for her to die. You acted so grief stricken, so at sea, that no one suspected you."

Standing on the very spot where Dr. Dana Dobbs had succumbed to death, her sister glared at me. "Who *are* you?"

"I'm the one who made the sweet tea, which you then poisoned. I'm the one you almost killed in the alley with the Dumpster." I felt anger surging, blooming in my chest with red heat. "I'm the one who knows for certain that Angie Kissel didn't kill your sister. That *you* did. And I'm the one who's going to make sure you go to prison for your crime."

Over her shoulder, Quinn managed to look skeptical, impressed, and amused at the same time. I didn't know if she recognized him in his casual clothes.

"I'm sure the police can find out all they need about the details, but I want to know why you did it."

She took off the hat and tossed her hair. "I don't know what you're talking about. Honestly, accusing me of killing my own sister."

"We just caught you in the middle of a break-in," I pointed out. "You're not exactly in a position of power."

Croft strode toward her and stopped a few yards away.

Fear flared on her face when she saw him; then it was replaced with calculation. "Mr. Barrow," she said. I could almost see her brain scrambling for an explanation. "I know this was wrong, but I was so desperate to find my wallet, you see. It contains something quite sentimental—"

"You told me you found it in your car," I said.

Croft made a rude noise.

She skewered me with her eyes. Opened her mouth. Closed it again.

"Let's see here," I said, starting to pace back and forth in front of her. It had helped me think earlier. Maybe it would now. I kept my gaze on her the whole time.

"The tarot spell book."

She blinked.

"And the candles. Not your sister's, were they? They were yours. And you're the one who left that little camp-fire on my front lawn in an attempt to bind me from looking for her killer."

Quinn's brow knit in puzzlement.

Phoebe's nostrils flared.

"But who did you want to . . . Oh." I stopped. "Oh, my. You're in love with Nate Dobbs."

Tears suddenly filled her eyes.

I shook my head. "You're *such* a good liar. The way you acted like you could barely stand him at the signing. The way you avoided him. I bet your sister, your *trusting* sister, never had a clue you two were having an affair."

Mimsey watched us with an unreadable expression, but over by the shelving units, Lucy's mouth was twisted into repugnance. Ben held her close to his side. Nearby, Angie gaped up at the tableau. Red fury rolled off Croft so strongly that I feared for his heart.

"We weren't having an affair," Phoebe whispered. "He was too good for that."

"Right. Isn't that why he wanted a divorce?" I asked.

"He wanted a divorce because my sister was watching

his every move. Because he couldn't stand it anymore."
Her voice grew louder. "Because he couldn't stand *her*
anymore. But she wouldn't let him go." She swallowed,
hard. "And I didn't have a chance with him unless he
was free of her."

"So you killed her," I said. Our eyes were locked.
The rest of the room seemed to have faded away. "The
red candles and tarot spell book you implied were
Dana's at the radio station—you tried to use them to
make Nate love you."

Her breath came in ragged gasps.

"And you saw the book open on the table when you
came back in with the police to see your sister before
they took her to the morgue. The book where Dana had
written his name."

A sob, and her hand came up to cover her mouth as
if she could keep the words inside.

I fell silent. Seconds ticked by.

And another piece fell into place.

"If it wasn't you, then it was Nate," I said airily. "I
guess Dana really did name her killer moments before
she died. I mean, he had access to the poison she was
killed with, and she wouldn't give him a divorce. Now
he has his freedom, and I'm betting he gets the majority
of her money, too." I broke eye contact and turned away.
"Maybe I was mistaken about what you told me about
your wallet. But if that's why you're here, then Nate
must be the killer. Croft, we need to call the police and
show them the book."

"No!" Phoebe wailed. "No, it wasn't him. I saw what
she'd written and knew the police would think he'd
killed her. I didn't know he worked with cyanide! I'd
never have made it if I'd known." She reached into her

pocket, and through the thick fabric, I saw her hand close around something.

"You're insane," Croft said, shuffling closer. His eyes blazed, and his hands were clenched into fists by his sides. "A heartless, murdering psychopath. You deserve to rot for what you did."

"Croft," I warned.

She pulled her hand out of her pocket and raised it to his face.

Quinn saw and started toward her.

"No!" I yelled. It was as much at myself as at Phoebe. A familiar power had flared to life beneath my skin, erupting at a cellular level. I struggled to contain it, hyperaware of Quinn's approach.

She grimaced and pressed down on the black plastic tube in her hand, squirting pepper spray into the bookstore owner's eyes. He screamed and covered his face with both hands, staggering backward toward the wall.

Ben rushed her next, and she spun toward him.

I watched as if it was all in slow motion. "No, no, no."

Spray erupted from the canister, heading straight for my uncle's face. I closed my eyes and reached out my hand. My intention coiled out to *grab* the aerosol droplets from two yards away and *fling* them back into Phoebe's face.

She cried out.

I opened my eyes.

My skin was still pulsing with an undercurrent of silvery light. A quick glance around revealed Angie staring at me with wonder, while Ben and Mimsey had turned their attention to Quinn. Lucy had rushed to Croft's side and was already leading him out front to the restroom, murmuring comfort.

"What the hell was *that*, Lightfoot?" Quinn thundered.

I swallowed and took a deep breath and pointed to Phoebe, who had fallen to her knees at his feet. "I told you I'd get a confession."

"Yeah, yeah. I recorded it. But that's not what I'm talking about." He looked wildly around. "Did you guys see that?"

Mimsey politely raised her eyebrows. "See what?"

Quinn took a pair of handcuffs from the pocket of his leather jacket. "Ben?"

"Don't know what you're talking about," my uncle said gruffly. "I'm calling an ambulance for Croft."

"She glowed," Phoebe said through her tears as Quinn helped her to her feet. Her face was swollen, and her eyes red. "She did it in the alley, too." She pointed a shaking finger at me. "She's a witch."

I forced a laugh. "Right. I love it when a murderer calls me names."

But Detective Quinn's look was speculative as he began the process of wrapping things up.

Chapter 25

For the first time in a week, I slept like a baby for three solid hours. We'd been giving statements and helping Croft shore up his back door for a good hour after Phoebe had been taken out. Angie had decided to go to her apartment after picking up her car at the carriage house. So it was just Mungo and me, snoring away until dawn crept through the windows to wake us. I honestly couldn't have told you the last time that had happened.

Justice had been served up hot. Dr. Dana's killer had been apprehended after giving a full confession right in front of Detective Quinn. Before she was led out, I'd asked her where she got the cyanide. She'd told me she'd found a video online that showed how to make it.

So Phoebe would be eating her turkey dinner in jail, while Quinn got to go home to his family. I felt bad for her on one hand, but on the other I was glad she'd be someplace where she couldn't hurt anyone. I had a feeling that if she'd gotten away with killing her sister, she might have tried to solve her problems the same way in the future. Nate was a lucky guy to have escaped her version of love.

Angie Kissel could go on with her life, and I'd fulfilled

my promise to Mungo. I had a rare day off and would be sharing a scrumptious meal with my favorite people in the world. Maybe best of all, I'd made another big decision. Maybe not everyone would like it, but that wasn't my problem.

As for Quinn seeing me glow? I wasn't sure what to do about that. He'd directed a lot of looks my way during the follow-up the night before. They'd ranged from curious to baffled to thoughtful. I had a feeling we'd be having an interesting conversation in the near future.

I puttered around the carriage house in my pajamas for a while. Declan got off his shift at nine, but I'd talked to him after all the excitement the night before, and they'd been kept busy with the usual idiotic holiday escapades. There had been two car wrecks, and a serious fire had resulted from the combination of faulty wiring and an over-the-top Christmas light display gone wrong. The firefighters had been out all night, and he hadn't had much sleep. His plan was to take a nap before meeting me at Lucy and Ben's for Thanksgiving dinner.

At least that's what he'd told me. I was sure he wasn't avoiding me.

Pretty sure.

I'd just fed Mungo his second breakfast of leftover chicken and potatoes when a knock sounded at the door. The wooden floor felt cool on my bare feet as I padded over to answer it. Angie stood on the front porch, grinning like a Cheshire cat on steroids.

"Hi, Katie!" She stepped in and closed the door behind her.

"You seem awfully chipper after hardly any sleep," I said.

"Chipper barely covers it. Oh, Katie, I'm so *happy*."

I smiled. "Nice not to have a murder arrest hanging over your head, huh. Coffee? Tea?"

"I'd love some tea." She shucked her purse and jacket and followed me into the kitchen. Mungo left his chicken to greet her, and she bent down to give his ears a good scritching.

"Hey, little guy." Her voice was tender.

The water heated in no time in the electric kettle, and I suggested we go out to the back patio to drink our tea.

"Let's just sit here, if that's okay. I can't stay long. I just came to pick up my things." She beamed.

"Okay," I said, getting a little suspicious. Putting a plate of apricot scones on the table, I sat down across from her.

She took one. "Oh, yum! These are so good. All the Honeybee pastries are just so delicious. I really loved working there."

"Is that what all this joie de vivre is about? You're looking for a job?"

She sat back and laughed. "Goddess, no. I have a job. I *love* my job."

Swallowing my tea, I narrowed my eyes. "Then what is going on? Are you this happy because we caught Phoebe?"

"Well, I am happy about that, of course. And thank you. Thank you from the bottom of my heart."

Yip! Mungo weighed in from where he was scarfing down the last of his breakfast.

"Don't bark with your mouth full," I said. "And you're welcome, Angie."

"And thank you for . . . for helping me to understand that I need to trust myself."

"How did I do that?"

She looked thoughtful. "I'm not sure. Maybe just by

being you. Someone tries to use sorcery to make you love them, and the same night someone tries to bind you with a spell, and you just take it all in stride."

I made a face. "I wouldn't exactly say that."

"The point is, you obviously trust yourself. And that made me think that I need to do the same thing. See, I stopped practicing magic because a spell backfired on me. It was my own fault, but instead of learning from it, I just stopped. From fear." She took a deep breath. "I've decided that I'm going to take up the Craft again."

YIP!

"I'm sure she appreciates that, Mungo." But my stomach was turning somersaults. What did that mean for Mungo? I forced myself to say, "And I'm happy for you. It's clear that you know your stuff and that you have real power as well."

She blushed. "Thanks." She drained her tea and stood. "I'll just grab my things."

As she left the room, she didn't so much as glance at my familiar. He largely ignored her as well. I heard Angie climb the stairs to the loft, and my shoulders gradually relaxed. Mungo and I belonged to each other now, and just because his former witch had decided to practice magic again didn't change that. Lots of witches didn't have familiars. Heck, Cookie hadn't had one until a few months before.

Taking a deep breath, I got up to put the teacups into the sink. "See? More good stuff," I said to Mungo. "There's a lot to be thankful for today." For good measure, I tried the little two-step Iris did when she was happy, but I stumbled and almost dropped the kettle. "Maybe I'll leave the happy dance to Iris," I said.

Angie appeared in the doorway with her bag in her hand.

"Heading over to your friend's for dinner now?" I asked, following her out to the living room.

"In a bit." She dropped the bag, and we hugged. Turning, she opened the door. "Come on, Mungo."

My breath stopped in my chest, while my heart started pounding double time. A fist of disbelief clenched my stomach.

No. She can't be taking Mungo! My Mungo?

He trotted out the door behind her, and I felt my legs crumple. As I caught myself on the back of the chair, my breathing started again—ragged, gasping, sobbing inhalations.

He's going with her.

MUNGO! I mentally shouted.

Yip!

He stood in the doorway, looking at me with quizzical worry.

"Katie, are you coming out?" Angie called from the yard.

Shaking, I rubbed the back of my hand across my eyes and straightened. "Mungo?" I croaked at my familiar.

He ran over and jumped up on the chair, scrabbling up the backrest until he was in my arms and frantically licking my face.

"Hey, you two. Come on. I want you to meet someone."

Trembling and sick to my stomach, I went out to the porch.

Angie was sitting in the grass near the front walk where she'd parked her car. The door was hanging open, and she was leaning over something.

Something very, very wiggly.

Angie looked up with a huge smile. "If I needed any more evidence that I'm supposed to follow my true nature, this is it. She found me this morning."

A tiny caramel-colored puppy tumbled out of her lap and gamboled toward us. I let Mungo down, and he raced to the newcomer. They rolled in the grass, and the baby dog barked, tiny and high and sharp. I sank to my knees next to Angie, tears welling despite the smile on my face.

"She's a cocker spaniel. My neighbor found her and was going to take her to the pound. But as soon as I saw her, I knew. Katie? What's wrong?"

"Oh, nothing. Nothing at all."

"Her name is Olivia."

"Hi, Olivia," I said softly.

She ran over and jumped in my lap, wiggling and wobbling and wagging. A giggle erupted from my chest.

"She's adorable," I said. "Welcome, Olivia."

Olivia blinked up at me, mouth hanging open in a doggy smile.

The sound of a car engine made us all look up. I recognized the Audi and stood. Mungo ran to stand beside me.

Angie saw our faces and bundled Olivia back into the car. "Who's that?"

"The furata guy," I said.

"Ooh."

Steve boiled out of the car and walked toward me, hands outstretched. "Katie, I'm sorry. I'm so sorry. You're right. I'm a jerk. I never should have tried the charm."

"Charm! That thing is a serious spell. Did you really think you could *make* me love you?"

"No, no. It was only a charm. Like the one you wear . . ." He trailed off, staring at my bare neck. Recovering himself, he said. "At least that's what the medicine woman I got it from told me."

"She told you wrong." Angie's voice was flat. "It's

far more powerful than a simple charm. It's a forcing spell."

Steve stopped. "Who are you?"

"A friend," Angie and I said at the same time.

"Which is more than I can say for you," I said.

He buried his face in his hands. "Oh, God. I'm so sorry. I've completely ruined it between us," he moaned.

Moaned.

I'd never heard Steve Dawes moan in my life.

"Oh, for Pete's sake, stop being so dramatic," I said. "You're a Dragoh at heart."

"I'm not—"

"You are." I barely stopped myself from stamping my foot. "You always have been, no matter how much you tried to deny it at first. It's in your blood, like my gift is in mine, and Angie's is in hers."

He dropped his hands and looked at my new friend.

My eyes cut toward her to see if I'd overstepped my bounds. She didn't seem upset. In fact, her eyes were glued to Steve.

And she didn't look very upset with him, either.

"I don't know, Katie," he said slowly. "Maybe you're right." He took a few steps toward us. "What was your name again?"

"Never you mind what her—"

"Angie," she said, stepping toward him.

I exchanged a look with Mungo. *Seriously?*

"Angie Kissel."

"Oh, I've heard about you from my friends in the police department. Congratulations on your freedom."

She ducked her head coyly.

"Our Katie here does good work, doesn't she?"

Angie nodded. "Without her help I'd probably be going to jail."

Steve met my eyes again. "I really am sorry. I don't know that you're right about me, but I'll think about it. At least Father is speaking to me again. Pretty sure my mother had something to do with that." A smile tugged at his lips. "Happy Thanksgiving to you both."

With one last, long look at Angie, he got back into his car and left.

She turned to me. "*That's* the guy who gave you the furata?" The look on her face reminded me of Iris' reaction to Steve.

"Mmm-hmm," I said wryly.

As she and little Olivia left, I had to admit Angie might be a good choice for Steve. And he for her?

Well, the jury was still out on that.

Honeybee met us at the curb in front of Ben and Lucy's town house. She rarely ventured outside, but on special occasions she took it upon herself to guide guests inside. Mungo and I greeted her and followed her elegant orange-and-white-striped tail up to the front door. I inhaled the scents of turkey, onion, garlic, sage, and cinnamon, and sure enough, my stomach growled.

Lucy had replaced the carved jack-o'-lanterns of Halloween with gourds and squash arranged on a series of hay bales around the front door. Herbs and flowers crowded into the small yard on either side of the front walk. Cornstalks leaned on either side of the door, and a Thanksgiving wreath of pinecones and dried leaves decorated the red door that led inside.

The door opened into a verdant oasis where Angie would have felt right at home. Houseplants stretched out of pots on the tables and floor and swung down from the high, bright ceiling. Ivy crawled up the bricks that surrounded the fireplace. Skylights and tall windows streamed November sunshine into the light, airy space.

The white sofas and chairs had been moved out of the center of the living room, and a long, many-leaved table filled most of the space. The white tablecloth and two-story white walls contrasted beautifully with the dark cherry-wood floors and boldly patterned rugs.

Mungo ran off with Honeybee to join the other familiars, who were gathered in the cheery, glassed-in breakfast nook. Clever them, staying out of the way of the busy humans, I thought as I joined the melee of furious activity that dominated the kitchen. The scarred wooden worktable where Lucy packaged the herbs from her garden and prepared food for canning was covered by dishes ready for the table. I added the biscuits I'd decided to bring instead of sourdough rolls, an urn of homemade strawberry jam, and three pies from the Honeybee.

Ben came over to help me unload the box in which I'd transported my loot. I looked sideways at him.

"Thanks for what you did last night," he murmured. "The pepper spray thing."

"Sure," I said. Another time I might have brought up his comment about protecting me, but it was Thanksgiving.

"I got a call from Bing Hawkins yesterday afternoon," he said.

"Uh . . ."

"I've decided on a trial run of one ad, three times a day for a week. We'll see if it brings more people in."

Barely keeping myself from laughing, I said, "He did bring up a lot of good reasons for advertising on the radio."

"I'll say," he muttered.

"Honey, can you reach that gravy boat on the top shelf?" Lucy asked her husband, and he went to help her.

Cookie and Oscar shared a glass of wine in the corner, and Gregory and Jaida leaned over the stove with their heads together. As I watched, he leaned down and whispered something in her ear. Ben passed by Lucy with the gravy boat, trailing his fingertips along the small of her back, and she turned to him and smiled. Bianca and little Colette sat at the table, mother helping daughter arrange pickled watermelon rind on a plate. Mimsey and her husband, James, stood on the periphery, his arm around her shoulders.

A movement in the other room drew my attention. It was Declan, coming down from the rooftop with the smoked turkey in a huge roasting pan. He entered the kitchen, and everyone cheered. We all moved aside to allow him to put the main attraction on the butcher-block counter.

"All right. Move aside. Carving is my domain," Ben announced.

Declan came over to where I stood in the doorway, a tentative smile on his face. "Hi."

"Hi." I put my hand on the back of his neck and pulled him to me.

His eyes widened, then closed as we kissed.

"Get a room!" squawked Mimsey's parrot, gliding through the living room.

"Heckle," the older witch gasped, then laughed.

I giggled as well, and I felt Declan's shoulders relax. Ben beamed his approval.

"Did you get some sleep?" I asked as we started moving dishes from the kitchen to the big table.

"Enough." He set a bowl of quivering cranberry

sauce next to the steaming mashed potatoes. Small talk to keep things light.

It took us a while to transfer all the food. Ben brought in the huge turkey on a platter as we took our chairs at the table. He sat down at his place at the head of the table and looked around at us. Taking Lucy's hand in his left, he held out his right to Declan. I fumbled in my lap for a moment as we all followed suit and joined hands.

"Lucy, do you want to start?" my uncle asked.

She gave a quick nod. "I'm thankful for you—every single one of you."

Ben quirked an eyebrow. "You always say that."

A gentle smile blossomed on her face. "It's always true."

My uncle said, "Well, I'm grateful for you, my dear. Everyone else here, too, but especially you. Declan?"

My boyfriend looked at me. "You guys are so sappy," he teased. "I'm grateful I got off work before all the fires start up from people not using their turkey fryers right."

"You are such a romantic," I said.

"Oh, I guess I'm thankful for you, too." He kissed my temple.

I took a deep breath. This was it. There was no turning back.

Slowly, I turned our clasped hands on the table so that mine was on top. The platinum filigree and sapphire on my finger winked, and I heard Lucy's quick intake of breath. I looked into the expanse of his blue eyes.

"I'm thankful that I'm going to spend the rest of my life with you."

He blinked. Looked down at the ring I'd slipped on when we sat down. And grinned.

"About time!" Heckle squawked.

Recipes

Katie's Greek Scones

Makes 8 large scones

2¼ cups all-purpose flour
1 tablespoon baking powder
½ teaspoon salt
1 teaspoon dried rosemary
6 tablespoons butter, cut into 1-inch pieces and
    chilled in the freezer for 15 minutes
⅓ cup sun-dried tomatoes packed in oil, rinsed and
    roughly chopped
¼ cup Kalamata olives, roughly chopped
⅔ cup Feta cheese, crumbled
1 egg
½ cup milk

Preheat oven to 400 F.

Set aside ¼ cup flour in a separate bowl. In a medium bowl combine 2 cups flour, baking powder, salt, and rosemary. Cut the chilled butter into the flour mixture by rubbing with your fingers or by using a pastry blender until the consistency is that of rough cornmeal.

Add the sun-dried tomatoes, the Kalamata olives, and Feta cheese to the ¼ cup flour and toss to coat. Shake it to remove excess flour and add to pastry mixture, tossing with your hands to evenly distribute.

Whisk together the egg and milk. Add to the flour

mixture, stirring lightly with a fork until the ingredients are moistened and just hold together.

Transfer to a lightly floured surface and knead twenty times. Add more flour to the surface if needed. Pat into an 8-inch circle that is slightly higher in the center than on the edges. Using a very sharp knife, cut eight equal wedges. Place scones on a baking sheet lined with parchment paper, an inch or so apart from one another. Bake for 12–14 minutes, until golden brown.

Iris' Pumpkin Spice Softies

Makes 48–60 cookies, depending on size

2 cups butter, softened
2 cups granulated sugar
2 teaspoons baking powder
2 teaspoons baking soda
1 teaspoon salt
2 teaspoons allspice
1 teaspoon ginger
1 teaspoon cinnamon
2 eggs
2 teaspoons vanilla extract
15-ounce can of pumpkin
4 cups flour

FROSTING
4 ounces (one stick) butter, softened
8 ounces cream cheese, softened
1 teaspoon vanilla extract
2 cups confectioners' sugar, sifted

Preheat oven to 350 F.

Beat the butter in a large bowl with an electric mixer until fluffy—about 30–40 seconds on high speed. Add the granulated sugar, baking powder, baking soda, salt, allspice, ginger, and cinnamon. Beat until thoroughly combined. Add the eggs and vanilla, and beat on medium until combined. Mix in the pumpkin. Slowly add the flour, beating it in on low until the mixture is smooth and even.

Using two spoons, drop dough onto a parchment-lined cookie sheet about two inches apart. Bake for 10–12 minutes until the tops are firm. Cool cookies on a wire rack.

For the frosting, combine softened butter and cream cheese with the vanilla extract in a mixing bowl. Beat on medium until glossy. Mix in the sifted confectioners' sugar until uniform. Spread the frosting on cooled cookies with a knife for a rustic look, or use a pastry bag for a tidier appearance.

Read on for an excerpt of the first book in
Bailey Cates's *New York Times* bestselling
Magical Bakery Mystery Series!

Brownies and Broomsticks

is available wherever books are sold.

This was a grand adventure, I told myself. The ideal situation at the ideal time. It was also one of the scariest things I'd ever done.

So when I rounded the corner to find my aunt and uncle's baby blue Thunderbird convertible snugged up to the curb in front of my new home, I was both surprised and relieved.

Aunt Lucy knelt beside the porch steps, trowel in hand, patting the soil around a plant. She looked up and waved a gloved hand when I pulled into the driveway of the compact brick house, which had once been the carriage house of a larger home. I opened the door and stepped into the humid April heat.

"Katie's here—right on time!" Lucy called over her shoulder and hurried across the lawn to throw her arms around me. The aroma of patchouli drifted from her hair as I returned her hug.

"How did you know I'd get in today?" I leaned my tush against the hood of my Volkswagen Beetle, then pushed away when the hot metal seared my skin through my denim shorts. "I wasn't planning to leave Akron until tomorrow."

I'd decided to leave early so I'd have a couple of extra days to acclimate. Savannah, Georgia, was about as different from Ohio as you could get. During my brief visits I'd fallen in love with the elaborate beauty of the city, the excesses of her past—and present—and the food. Everything from high-end cuisine to traditional Low Country dishes.

"Oh, honey, of course you'd start early," Lucy said. "We knew you'd want to get here as soon as possible. Let's get you inside the house and pour something cool into you. We brought supper over, too—crab cakes, barbecued beans with rice, and some nice peppery coleslaw."

I sighed in anticipation. Did I mention the food?

Her luxurious mop of gray-streaked blond hair swung over her shoulder as she turned toward the house. "How was the drive?"

"Long." I inhaled the warm air. "But pleasant enough. The Bug was a real trouper, pulling that little trailer all that way. I had plenty of time to think." Especially as I drove through the miles and miles of South Carolina marshland. That was when the enormity of my decisions during the past two months had really begun to weigh on me.

She whirled around to examine my face. "Well, you don't look any the worse for wear, so you must have been thinking happy thoughts."

"Mostly," I said, and left it at that.

My mother's sister exuded good cheer, always on the lookout for a silver lining and the best in others. A bit of a hippie, Lucy had slid seamlessly into the New Age movement twenty years before. Only a few lines augmented the corners of her blue eyes. Her brown hemp skirt and light cotton blouse hung gracefully on her short but very slim frame. She was a laid-back natural beauty rather than a Southern belle. Then again, Aunt Lucy had grown up in Dayton.

"Come on in here, you two," Uncle Ben called from the shadows of the front porch.

A magnolia tree shaded that corner of the house, and copper-colored azaleas marched along the iron railing in a riot of blooms. A dozen iridescent dragonflies glided through air that smelled heavy and green. Lucy smiled when one of them zoomed over and landed on my wrist. I lifted my hand, admiring the shiny blue-green wings, and it launched back into the air to join its friends.

I waved to my uncle. "Let me grab a few things."

Reaching into the backseat, I retrieved my sleeping bag and oversized tote. When I stepped back and pushed the door shut with my foot, I saw a little black dog gazing up at me from the pavement.

"Well, hello," I said. "Where did you come from?"

He grinned a doggy grin and wagged his tail.

"You'd better get on home now."

More grinning. More wagging.

"He looks like some kind of terrier. I don't see a collar," I said to Lucy. "But he seems well cared for. Must live close by."

She looked down at the little dog and cocked her head. "I wonder."

And then, as if he had heard a whistle, he ran off. Lucy shrugged and moved toward the house.

By the steps, I paused to examine the rosemary topiary Lucy had been planting when I arrived. The resinous herb had been trained into the shape of a star. "Very pretty. I might move it around to the herb garden I'm planning in back."

"Oh, no, dear. I'm sure you'll want to leave it right where it is. A rosemary plant by the front door is . . . traditional."

I frowned. Maybe it was a Southern thing.

Lucy breezed by me and into the house. On the porch, my uncle's smiling brown eyes lit up behind rimless glasses. He grabbed me for a quick hug. His soft ginger beard, grown since he'd retired from his job as Savannah's fire chief, tickled my neck.

He took the sleeping bag from me and gestured me inside. "Looks like you're planning on a poor night's sleep."

Shrugging, I crossed the threshold. "It'll have to do until I get a bed." Explaining that I typically slept only one hour a night would only make me sound like a freak of nature.

I'd given away everything I owned except for clothes, my favorite cooking gear, and a few things of sentimental value. So now I had a beautiful little house with next to no furniture in it—only the two matching armoires I'd scored at an estate sale. But that was part of this grand undertaking. The future felt clean and hopeful. A life waiting to be built again from the ground up.

We followed Lucy through the living room and into the kitchen on the left. The savory aroma of golden crab cakes and spicy beans and rice that rose from the take-out bag on the counter hit me like a cartoon anvil. My aunt and uncle had timed things just right, especially considering they'd only guessed at my arrival. But Lucy had always been good at guessing that kind of thing. So had I, for that matter. Maybe it was a family trait.

Trying to ignore the sound of my stomach growling, I gestured at the small table and two folding chairs. "What's this?" A wee white vase held delicate spires of French lavender, sprigs of borage with its blue star-shaped blooms, yellow calendula, and orange-streaked nasturtiums.

Ben laughed. "Not much, obviously. Someplace for

you to eat, read the paper—whatever. 'Til you find something else."

Lucy handed me a cold sweating glass of sweet tea. "We stocked a few basics in the fridge and cupboard, too."

"That's so thoughtful. It feels like I'm coming home."

My aunt and uncle exchanged a conspiratorial look.

"What?" I asked.

Lucy jerked her head. "Come on." She sailed out of the kitchen, and I had no choice but to follow her through the postage-stamp living room and down the short hallway. Our footsteps on the worn wooden floors echoed off soft peach walls that reached all the way up to the small open loft above. Dark brown shutters that fit with the original design of the carriage house folded back from the two front windows. The built-in bookshelves cried out to be filled.

"The vibrations in here are positively lovely," she said. "And how fortunate that someone was clever enough to place the bedroom in the appropriate ba-gua."

"Ba-what?"

She put her hand on the doorframe, and her eyes widened. "Ba-gua. I thought you knew. It's feng shui. Oh, honey, I have a book you need to read."

I laughed. Though incorporating feng shui into my furnishing choices certainly couldn't hurt.

Then I looked over Lucy's shoulder and saw the bed. "Oh." My fingers crept to my mouth. "It's beautiful."

A queen-sized headboard rested against the west wall, the dark iron filigree swooping and curling in outline against the expanse of Williamsburg blue paint on the walls. A swatch of sunshine cut through the window, spotlighting the patchwork coverlet and matching pillow shams. A reading lamp perched on a small table next to it.

"I've always wanted a headboard like that," I

breathed. "How did you know?" Never mind the irony of my sleep disorder.

"We're so glad you came down to help us with the bakery," Ben said in a soft voice. "We just wanted to make you feel at home."

As I tried not to sniffle, he put his arm around my shoulders. Lucy slipped hers around my waist.

"Thank you," I managed to say. "It's perfect."

Lucy and Ben helped me unload the small rented trailer, and after they left I unpacked everything and put it away. Clothes were in one of the armoires, a few favorite books leaned together on the bookshelf in the living room, and pots and pans filled the cupboards. Now it was a little after three in the morning, and I lay in my new bed, watching the moonlight crawl across the ceiling. The silhouette of a magnolia branch bobbed gently in response to a slight breeze. Fireflies danced outside the window.

Change is inevitable, they say. *Struggle is optional.*

Your life's path deviates from what you intend. Whether you like it or not. Whether you fight it or not. Whether your heart breaks or not.

After pastry school in Cincinnati, I'd snagged a job as assistant manager at a bakery in Akron. It turned out "assistant manager" meant long hours, hard work, no creative input, and anemic paychecks for three long years.

But I didn't care. I was in love. I'd thought Andrew was, too—especially after he asked me to marry him.

Change is inevitable . . .

But in a way I was lucky. A month after Andrew called off the wedding, my uncle Ben turned sixty-two and retired. No way was he going to spend his time puttering around the house, so he and Lucy brainstormed and came up with the idea to open the Honeybee Bakery. Thing was, they needed someone with expertise: me.

The timing of Lucy and Ben's new business venture couldn't have been better. I wanted a job where I could actually use my culinary creativity and business know-how. I needed to get away from my old neighborhood, where I ran into my former fiancé nearly every day. The daily reminders were hard to take.

So when Lucy called, I jumped at the chance. The money I'd scrimped and saved to contribute to the down payment on the new home where Andrew and I were supposed to start our life together instead went toward my house in Savannah. It was my way of committing wholeheartedly to the move south.

See, some people can carry through a plan of action. I was one of them. My former fiancé was not.

Jerk.

Lucy's orange tabby cat had inspired the name of our new venture. Friendly, accessible, and promising sweet goodness, the Honeybee Bakery would open in another week. Ben had found a charming space between a knitting shop and a bookstore in historic downtown Savannah, and I'd flown back and forth from Akron to find and buy my house and work with my aunt to develop recipes while Ben oversaw the renovation of the storefront.

I rolled over and plumped the feather pillow. The mattress was just right: not too soft and not too hard. But unlike Goldilocks, I couldn't seem to get comfortable. I flopped onto my back again. Strange dreams began to flutter along the edges of my consciousness as I drifted in and out. Finally, at five o'clock, I rose and dressed in shorts, a T-shirt, and my trusty trail runners. I needed to blow the mental cobwebs out.

That meant a run.

Despite sleeping only a fraction of what most people did, I wasn't often tired. For a while I'd wondered if I was manic. However, that usually came with its opposite, and despite its recent popularity, depression wasn't my thing. It was just that *not* running made me feel a little crazy. Too much energy, too many sparks going off in my brain.

I'd found the former carriage house in Midtown—not quite downtown but not as far out as Southside suburbia, and still possessing the true flavor of the city. After stretching, I set off to explore the neighborhood. Dogwoods bloomed along the side streets, punctuating the massive live oaks dripping with moss. I spotted two other runners in the dim predawn light. They waved, as did I. The smell of sausage teased from one house, the voices of children from another. Otherwise, all was quiet except for the sounds of birdsong, footfalls, and my own breathing.

Back home, I showered and donned a floral skort, tank top, and sandals. After returning the rented trailer, I drove downtown on Abercorn Street, wending my way around the one-way parklike squares in the historic district as I neared my destination. Walkers strode purposefully, some pushing strollers, some arm in arm. A ponytailed man lugged an easel toward the riverfront. Camera-wielding tourists intermixed with suited professionals, everyone getting an early start. The air winging in through my car window already held heat as I turned left onto Broughton just after Oglethorpe Square and looked for a parking spot.

ABOUT THE AUTHOR

Bailey Cates believes magic is all around us if we only look for it. She is the *New York Times* bestselling author of the Magical Bakery mysteries, including *Magic and Macaroons*, *Some Enchanted Éclair*, and *Charms and Chocolate Chips*. Writing as Bailey Cattrell, she is also the author of the Enchanted Garden mysteries, which begins with *Daisies for Innocence*. Visit her online at baileycates.com.

From *New York Times* bestselling author

Bailey Cates

The Magical Bakery Mystery Series

Katie Lightfoot helps her aunt and uncle run the HoneyBee Bakery in Savannah's quaint downtown district, where delicious goodies, spellcasting, and the occasional murder are sure to be found...

Brownies and Broomsticks
Bewitched, Bothered, and Biscotti
Charms and Chocolate Chips
Some Enchanted Éclair
Magic and Macaroons
Spells and Scones

"An attention-grabbing read that I couldn't put down."
—*New York Times* bestselling author Jenn McKinlay

"Charming and magical."
—Kings River Life Magazine

"A top-notch whodunit."
—Gumshoe

Available wherever books are sold or at
penguin.com

facebook.com/TheCrimeSceneBooks

OM0161